D1714986

Celeste Barclay
Visit my website at www.celestebarclay.com

Printed in the United States of America

First Printing: Nov 2018
Celeste Barclay

ISBN-13 9781730708008

His Highland Prize

The Clan Sinclair Book Three

Celeste Barclay

This is novel is dedicated to "Birdie" for twenty plus years of being best friends and her constant encouragement to take one more step, to try again one more day, to reach for one more dream, to write one more book.
~Happy Reading~
Celeste

The Clan Sinclair

Book 0 *Their Highland Beginning, Prequel Novella*
  Liam Sinclair and Kyla Sutherland
  FREE
  Book Funnel
  My Book Cave
  Prolific Works

Book 1 *His Highland Lass*
  Mairghread Sinclair and Tristan Mackay

Book 2 *His Bonnie Highland Temptation*
  Callum Sinclair and Siùsan Mackenzie

Book 3 *His Highland Prize*
  Alexander Sinclair and Brighde Kerr

Book 4   TBD- Magnus Sinclair and Deirdre Fraser

Book 5   TBD-Tavish Sinclair and Ceit Comyn

The Clan Sinclair

Liam Sinclair m. Kyla Sutherland

    b. Callum Sinclair m. Siùsan Mackenzie (SH-IY-oo-san)
        b. Thormud Seamus Magnus Sinclair (TOR-mood SHAY-mus)
        b. Rose Kyla Sinclair

    b. Alexander Sinclair m. Brighde Kerr (BREE-ju KAIR)

    b. Tavish Sinclair m. Ceit Comyn (KAIT-ch CUM-in)

    b. Magnus Sinclair m. Deidre Fraser (DEER-dreh FRA-zer)

    b. Mairghread Sinclair m. Tristan Mackay (Mah-GAID)
        b. "Wee" Liam Brodie Mackay

Chapter One

I just need to make it to the light. Heavenly Father, please let there be a light over this hill. I canna go much farther. I must go farther. Will there never be a village or a keep nearby? I dinna think I will last much longer. Please, in the name of the Father and all the heavenly saints, just let me find someone who can help me.

Brighde Kerr pushed her sopping wet hair from her eyes as she stumbled onward. She lost her shoes days ago after they had fallen apart while on the run from her pursuers. Her kirtle, which had once been a daffodil yellow was now a murky shade of beige with a ripped sleeve, frayed hem, and at least two holes that she had noticed in the skirts. Brighde ached all over. Her feet were raw from walking and running for nearly two weeks. Her legs protested taking even one more step, and her chest burned from trying to breathe through her efforts and the torrential downpour in which she once again found herself.

Light! I'm sure of it. I can finally see it coming from a keep. Dear God above, please allow me in. I just need---

Brighde slipped as she crested the last hill that kept her from reaching Castle Dunbeath and the Sinclairs. She landed heavily on her knees and rolled a couple of feet before she was able to right herself. She tripped over the torn hem of her gown and almost went head over heels again. The night was so dark that she could not even see the hand she raised in front of her. Only the brief flashes of lightning told her she was still headed in the right direction. The sound of thunder had long since drowned out the crash of the waves she had used to guide her along the coast. The light she did see was merely a faint haze, but it was enough to drive her onward.

Stumbling and weaving like someone who had been at a barrel of whisky for too long, she made her way forward. As the keep came into focus more clearly, she could just make out the faintest of movements on the wall walk. She tried to call out, but her voice was hoarse from lack of use and lack of water.

"Who goes?" called one of the guardsmen from above.

She opened her mouth again and could only mouth the word *help*. No sound came from her. She took two more faltering steps before falling to her knees.

"Sir Alexander! There's a woman at the gate! She looks to be in a right state. Do we let her in?"

Alexander Sinclair, the second son of Laird Liam Sinclair, moved to the front of the battlements closest to the gate. He leaned far over the wall to see but could only, barely, make out what looked like a rock that he knew had never been there before. And now, the rock shifted. As a crack of lightning illuminated the shifting mass, Alex caught sight of hair that was so fair that it was almost white. It glowed around the woman like a halo. Alex could not help but shake his head and rub his eyes. The huddled woman leaned back and looked up at the wall. Another flash of lightning made it possible for him to see part of her face and that her mouth moved. He could not see all her face, nor could he make out what she was saying, but she clearly needed help. Highland hospitality required that they let her in, but more than that, something about her called to Alexander.

He made his way as quickly and carefully as he could down the slick stairs calling out for the gatekeeper to raise the portcullis. By the time he made it down, the gate had risen high enough for him to bend down and pass through. He jogged over to the woman, wary in case of a trap. When he reached her, Brighde was kneeling but nearly unable to keep her head up. She swayed as she had no energy left to fight the wind that rattled the windows and made her teeth clack together as she shivered. Alex sat on his haunches as he looked at the woman. Brighde looked into Alex's eyes and thought she was seeing an angel.

"Am I dead now after all of this? Which clan are ye?" she croaked.

"Sinclairs. Who are ye, lass? What are ye doing out here alone in this gale?" Alex could not resist the urge to reach out and brush away the hair that was plastered to her face. The light from the wall walk made it only slightly easier for him to see her. As he moved her hair away, she pitched forward as her eyes rolled back. Alex caught her against his chest and could feel the tremors that shook her slight frame. He could feel how her sodden clothes clung to her. He leaned her back slightly and supported her with his knee. Her lashes fluttered briefly.

The last words she managed to squeeze out were, "help me, please. *Help.*" With that, her eyes shut again. Alex was not sure if she lived or just died in his arms. He pressed his head forward and rested his ear against her lips. When he felt the soft puff of air, he felt himself shudder with relief. He lifted Brighde into his arms and ran back to the gate. As he rushed into the bailey, he began calling orders.

"Someone fetch Hagatha! Go for the healer. I dinna care what she is doing. Unless she's delivering a bairn or sewing someone shut, she's to come to the keep. *Now!*" he bellowed.

Alex sprinted up the stairs leading to the massive doors that would allow him entrance into the Great Hall. He had to shift Brighde slightly to free a hand to open the door and then used his shoulder to nudge it open. He was relieved when the

2

wind helped him push it wide. He ran across the Great Hall once again calling out orders.

"Elspeth! Elspeth! Bring something warm to drink! Someone bring up the tub."

When he reached the stairs, he took them two and three at a time. He did not give a second thought to where he was taking her. He jogged down to the door of his chamber and shouldered that open too. He left the door wide open in his hurry to get her somewhere warm and safe. He gently laid her on his bed and turned to stoke the fire. After the flames began to blaze, he rushed back to the bed. He thought to remove her shoes and stockings, but only then did he realize she was not wearing any. He could see that her ankles were swollen, and when he looked at her soles, he almost retched. They looked like someone had carved into them. Some of the cuts were so deep that they had become infected. There were scratches across the top of her feet, and he could see the beginnings of some that reached up her calf. He once again lifted her into his arms and moved to the chair in front of the fire. With his foot hooked around the leg, he pulled the chair as close to the fire as he dared.

He had just settled into the chair when Hagatha bustled into the room with Laird Liam Sinclair on her heels. Alexander could barely spare a glance at either as he intently stared down at the unconscious form in his arms. Absentmindedly, he rubbed circles on her back in hopes of warming her even a little bit.

"She collapsed in ma arms after asking where she was. When I told her, she thanked God and then shut her eyes. They havenae opened since." He continued to stare at her intently. With the light of the fire and her hair out of the way, Alex could finally completely see her face. She was lovely. Beautiful.

She may well be the finest woman I have ever seen. What could have befallen her that she turns up on our doorstep in this weather and in this condition?

Alex took in her features. Her eyes were slightly wide apart and tilted up at the corners like a cat. Her button nose was straight and proportionate to her face. Her mouth had full lips and was wide as well. Her individual features might not have been the mark of beauty, but when put together, she was exceptionally good looking. Alexander had been right in his estimation of her hair. It was like wet spun flax. Parts were so light that they almost looked white. Her skin was nearly alabaster, but he suspected that was more from her current condition than her true coloring. She had a light smattering of freckles that led him to think she usually spent time in the sunshine.

"Did she say who she was? Or why she was traveling alone so far north?" Laird Sinclair asked.

"Nay. I told ye all that she said. I dinna see aught plaid, so I dinna ken her clan. She didna even say her name." Alex still had not looked up, so he could not see the speculative look on his father's face. "She just asked for help."

Alexander was the most serious of all of Laird Sinclair's five children. Only his daughter, Mairghread, could sometimes match his reserve. None of his other three sons were quite as introverted as Alexander tended to be. To see him now, with worry and concern etched across his face, Liam Sinclair knew that this was no passing fancy. Alex was never fickle about women and generally gave them only a passing glance. The Sinclair knew his son to be like any other healthy young man, but he did not chase women as Callum and Tavish did. His youngest son, Magnus, did not have to chase women as they seemed more apt to chase him. The laird watched Alexander's gentleness with the unknown lass. He watched as his son unfastened the extra length of plaid from his shoulder and wrapped their mystery guest in it as they awaited the tub that had just been brought in to be filled. His eyes shifted to the pair of bare feet that stuck out from the clearly destroyed gown. He noticed that the material was finer quality, or at least had been once upon a time. He did not need to move closer to see the damage that had been done to her feet. He wondered what could have made their guest travel so far as to injure herself so badly. The one thing he knew about her, at this point, was that she must have a will of steel to have traveled so far, alone, and in what had to be excruciating pain. A small smile played at the corner of his mouth as he thought to himself, *and so another one has found a match that will be a challenge, but that only makes the reward all the sweeter.*

Alexander finally looked up and scowled when he saw the smile playing around his father's mouth.

"I dinna think there is much to grin at here. She could vera well die, and we dinna even ken what name to put on the headstone."

"Ye dinna need to be so morbid, Alex. Ye were always such a grim child," Hagatha stated as she moved about the room. The older woman was the head of the household and had been with the Sinclairs since well before he was born. Alex looked over his shoulder and could see that there were drying linens stacked on the bed next to a flannel nightgown and two extra plaids. "Ye and the laird can step out now. The women and I will take care of her." When Alex did not make a move, Hagatha put her hands on her hips. "Ye canna vera well stay here. We need to give her a warm bath to get her blood pumping."

Alex looked from the unconscious form in his arms, to the women standing around the room, to his father, and back to the tangled and freezing mass in his arms. If he had not felt her shivering so badly, he was not entirely sure he would have released her. He could not figure out why he had such an overwhelming need to hover and ensure her wellbeing. He knew himself well enough to know that it was not a pretty face that drew him. He had seen plenty of them in his lifetime. No, it was something entirely different. There was an energy that radiated from her even in her current position. He could not help but admire the fortitude he knew was needed to endure what she clearly had. He was concerned that there was far more to worry about than what they could currently see.

"Give her here and be gone with ye." Hagatha made a shooing motion with her hands as she reached for the woman. If it had been anyone else who spoke to him in such a way, they would not have lasted long in the Sinclairs' employ, but Hagatha was like a much loved and very revered older aunt. She was as much a part of the family as any servant could be. Alexander trusted her with his life, and so he finally stood with the woman and entrusted Hagatha with her. Two other women came forward to help support the limp body.

"I will let ye ken as soon as she is respectable again. Dinna fash, lad." Hagatha patted his arm and turned back to work. Alexander reluctantly walked to the door and followed his father out.

"Is there a reason that ye brought her to yer chambers instead of taking her to one of the guest chambers?"

"I didna give it any real thought. I just wanted to get her warm and dry as quickly as I could. I didna want to wait to take another flight of stairs and wait for a fire to be lit."

"Ye could have taken her to Mairghread's chamber."

"Nae, Callum has laid claim to it." This made the Sinclair raise an eyebrow. "He doesnae want to be reminded of the arse he was in front of Siùsan."

This made the Sinclair chuckle as he nodded his head.

"Besides, none of the fires have been lit in the other chambers now that Mairghread lives at the Mackay keep with Tristan, and with the others chasing after Siùsan." At this, he could not contain his own chuckle, "none of their chambers have been warmed either. It just seemed logical to take her to mine."

Liam Sinclair looked at a face that was so like his. Chestnut hair framed an angular face with a strong jaw and straight nose. Deep brown eyes, level with his own, looked back at him. He almost shook his head as he realized just how grown up all his children were. Mairghread was married and lady of her own keep and clan. Callum, God willing and with some common sense, would be married to Siùsan soon too. It seemed that all his children were not really children anymore.

"Do as ye think is right, for now. Once she's even a mite better, she'll need to be moved to her own chamber. She doesnae need to begin her stay with us with a tarnished reputation."

"Aye, Da."

Liam Sinclair began to walk towards the stairs down to the Great Hall and his solar, but he looked back when he noticed he was walking alone. Alexander simply shook his head and slid down the wall. He stretched out his long legs, crossed his arms, and tilted his head back against the wall. There was no point in arguing. Alexander was not going anywhere.

Alexander would have sworn his last penny that he waited hours before the door to his chamber opened, but he knew that it had to have been less than one. There was a startled gasp from one of the servants as she almost tripped over Alexander's legs which were currently a roadblock to her exit. He pulled his legs in and sprang up. At his height of six and a half feet, he could clearly see over the heads of the women who were trying to leave. He saw Hagatha tucking the blankets high around the woman's shoulders. Aileen, the healer, who came shortly after Alex took up camp outside his door, was slowly spooning a liquid between her patient's cracked lips. Alex looked around the room and saw that all the linens and soaps and whatever else women used had been cleared away. The sodden and ruined clothes that their mystery guest arrived in were in a basket near the fire. Steam was rising off them, but he wondered if they were just destined for a fire somewhere else. There seemed to be little left to salvage. His eyes returned to the woman who was sleeping so deeply in his bed. He had never brought a woman to his chambers rather preferring to have his liaisons elsewhere. The men of the Sinclair clan were known for their steadfast loyalty, and within the laird's family that always extended to their wives. He had never had any desire to bring a woman to his chambers as he believed it was a space reserved for the wife he would one day have. Seeing the blonde hair strewn across his pillow was somewhat a surprise after having so assuredly avoided sharing his bed with anyone.

I amnae sharing ma bed with her. She is in ma bed, and I am here near the door. She can have it for as long as necessary. It's Highland hospitality and naught more.

Even in his own head that sounded ridiculous. By now, Hagatha probably had a fire lit in one of the other chambers with the intention of having her moved. He could easily carry her to another chamber, but the way she was tucked in and resting made him averse to the idea of moving her, and away from him.

"I see ye couldnae be patient even a moment longer. How did ye ken she wasnae still in a state of undress and not ready to receive visitors? Ye should be in the passageway and not gawking like a trout with its mouth open." Alex looked down at Hagatha who had moved quietly to stand before him. "She can rest here while I finish having a chamber prepared for her. I had a fire lit and a bed turned down for her. The room only needs a little longer to warm."

"Nay."

"What do ye mean 'nay'?"

"I mean just that. Nay. She isnae to be moved until she is awake and able to move on her own. I dinna want her jostled or disturbed. She's obviously been through quite a trial already. If she isnae bothered by being in here, then neither am I. She stays." Alex assumed the most natural position for all the Sinclair men, feet hips width apart and arms crossed.

"Dinna start with that. Ye dinna intimidate me. Nae when I used to change yer dirty nappies. She canna stay in yer chamber. She's barely more than a lass, so it isnae proper for a maiden to be in here. By now, the entire keep, if nae the entire clan, kens ye brought her in here."

"Aye, they all ken that she is unconscious as well. Does anyone truly believe I would molest an unconscious lass?" Alex looked duly insulted.

"Nay, I suppose they wouldnae." Hagatha began to move around the immobile monolith that was Alex, but he reached an arm out. He pulled her in for a loose embrace having hugged her his entire life.

"Thank ye for tending to her. Do ye ken if she will make it?"

"I wouldnae have set aboot having a chamber prepared for her if I thought it wouldnae get used." She tsked as she patted him on the back and moved to the door.

Alex walked silently to the bedside opposite from where Aileen leaned over her patient. She looked up when he stopped.

"She will be well, ma lord, as long as a fever doesnae set in. She doesnae have one yet, but it vera well could come on during the night. If it does, I expect it will be fierce, and I canna say yet what will happen."

Alex simply nodded his head. He moved to the fireplace and lifted the chair in which he had sat holding his guest. He could not think of anything else to call her at this point. He brought the chair close to the bedside and sat down.

"I will stay with her, ma lord. Ye dinna need to."

Alex simply shook his head as he bent forward to press the back of his own hand to her forehead. He was only mildly reassured that there was no fever, but she was still unnaturally cold and pale.

"Why isnae she warm yet? Did ye nae let her soak long enough in the warm water?"

"We did, but we couldnae keep her in there too long for fear of her temperature changing too rapidly, too soon. Hagatha put two heated bricks in the bed with her, and she had a plaid wrapped around her beneath the covers as well as the three ye can see on top."

Alex simply nodded his head as he kept watching her. Aileen moved about silently collecting her things and put them back into her bag from which she also drew an extra length of plaid. She walked over to the hearth and was about to sit down when Alex spoke again. His voice was so low that he barely heard himself.

"Ye dinna need to stay. I ken ye have worked hard. Go to the Hall and get something to eat. Hagatha can arrange for ye to sleep with the other women tonight. I will call for ye the moment there is a need, but I dinna think she will move much tonight. Between exhaustion and being battered by the weather, I dinna think she will on the morrow either."

The healer began to shake her head and disagree, but Alex's dark eyes and set jaw made her stop before she even started. It was clear that he would not budge and that his words were more an order than a suggestion. She nodded and moved to the door.

"There is willow bark tea on the table beside the bed. If she seems restless, ye can give her a few spoonfuls. If she'll take it, give her small sips of water too. Nae too much or she will retch or choke. The honey is for her cracked lips, and the salve is for her feet. She'll need that reapplied every couple of hours." With that, she quietly opened the door and stepped out. She left the door slightly ajar. Even if Alexander was not worried about propriety someone had to be for the girl's sake.

"Who are ye, lass? How did ye find yerself alone? What happened?" Alex asked these questions but knew no answers would be forthcoming. He watched as she slept peacefully. Eventually, his own eyes began to drift closed. He rested his head on his arm on the bed as he continued to face her. His last thought before drifting off was that he would find out what happened as soon as he could. No one, especially a young woman, traveled alone in such weather in the northern Highlands. Not unless it was dire.

Alex awoke to a subtle shifting of the mattress under his arms and head. He looked around and rubbed the sleep from his eyes. His eyes settled on the sleeping woman in his bed. Brighde was shivering uncontrollably. It was even worse than when he brought her inside from the storm. He moved forward to check her forehead for a fever. Her brow was frigid to his hand, so he moved his palm along her cheek and down her neck. He pulled back the covers just enough to draw her hand out. Her nails matched the blue tinge of her lips.

"Shite."

With no fever, he knew there was nothing else the healer could do except for the only thing he could do. In the back of his head, he knew he should probably call Aileen or any other woman to help him, but something compelled him to be the one to warm her. He moved over to the fireplace and threw two extra bricks of peat and three pieces of wood into the flames. He brought two more lit candles to the bedside tables, then looked over at the door. The draft through the passageway must have pushed it halfway open, so he mostly closed it, leaving it only ajar. He moved to the empty side of the bed and unpinned his plaid from his shoulder. He looked at the door one more time before he unbelted his plaid and caught it before it landed on the floor. He hesitated for only a moment before he pulled his leine over his head and drew back the covers far enough for him to climb in. He scooted close to the shivering, sleeping form and gently unwrapped the plaid before he reached for the hem of her nightgown. He had a momentary pang of guilt when he thought how she would react if she awoke. He did not want to scare her or make her worry that he had taken advantage of her but using his body heat against Brighde's skin was the only way that she would warm up. He gently lifted the front of her nightgown up to her waist and then rolled her to her side. He was then able to lift the back up to her shoulders. He tried to leave the front of her nightgown hanging as far down her body as he could. He drew himself close to her and wrapped his arm around her front on top of the flannel. His body reacted immediately to the soft curves that filled his arms and pressed against his front. He willed his cock to relax and not swell as it clearly longed to do. He was not there to molest the woman or indulge in any sexual fantasies, but his body seemed to be of a different opinion from his head. He breathed in the light floral scent of the soap the women must have used. It was the lemongrass that his mother had preferred. As soon as he recognized the scent, he thought his body would calm. Normally, nothing would shut down his ardor like a woman who smelled like his mother, but this woman seemed to be an entirely different story. Despite recognizing the scent, his cock remained at attention.

"Bluidy hell," he muttered. "This isnae what I intended. It has clearly been too long since I've been with a lass."

Alex knew that putting any space or any material between them would defeat the point. He took several deep breaths and tried to think of anything else besides the feel of her round bottom pressing against his groin. He shifted his body slightly so that he could move his hips away and press his chest more firmly against her back. As the hair on his chest brushed her back, Brighde moaned softly. It was not a moan of pleasure. It was clearly pain. Alex leaned back slightly to allow the light from the fire and the candles to illuminate her back. It was covered in bruises and some scratches. Alex sat bolt upright and reached for one of the candles. Nothing could have cooled his ardor as quickly as what he saw now. He lifted the flannel gown high enough that he could see her entire back. It was riddled with bruises in various shades of healing. He could tell they were a couple of weeks old, but their distinct and dark coloring only proved how horribly she had been beaten. He only now noticed that a bandage was wrapped around her ribs, and it must have been the pressure against her bandage that made her moan. He gently rolled her onto her back. Yet again, he looked towards the door to make sure no one was near. He felt a bit like a naughty lad peeking at the lasses while they swam at the loch. He slowly lifted the front of her gown and tried to keep his gaze averted from the thatch of blond curls that lay at the juncture of her legs and hips. His eyes instead landed on the dark bruises that covered her breasts and chest. These were clearly the result of someone pinching her, and pinching hard. He looked back down to where the bandage was wrapped around her middle. He could see bruises peeking out from the top and the bottom. He pulled the nightgown back down. He had seen more than enough. He felt rage swelling in his chest, and his ears began to ring. Someone, no some man, had beaten this woman within inches of her life and very well may have raped her. Alex forced himself to take several deep breaths before he gently rolled her back onto her side. This time, when he lay next to her, he was exceedingly careful about how he wrapped himself around her. After only a moment or two, he heard her sigh and felt her body relax against his. He, too, relaxed and drifted off once again with his arm lightly but securely wrapped around her middle.

The sky was just starting to soften from the darkness of night when Alexander felt like he was on fire. As he came awake, he could not understand why he felt like flames were licking at the front of his body and legs. As his eyes opened, he remembered where he was and, more importantly, who he was with. He looked down and saw blonde hair that was drenched in sweat. The lass's back was damp with perspiration too. Alex knew immediately that this was not from him making her too hot. He knew he could be like a furnace when wrapped under too many covers, but this was clearly a vicious fever that took hold. He reached around and pressed the back of his hand against her forehead and then cheek. She was blazing hot.

Alex climbed out of bed and wrapped his plaid around his waist. He did not bother with his belt but just tucked it closed. He rushed to the door and pulled it all the way open. Stepping into the passageway, he grabbed one of the lit torches from the sconce by his door. He moved across the landing to the top of the stairs. A few people had begun to move about in the Great Hall and others were beginning to awake.

Spying Elpeth, Hagatha's sister and head cook, he called down to her as quietly as he could.

"Elspeth. Elspeth."

"I hear ye, lad, and so will everyone else if ye keep squawking."

"Can ye fetch Aileen and Hagatha? She's spiked a high fever. She's drenched in sweat and feels like she's on fire." He turned back towards his chamber without waiting for Elspeth to respond. He knew Aileen and Hagatha, and probably a small army of women would soon be in his room. When he arrived, he pulled his leine over his head and rewrapped his plaid around his waist still not bothering to properly pleat it or to use a belt. He spotted the cup of now completely cold willow bark tea on the bedside table and felt horrible that he had completely forgotten to give it to her or to follow any of Aileen's instructions. He had fallen asleep twice without thinking about what the woman truly needed. He found the melted ice chips in a small bowl and gently lifting her head, he tipped the cold water to her lips. Brighde parted them as soon as she felt the liquid and allowed it to dribble down her throat. She seemed able to swallow even though she was not aware of what she did. Alex was careful not to give her too much as he remembered Aileen's warning that she could choke or retch if given too much at once. He had just resettled her on the pillow when Aileen, Hagatha, and his father entered the room.

All three took in his semi-state of undress and the clear indentations on the second pillow on the bed. As a one, they turned to look at him.

"Da, I didna do aught wrong. Well besides forgetting to give her the willow bark tea," he noted the last part as Aileen peered into the cup and shook her head. "I dozed off while sitting with her and woke in the middle of the night to her shivering. She was almost as cold as when I brought her inside. I stoked the fire and climbed into bed next to her. But only to share ma body heat. She seemed comfortable enough, and I must have fallen back to sleep. I awoke just moments ago to her feeling like she was on fire."

"This is exactly why I planned to stay here last night. The willow bark would nae have only eased her discomfort but helped lower a fever." Aileen looked up at him. While her words sounded accusatory, her tone was anything but. She looked from Alex's worried face to the woman and simply shook her head. "Ye didna do aught wrong. By warming her, ye probably saved her life more than the tea would have. The fever means her body is trying to fight off the infections. If she had frozen overnight, well—" Aileen trailed off as she moved about preparing a fresh cup of tea.

Alex moved out of the way of Aileen and Hagatha as they tended their patient. He ran his hand through his hair making it stick up on end. He desperately wanted to pace but knew that would not help anyone and would only cause him to be in the way. He looked over to his father who was intently watching him rather than the women with their patient. All he could do was shrug. He did not know what else to say to his father. He felt incredibly useless and not entirely convinced by Aileen's somewhat lackluster words of reassurance.

The Sinclair moved over to his son and draped his arm across his back drawing him towards the window. They stood looking at the bailey below as it began to come alive for yet another morning.

"Da, someone has beaten her. I dinna ken how she survived such a thrashing and then to have walked from God kens where to here. Those bruises are a couple of sennights old. I canna imagine where she came from or how far she walked, but she seemed intent to reach us for some reason. She seemed relieved to hear we are the Sinclairs."

"I ken, Alex. Hagatha and Aileen filled me in when they came below stairs. They said that she has been awfully mistreated, and it is a wonder that she made it here in one piece."

"Da, mistreated doesnae even begin to describe what I saw."

To this, Laird Sinclair raised one eyebrow.

"I'm telling ye, I didna do aught wrong. When I awoke the first time, she was shivering so hard that her small body was able to shake the bed. I kenned the only thing to do was for me to share ma body heat with her. I could have called Aileen or any of the other women, but truth be told, none of them would have provided as much warmth as I could. I took off my plaid and leine and climbed into bed next to her. Without lifting the covers, I was able to pull her nightgown up and rolled her onto her side. I kept my hands on the outside of the gown, but it was as I brushed my chest against her back that I heard her groan. Da, I barely touched her. I brought the light over and looked at her. Her back is covered with scratches and bruises. I rolled her onto her back and, aye, I did lift up her nightgown, but the sight that met me was the last thing I ever wanted to see. It's clear that someone did more than just beat her. They may have raped her, Da. She has pinch marks around her breasts, and now that the sun is coming into the chamber, I could see bruises around her neck from someone trying to strangle her."

"Alex, I ken all of this already. Aileen examined her thoroughly. She doesnae think the lass was raped, but it has been long enough now that she canna be sure until the lass can tell us herself."

"But who would have done something like this to her? Why? She looks to be tall and strong, but clearly no match for a mon."

"I suspect that whoever beat her did so because she rejected him. There are few times where even an angry mon would do so much damage. This looks like wounded pride along with anger. This was punishment." The Sinclair looked back over his shoulder and shook his head. It was close to only a year ago that his own daughter had been abducted and beaten by a rejected suitor, but even Mairghread's injuries seemed inconsequential compared to what he could see and had heard of this woman's condition.

"What're we going to do then?" Alex felt helpless for the first time since his mother had grown ill and then passed away. He and his brothers easily stood taller and broader than most men. Alone, they were each a force to be reckoned with, and as a team, they were virtually unstoppable. The only time they had not been able to win was as their mother lay dying. Alex had the same feeling now as he looked back at the slight form that was covered with a mountain of blankets and plaids. She seemed so tiny all of a sudden. As though she had shrunk in just the few minutes that he had turned away.

"We will tend to her for as long as she needs and then offer sanctuary for as long as she wants."

"And if whoever did this finds her and comes for her?"

"Find whom?" Alexander's father gave him a pointed look.

"Thank ye, Da." He allowed his father to pull him in for a bear hug. Unlike most men or even most noble families, the Sinclairs never shied away from showing their affection to one another. Even at almost a score and a half, Alexander still felt comfort and safety when embraced by his father. Nothing had changed since he was a lad. He had a healthy fear and respect for the man who could still thrash him and his brothers in the lists, but he also knew that his father would give his life without a second thought for him and his siblings. Alex admired his father and hoped one day to be the kind of father and husband Alex had seen modeled all of his life.

Chapter Two

The next fortnight was merely a blur to Alex. His brothers had returned with Siùsan who seemed much more enamored with his older brother, Callum, than when she ran off. They had come to some type of truce before they returned to the castle. He was aware that life was being lived beyond his door and that he was missing much of it, but he could not tear himself away. He found that his feelings were often conflicted these days. One moment he regretted alienating his family and ignoring his other responsibilities, and in the next moment, he felt completely justified in staying in his chambers to tend to his ward. Sometime after the first day, he had come to think of her like that because he could not think of a better word. He felt a need and duty to protect her that compelled him to stay by her side. If anyone asked him to describe his idea of a ward only a fortnight ago, he would have said a young child or an old widow. The woman who lay still unconscious in his bed was certainly neither of those.

The fever raged for nearly a full fortnight before breaking. Then it often came back at night. Ice baths, cold compresses, and willow bark tea barely put a dent in the fire that latched onto a body that seemed to be fading away more and more each day. Alex had seen for himself that Brighde was already exceedingly slim when she arrived, but after two sennights of being bedridden, she was painfully thin. The healer gave her as much beef broth as Brighde could manage, but there was little more that could be given to her without her casting up her accounts. Even watery porridge came right back up. Milky mashed potatoes worked the first two times it was given to her, and then it, too, began to come back up almost as soon as it was fed to her. Elspeth had even sent up blancmange hoping that its smooth consistency would stay down, and its sweetness would revive her a bit. Nothing worked. Alexander stood or sat helplessly watching her shrink before his eyes.

Brighde mumbled often in her delirium, but her words were never intelligible. She thrashed about when in the throes of her fever. Sometimes it appeared that she was trying to escape from an unseen foe, and other times she was fighting against some invisible enemy. It was during those times that Alexander truly feared what he might learn once she awoke. Her moans were ones of pure anguish, and Alex felt more and more useless by the day. The best that he could do was to keep cool compresses on her head when her fever spiked and spoon Aileen's concoctions into her. The tinctures progressed beyond willow bark tea. To relieve the pain that was obvious whenever Brighde moved and to fight the fever, Aileen made a mixture of henbane, mandrake, hops, and cloves. She refused to even consider using wolf's bane or nightshade since Brighde lost so much weight so quickly. Aileen was not convinced that there was a small enough dose of either that would still be safe. For the wounds on Brighde's feet, salves of yarrow and wormwood were made and applied multiple times throughout the day and night. She used honey to bind the ingredients and to draw out the puss from the infected cuts. Honey was also liberally used to help the tinctures go down.

Aileen ordered ice baths be brought up to Alex's chambers every night in preparation for the inevitable onslaught of fever. While Alex stepped out of the room multiple times a day to allow Aileen and the other women to tend to Brighde's more private needs, he remained to assist with moving her in and out of the tub. He tried his best to avert his eyes when he lifted her from the tub. The white chemises that were lent to her became barely more than gauze once they were wet. They left nothing to the imagination. As a healthy and warm-blooded man, he caught himself more than once looking where he knew he should not. Guilt for taking advantage of his ward when she could do nothing to defend herself made him sick and brought on a self-loathing he had never felt before.

During these first two sennights, Alexander ate little and only left his chambers when he absolutely had to. It was only at his new sister's-by-marriage insistence that he went onto the wall walk at least twice a day for some sunshine and fresh air. It was Siùsan's steadfast agreement to not leave the room until he returned that convinced him to go. She swore that she would only leave if it was to find him if anything changed. The stress and strain were beginning to take their toll on him.

After the first fortnight passed, there were moments when her eyes flashed open, and she seemed to look around, but her eyes were still fever hazed, and she never said anything. She drifted back to sleep almost as abruptly as she awoke. These glimpses of hope that were then dashed when she slipped back into unconsciousness were the hardest moments that Alex could ever remember. The false sense of hope that they gave was brutally ripped away when it was days between these wakeful moments.

Alexander barely noticed that his brothers were planning another journey with Siùsan. It barely registered that this meant the only other caretaker that he trusted besides Hagatha and Aileen would no longer be able to help. Nothing that did not pertain to the ill woman in his bed seemed to permeate his mind.

Nearly a month had passed since his unexpected guest's arrival when he was summoned to his father's solar. He was wary of leaving Brighde and what he would hear once he was there. He was in no mood to hear any more teasing about his infatuation, obsession, inexplicable drive to be near his mystery guest, or whatever it was that he felt. However, he knew it would be far worse if he did not make an appearance.

Alexander entered the solar with a scowl on his face that made even his brothers take a step back. Alex might have tended to seem withdrawn at times, but that was generally because he was observing and assessing his surroundings before making any decisions or taking any actions. His mood now was entirely different. It was withdrawn and defensive. An aura of frustration and anger exuded from him, and there was a restlessness that his family had never seen before.

"I'd like the four of ye to travel with Siùsan and at least half a score of guards. I dinna want to take any chances with another attack."

Alex was having a hard time following his father's words. *An attack? Och, Christ on the cross! How could I forget that Callum and the others were ambushed while returning with his little runaway bride? Wait. He wants the four of us. Like bluidy hell, I'm going anywhere.*

Alex was only vaguely aware of the conversation continuing around him until all eyes seemed to be on him. He only then noticed that his hands kept fisting and unfisting. *I canna deny Da, but I sure as shite am not leaving here.* Alex could feel his temper rising the longer they all stood about especially with four sets of eyes staring at him.

"Da, ye ken I am the only one here that she really kens. With Siùsan leaving, there is nay body else to care for her. I dinna want her frightened when she awakes if I turn up gone and she feels trapped in an unfamiliar keep with an unfamiliar clan." Alex stared at his father and held his breath.

"Ye can stay."

Those three words felt like a punch in the gut and a hug all at the same time. He had been prepared to launch into an argument with anyone who would listen, so to hear his father so readily agree with him nearly stole the breath from his lungs. Somewhere in the background, he could hear Tavish speaking. It was the next words from his father that finally registered.

"I ken now that he's serious enough aboot the lass to put up and argument against leaving her somewhere unknown. I ken more from watching him than from his words."

Alex was the last to leave his father's solar. He regretted the feelings of anger and the temptation to deny his father. He knew that if ordered, he would have refused his father for the first time in his life. This realization was confusing and disconcerting. The woman had barely said more than ten words to him, and yet he was willing to put aside his duties to his family for her.

"Son, dinna fash over wanting to stay here. I kenned how ye felt before I said aught, but I wanted to be sure. What I dinna ken is why ye feel so strongly."

"Da, I honestly canna say. She was so desperate to reach us, and when I went out to meet her by the gate, something about her took ma breath away. She was clearly beautiful even in such a bedraggled state, but it was more than that. The determination and helplessness should not have gone together, but I could feel them. Having seen the extent of her injuries, I feel a mixture of savage rage towards whoever did this to her, regret that I did not ken her to protect and prevent this, and an overwhelming admiration and respect for the willpower she needed to survive. I dinna ken how else to describe it. I feel so useless. Besides when Mama got sick, this is the only time in my life where neither reason nor brute force can solve the problem. I canna will her better. I canna fight the imaginary demons that she battles. I was the only Sinclair that she met, and the last face she's seen in almost a moon. I dinna want one of these times she awakes to be the one time she understands what is happening and nae have anyone she might recognize be there."

"Ye dinna need to explain any more to me, Alex. I understand more than ye realize. I dinna think many people remember, but yer Mama fell ill within sennights of our wedding. Ye ken that ours was an arranged marriage, and we had only gotten to ken each other for a brief time before we wed. Something drew me to yer Mama during those few short weeks, and I was beguiled by her during our wedding, but we didna have much chance to be married before she became gravely ill. I thought I was going to lose ma wife before I even had a chance to completely get to ken her. I was just as ye are. No one could convince me to leave her side. Everyone thought I was just a young and devoted husband. That I was enamored with her because of her beauty and whatever we may have done in our chamber. But that had absolutely naught to do with it. Aye, yer Mama was to this day the bonniest woman I have ever seen, but it was something more that drew me in. It was more of what I kenned she must have endured while with her own clan. Her father, the old Sutherland laird, was a hard and unforgiving mon. He wasna kind or patient with anyone. I saw the scars yer mama tried to hide. I saw the fading bruises that she thought had healed. I kenned she must have survived much before she arrived here. I admired her strength and grace because she survived her father's beatings, her brothers' taunting, her mother's willingness to overlook what befell ma Kyla, and was still kind and big-hearted to all those who were around her. The good Lord works in ways we may never understand, and sometimes He brings people to us without an obvious explanation. I think this woman may vera well be yer Kyla, lad. If she is, then I pray ye have a long and happy life together. But just be prepared, son. She might nae recognize ye or remember ye. She might nae be as eager to form an attachment as ye are. Ye must be prepared to give her space."

"Aye, Da. I didna ken all of that aboot ye and Mama. It makes sense though. I will take yer words to heart."

Chapter Three

*H*ow am I so hot again? Will I never get away from this fire? I canna see the flames, but they are eating me alive. Where is it coming from? Why willna anyone move me away from it? Dinna they hear me? I canna scream any louder.

The pleas for help rattled around in Brighde's head but never escaped her mouth. The intense pain that seemed to just seep throughout her body was more than she could bear most of the time. The blackness that engulfed her over and over was the only relief.

Holy witch's tits, that's bluidy cold! What is happening to me? I didna see a loch nearby, so how could I have fallen into one? If I could just open ma eyes. If I could just see through this infernal darkness. Hasnae that storm ended yet? I must make it to the Sinclairs. They can help me. But what if they dinna want to? What then? Where do I go if they willna take me in? So many questions. I just need to rest. More sleep is all I need.

Brighde thrashed about trying over and over again to climb out of the frozen loch she must surely have fallen into. Her mind could not resolve the freezing water to the summer storm she last remembered.

I must eat. I am starving. How long has it been since I last ate? Berries. Berries the day before the last storm. I ate some of those. Perhaps they didna agree with me, and that is why ma mind plays such tricks on me. Mayhap they were those berries that Mama warned me about. The ones that would make me see hobgoblins and wraiths. There are nay such things as ghosts and ghouls. It must have been the berries. They've left such a bitter taste in ma mouth. I canna find anything to drink to rinse them away. Why do they sometimes taste like potatoes?

Brighde was so hungry that she was sure that her belly was slowly eating her from the inside out just so she could stay alive. Her thirst overwhelmed her to the point where she once again welcomed the dark to escape one more source of discomfort.

Where is that light coming from? Where are the people I can hear? That mon's voice is so familiar. I canna place where I ken it from. I ken he isnae from ma clan. I ken I havenae heard the voice often, but it is so clear to me. I can hear him so often, but I canna seem to remember what he says. Why canna I answer him? Do I answer him, but he doesnae hear me?

Time and again, Brighde thought she recognized the voice, and she even thought it might belong to that handsome angel she saw just before she passed through the earthly veil. After all, she asked herself over and over, where else could she be where she could hear voices and sense people nearby but could not see anyone. She had always imagined heaven to be much brighter. The darkness made her wonder if her sins had sent her to purgatory or hell instead of heaven to be with her mama and grandmama.

How much longer must I wander in the dark? Even Jesus had light when he was in the desert. Have I been here for forty days and forty nights? Is this God's test of ma faith? I havenae forsaken ye, oh Lord, I just dinna obey ma earthly father. If I agree to ma father's demands, will that be enough, Lord? Heavenly Father, please dinna make me. Please, isnae there aught else I can do? There's that voice again. God, is this mon speaking to me? Why can I hear him, but he canna hear me? I answer him every time, but he talks over me as though he doesnae ken I'm talking. He doesnae answer ma questions even though I answer his.

Brighde's mind rebelled against the darkness that enveloped her day after day, night after night. Her mind knew that much time had passed, but she could not begin to reason just how long. She felt herself running towards the light that always seemed to vanish just as she reached it. At other times, she felt like she was walking with a veil over her head that was too thick to see through. The people around her could see her, but she could not see them. Her body felt like a led weight. As hard as she tried to lift her arms, they never seemed to cooperate. She could not fight the frustration, anger, and fear that seemed to progressively suffocate her. Just when she thought she could take no more, she began to see people when she reached the light.

I see them! I think they can see me too. They speak to me, but why dinna they listen to me when I talk. They keep asking me the same questions but dinna listen when I answer. This is so exhausting. I canna keep ma eyes open for long. Ma body aches everywhere, but at least I dinna feel on fire as often anymore. That is one small relief. Mayhap tomorrow I will keep ma eyes open for just a moment longer. Mayhap tomorrow I will talk just a little louder.

This semi-aware state persisted for a fortnight. During this time, Brighde found she was able to see a little more each time she opened her eyes. Her thoughts came to her faster, and it did not feel like her mind was mixed with pea soup. But no one ever seemed to listen to her. Brighde was surprised that these angels wore the same clothes as she had before she died. She thought they might all wear white robes. She was pleased that these celestial beings spoke the same language as she did, but she wondered if she was talking tongues, just like the Bible story.

Mayhap that is why they dinna understand me. Mayhap they speak in tongues, and I can understand them just as the apostles and disciples understood one another. But that doesnae make any sense. If I can understand them, they should be able to understand ma tongue. Pentecost would surely explain the never-ending, infernal heat. Or mayhap those really were the flames of hell. Purgatory. I truly am dead and caught between heaven and hell. That is the only answer.

~~~

Alex's hand twitched. As he slowly came awake, he thought it was a fly that landed on his hand, and in his sleep, he shooed it away. Except it was not his hand twitching. It was the feel of someone squeezing it ever so softly. With this realization, Alex came fully awake. He looked up to see a pair of light grey eyes staring at him. They were so light that they looked almost translucent and silver. He had seen these eyes several times before, but now they were not clouded by fever and pain. He looked down at his own hand that held such a frail and tiny one. He felt the light pressure once again. He shook his head in disbelief. She was awake. More than that, this mysterious woman who had spent nearly a moon unconscious in his bed was trying to tell him something. Something that he could actually make out as words rather than just sounds.

"Water," was what he heard whispered. Once again, he looked down at their joined hands. Sometime during her first sennight there, he had made a habit of holding her hand while they slept. He sat in the chair next to the bed and rested his head on the mattress. He held her hand and could feel when she became agitated from fever. It was this habit that made him aware that she was finally conscious.

"Aye. Just a moment, lass."

Alexander let go of her hand to reach for the cup that was always beside the bed. He reached over and gently lifted her head from the pillow as he brought the cup to her lips. He slowly tilted it to her, but after only a sip, he began to pull away. Her tiny hand grasped his with a surprising strength as she tried to press the cup back to her mouth.

"Nay, lass. I ken ye must be dying of thirst, but too much too fast after so long will only make ye sick again."

"How can I be so thirsty when I am dead?" Her voice was so hoarse from a month of disuse that she did not recognize the croaking sound she made.

"Aingeal, ye are nae dead." Alex could not help the small smile that played around the corners of his mouth. He had never felt such relief as he did now that he was having a conversation with the person who filled his every waking and most of his sleeping moments for the past moon.

"If I amnae dead, then why call me an angel?"

"Ye be the fairest sight I have ever seen. Only heaven could have created , something so lovely." Alex could have swallowed his tongue as he listened to what he said. *When the hell did I become a bluidy bard?*

Brighde was too weak to do little more than nod her head.

"If I amnae dead, then where am I? Werenae ye the mon I met by a gate? Ye're a Sinclair?"

"Aye to both of yer questions. I am the mon who came to meet ye at the gate. I am Alexander Sinclair. Alex. I brought ye inside from the storm. Lass, ye have been vera poorly for nearly a moon. Do ye remember aught of what has happened?"

Brighde shook her head, but it only made it hurt. She reached up to grasp her forehead and moaned.

"Rest, mo aingeal. There isnae any rush to remember. We can speak more later when it is morn."

"Nay," she rasped. She shook her head slightly. "Too much sleep."

"Ye still have a ways to go before ye are fully well. Ye still need rest."

"Nae more rest. Food." Brighde could barely produce more than a whisper. Alexander struggled to hear everything that she said and had to guess a few times.

"I will call the healer, and she can decide what ye might be able to have. Just a moment."

Alexander rushed into the passageway but did not have to go far before he ran into Aileen who had a fresh tincture in her hands.

"She's awake, Aileen. She's spoken to me and made sense."

Alex turned around and returned to his chamber before Aileen could respond. He resumed his seat next to Brighde. He noted that she watched keenly as he moved about the room and eyed Aileen like a hawk when she passed through the doorway.

"Lass, we are so glad ye are awake now. We have all been vera worried about ye. How do ye feel?"

Brighde looked first to Alexander and then to a woman whose voice she recognized but could not recollect her face. When she looked back at Alex, he nodded and encouraged her to speak by squeezing her hand. They both looked down in surprise at where their hands were joined. Neither had noticed; it just seemed natural after so many nights spent with her hand in Alex's.

"I feel quite a bit better, I suppose."

Alex's head jerked up when he heard her speak. Not only was this the most she had said so far and her voice was growing stronger than it had been, she suddenly had a very different accent.

"Aye. I'm vera glad to hear that. I imagine ye are more than a mite peckish after all this time. I will bring up some pottage, but ye canna have too much as first. Ye havenae had a real meal in more than a moon, so too much will make ye feel vera ill. Ye willna keep it all down if ye rush." Aileen moved about the bedside as she checked

Brighde's head for any lingering signs of fever. She also looked at the soles of her feet. Most of the cuts had nearly healed over with only a few still having scabs.

After Aileen left, Alex watched Brighde very closely. He was completely confused by what he heard. Her voice had not been strong when she awoke, but he was certain he heard her speak with a Scottish accent both that day and just before she collapsed in his arms. He did not have a chance to question her because Hagatha appeared with a team of women.

"Out with ye, Alex. Ye can see she is far better than she was and probably would like to refresh herself. She canna do that with ye hovering like a mother hen." Hagatha tugged none too gently on his leine. When he stood, she pushed him towards the door. Before leaving, he looked back over his shoulder and found Brighde watching him even with the flock of women fussing over her.

Chapter Four

$\mathcal{A}$ lexander made his way to the Great Hall for the first time in what felt like forever. He joined his father on the dais. As he looked around the clansmen and women who had bedded down for the night, he was struck with a sense of how far removed he had become from the people he had known his entire life and who he normally saw daily.

"I hear yer lass is finally awake and nae just the hazy stare she's had for the past sennight or so. How does she fair?"

"I wouldnae say she is ma lass, Da. We dinna ken each other, and I dinna think she would care for that title when she isnae even sure who I am beyond ma name." He shrugged and looked back over his shoulder to the stairs that led to his chamber. "But she is awake and speaking. She hasnae said much beyond being thirsty, hungry, feeling better, and wondering where she is. I suppose all the basics considering the situation. I dinna ken much more than that."

"I'd say that's quite a good deal of information considering she hasnae spoken in over a moon, and we were nae too sure she would make it."

"I suppose more will come with time."

"Ye have the right of it. In the meantime, ye could do with a hearty meal and a good long bath of yer own." The Sinclair chuckled as he watched his son try to discreetly give himself a sniff. "Ye arenae that bad, but a sluice down wouldnae be remiss. Besides, the lass isnae the only one who is fading away. Ye've lost quite a bit of weight too. I dinna ken if ye'll be able to lift yer sword in the lists tomorrow."

Alex looked at his father and the twinkle in his eye matched the one in his father's.

"Alright, auld mon. Dinna get too carried away. Ye ken that pride goeth before the fall. I will hold ma own against ye or any mon any day of the sennight and twice on Sundays."

Alex could not hold back a laugh. He had not realized how much he missed laughing until he heard how rusty his voice sounded. It felt good to be lighthearted about something after so much worry.

"What're ye doing up so late, Da?"

"Ah well, with yer brothers away and ye busy, I havenae had enough activity to wear me out. I amnae chasing after any of ye or breaking up yer spats."

"We arenae exactly bairns anymore, Da. Ye make it sound like we're still in short pants."

"None of ye are too braw for me to take a strap to ye." Once again, Alex laughed. Among him and his four siblings, they had often driven their father nearly to the brink, but he had never once thrashed any of them. A wee paddling with his hand from time to time, but that had not happened in nearly a score of years.

"Ye have to catch me first!"

"Dinna tempt me. I was enjoying a dram in peace before ye came down. Now either hie yerself off for a bath or to eat, or ye can pipe down and keep me and ma whisky company."

"Canna I do both? That is eat and keep ye company?"

"Of course, lad. Elspeth will have something brought out for ye."

Alexander and Liam settled into a casual conversation about all that had been happening in and around the keep since Alex's self-imposed sequestration. He had not realized just how much of life had passed him by while being nursemaid to his ward. He had only been out to the lists a handful of times while Brighde was in residence, worrying that she might awaken while he was away. He missed the time spent with the men, and he knew he had not been pulling his fair share of guard duty. Once again, part of him felt guilty for not keeping up with his responsibilities, but another part of him could not feel badly for caring for a woman that seemed so desperately in need of a champion and protector. Alex was determined to spend more time in the coming days overseeing the responsibilities that he was meant to have in his brother's stead, and he knew for his own wellbeing, he needed to go back to the lists and keep up on his training. A warrior never could tell when his skills might be tested. Being rusty was not an option. Time passed faster than he anticipated because he began to see his father stifle yawns, and his eyes were growing weary.

"Da, I think I will see if Hagatha will allow me to bathe in the kitchen. I will turn in shortly after that. I plan to be in the lists bright and early."

"Aye, well a little shut-eye does sound rather good. Goodnight, son."

"Goodnight, Da. And Da, thank ye."

Father and son looked at each other. For Liam, looking at his sons was like looking back in time to when he was younger. For the Sinclair brothers, looking at their father was like catching a glimpse of their future. Father and son embraced and moved off in separate directions. Alex made his way to the kitchens.

Hagatha and Elspeth were the last two in the kitchens. The sisters were sharing a hobnob and a warm chamomile drink. They looked up as he entered the kitchens.

Both women had been working in the keep since well before he or his older brother, Callum, were born. After his mother died, they stepped in to care for four children whose father was grieving and ruling a clan. While Liam Sinclair made more time for his children than most of his noble peers, there were many duties that imposed upon his time. Hagatha and Elspeth saw four children who were hurting and in need of love and guidance that only a mother could offer. Neither sought to replace the lady of the clan, but they both became more like much loved and respected aunts. Even though they maintained their status and duties as servants, all of the Sinclair children adored the women and loved them like family.

"Ladies, would it be too much of an inconvenience for me to bathe in here?"

"Ladies. Do ye hear the silver-tongued devil, Hagatha? Dinna need to flatter us. Ye ken we wouldnae say nay."

"Mayhap so, but it doesnae hurt to keep me in yer good graces." He walked over to both women and pecked them on the cheek.

"Get an ear full of his nibs." Elspeth could not help but smile despite trying to look stern. Both Hagatha and Elspeth were relieved to see Alexander leave his chamber and banter with them. "Hie yerself off and leave us to our chatter."

Alexander smiled over his shoulder as he moved to the far side of the kitchens and filled the metal tub that was permanently stored near the hearth. When he was dry, he realized he had not brought any clean clothes with him, so he wrapped his plaid around him and went up the back stairs to his chamber. He eased the door open and slipped into the room. He did not want to disturb Brighde nor startle her now that she was back in the land of the living.

The room was dimly lit only by the low fire behind the grate and a candle on one of the bedside tables. He crept in and moved silently to his trunk. He lifted the lid and cringed when it squeaked. He popped his head up to check and found himself staring into deep grey eyes that were wide with surprise but curious.

"Dinna fash. I dinna mean to wake ye, lass. I just came for fresh clothes." He pulled a clean leine from the stack and stood up. He almost laughed when her eyes widened even more. It would have been comical, but he did not want to embarrass her.

"What are you doing with clothes in here?" She looked around the room as if seeing it for the first time. "This is your chamber." She shook her head and looked around again.

"You gave up your chamber for me. Why would you do that?"

"Dinna ye remember what happened when ye arrived outside our gates?"

She only shook her head.

"Ye asked for help and asked which clan we are. After I told ye we are the Sinclairs, ye collapsed in ma arms. Ye were soaked through and shaking while unconscious. I didna give it much thought beyond getting ye to the closest chamber where there was a fire and ye could be tended to by the healer. None of the guest chambers on the next floor had a fire lit. My brothers arenae here now, so none of their chambers had fires lit either."

"But I have been here quite some time now, haven't I?"

"Aye, aboot a moon."

"A month? I've been ill for almost a month? I never get sick let alone for that long."

"Well, ye seemed to have been out in the elements for a good long while before ye made it here. And ye looked a little worse for wear."

A look flashed across Brighde's face that made it plainly clear to Alex that she did not appreciate his assessment of her condition when she arrived.

"Yes, well, it was a long and eventful journey to get here." Alex was about to ask her why she came and how she had come to be traveling alone, but she spoke before he could. "If you don't mind, I would like to go back to sleep. I know I have spent the last month asleep, but I am suddenly very tired again."

"Of course, lass. I dinna mean to disturb ye." Alex turned to walk out of the door but was stopped when he heard her raspy voice.

"If this is your chamber, where have you been sleeping?"

Alex slowly turned around. He saw the genuinely perplexed look and was not sure quite how to explain his actions of the past month. He walked back towards the side of the bed on which she was now propped up.

"I stayed in here most of the time. Ye were vera poorly and required constant observation."

"And you believed that should have been you? Do you not have any women here? I met your healer and housekeeper. Are there no others? You must be quite a small clan in that case." Alex could hear the touch of steel in her voice and the disapproval was clear.

"Nay. We have enough women here. I stayed because I didna want ye to wake and not recognize or ken anyone around ye. I thought mayhap ye would recognize and remember me. I thought it might reassure ye that ye are safe here." Alex watched for her response to decide if he should tell her anymore.

Brighde simply nodded and looked at the giant of a man who had been by her side when she awoke. She had been very confused, but she also recognized his voice immediately, not from when she arrived at the keep but while she was in her deep slumber. She also recognized his scent wafted to her when he left the chamber earlier that evening. She could smell it even more clearly now that he was freshly bathed. There was something deeply reassuring and grounding about recognizing it. She could see the water dripping from the ends of his hair. Her eyes traveled from the hair that brushed the back of his neck to his broad shoulders. They traveled over his expansive chest down to the rippled muscles of his abdomen. When they arrived at his trim waist with a plaid tucked around it, she dropped her eyes down and saw his bare calves and feet. She almost yelped when she saw him wiggle his toes. Her head shot back up to see him smiling at her. She shook her head slightly to clear her mind.

"Once you knew I was no longer in danger from the fever, why did you not move me to another chamber? And you said you stayed here, but you didn't say where in here?" Her eyes narrowed slightly, and her shoulders crept up in a defensive posture.

"I slept in this chair most nights," Alex rested his hand on the back of the chair next to him, "or I slept near the hearth. I didna have ye moved because ye were vera poorly until just a day or so ago. Yer fever kept coming back at night. I didna want ye jostled or disturbed."

"You didn't." She raised one eyebrow. "Doesn't your healer usually make those decisions?"

"Aye, and she agreed with me." Alex was beginning to feel a little defensive. He reverted to his usual stance which was his feet hip-width apart and arms crossed. He knew it was intimidating, but he also knew that he felt most comfortable and guarded in this position.

Brighde could not take her eyes off the muscles that rippled through Alex's chest, shoulders, and arms as he stood looking down at her. Somewhere in the back of her mind, it registered with her that she should be intimidated by such a large man looming over her when she was in such a compromised position and alone with him. However, there was something about this man that brought her more reassurance than fear. She felt safe in a way that she had not since she was a child. She could not quite pinpoint what it was about him that made her positive that he would never harm her, but she felt it as deeply as she had the fear that drove her to the Sinclairs.

"You don't need to stand there like that."

"Like what?" Alex was intentionally being obtuse.

She waved a hand in his direction before looking up at his whisky brown eyes.

"Like you might intimidate me. I already know you won't hurt me, so you don't scare me."

"Ye are either vera foolish or vera naïve to underestimate a mon."

"I don't underestimate you at all. How could I when almost every muscle is on display." She waved her hand in his direction again. "No, I meant that I know you would not hurt *me*. You might hurt someone else, but if you wanted to hurt me, you would have already. No, I believe you mean me no harm. You brought me into your home and gave up your chamber for me, and not for a short time either. That does not seem to be the behavior of a man who is trying to intimidate or harm me. I'd say just the opposite." With that Brighde clamped her mouth shut. It was one thing to

28

assert herself, but it was entirely another to say enough to antagonize him. She had no intention of testing her theory.

"Aye, ye may have the right of it." He uncrossed his arms. "But nae all men are like the Sinclairs. We dinna abide by anyone harming women, be they our clan's women or nae. But nae everyone is of the same mind. Dinna let yer guard down until ye ken for sure the mon can be trusted."

"Does that mean you believe I think you can be trusted?"

"Ye arenae screaming bluidy murder to find a strange mon in yer chamber."

"True, and it is your chamber after all. There is just something very familiar about you. I feel like I know you somehow. I recognize your voice from when I was ill. I feel like I heard it often."

"That would be a possibility since I was here often, and I spoke to ye throughout the day. The healer believed that ye could hear those around ye, and that might help ye fight back to life."

Brighde tried to stifle a yawn behind her hand and nodded. Alexander walked towards the fire and added another block of peat. He went to the door and paused.

"Lass, ye have me at a bit of a disadvantage. Ye already ken I am Alexander, Alex, Sinclair, but I dinna ken who ye are."

"Mary."

Alex raised an eyebrow and cocked his to the side waiting for her to elaborate, but when nothing was forthcoming, he nodded his head.

"Sleep well and dinna hesitate to call out if ye need aught."

"If I called out, who would hear me? There isn't anyone else here."

"I will be just outside the door."

"You will? Why?"

Alex shrugged. "Ye are awake now. I canna vera well stay in here, but ye havenae been awake long. If ye need something, someone needs to be close by."

"Then why not the healer or the housekeeper? What was her name again?"

"Hagatha and they have all sought their beds already. Goodnight, lass."

"Goodnight," Brighde whispered.

~~~

"*Nay! Nay! Dinna!*"

Alex awoke with a start. He shook his head and looked around to determine what woke him. He scrubbed his hands over his face and yawned. He was just about to close his eyes again when he heard a blood-curdling scream come from within his chamber. He was on his feet before he realized it and was already pulling his sword from its scabbard. He put his ear to the door but could not hear anyone moving about. He could hear whimpering and his heart began to pound in double time.

29

Cautiously, in case there was someone in the chamber, he pushed the door open. He scanned the room, but there was no one in sight other than the small form that lay thrashing on his bed. He lowered his sword and looked around once more. Convinced that they were alone, he returned his sword to its scabbard and leaned it next to the foot of the bed. He walked over to the side of the bed and gently placed his hand on Brighde's forehead. He did not feel any signs of fever.

"Lass." He tried to gently shake her shoulder, but she was too deeply in the throes of her nightmare. "Mary." He shook her a little harder hoping that he could wake her from whatever was terrorizing her sleep.

"Nay. Dinna take me." Alex had to lean forward to hear what Brighde now whispered. He could barely hear her. She continued to thrash about in her sleep, but now Alex could see big, fat tears leak from the corners of her eyes. Her thrashing suddenly ceased, and she began to whimper. Alex was at a loss as to what to do. As her whimpers became sobs, he made a decision and scooped her into his arms. He sat down on the bed with his back against the wall and cradled her in his arms.

"Shh, lass. Ye're alright now. I have ye. I willna let aught happen to ye. Shh, aon bheag." She did seem like a little one as he gently rocked her until her tears slowed, and she finally began to breathe evenly. Her eyes gently fluttered open, but Alexander could see that her vision was still hazy. She blinked several times and took a deep breath. As Alex's fresh scent filled her senses, she nuzzled into his chest, burrowing her head against his shoulder. Her hand slowly reached for his chest, and when it brushed against his skin, Alex felt a tingle race through his entire body. Brighde's eyes drifted closed as her hand slid back and forth. The motion seemed to soothe them both, and Alex felt both of their bodies relax.

"Mary, lass. Are ye well?" Alex whispered next to her ear.

Brighde's hand stopped, and she opened her eyes. Alex watched her as she became alert to where she was. She leaned far enough away to be able to clearly see Alex's face, but she did not pull away.

"What happened? Why are you here?" Brighde suddenly felt very much awake as she realized that she was tucked into Alex's arms and sprawled across his lap.

"Ye were having a nightmare, mo leannan. I heard ye crying out while I was in the passageway. I came to be sure there wasna anyone harming ye, and when I saw nay one in here, I checked to see if yer fever returned. Ye were cool to ma hand, but ye began to cry. I didna ken what else to do, so I held ye. I dinna want ye to ever be scared while ye are here. I dinna ken what brought ye here, but I ken someone mistreated ye vera badly before ye arrived, and ye murmured quite a bit while fevered. Now ye've had a nightmare." He brushed the hair from her face while looking down into her silvery gray eyes. "I willna ask ye what happened, at least nae now, but I will make sure ye are always safe while ye are our guest here."

Brighde was so shaken by the nightmare, which she could only piece back together in her mind, and the gentleness of the man holding her that all she could do was nod. Alex's gaze traveled over her as if to reassure himself that she was truly well. He shifted and began to place her on the bed next to him. She grabbed the front of his leine and shook her head.

"Not yet. Please don't leave me yet." Brighde could not believe her ears that she was begging this man that she barely knew to stay in a bedchamber with her, alone, but she was too overwhelmed to let go of the only anchor she had. She felt more grounded when Alex was near. She did not understand the calm and excitement that alternately coursed through her when Alex was near, but she knew at that moment that she needed him and his strength.

"I willna leave ye. I will wait until ye drift back to sleep, then I will sleep next to the fire. I will leave before the sun rises and move back to the other side of the door. I dinna want anyone to talk out of turn about ye."

"Thank you," was followed by a yawn, and Brighde's eyes fluttered shut. She quickly settled into a deep sleep, and when Alex felt her breathing slow, he gently placed her back onto the mattress. He covered her with the sheet and a plaid and made his way over to the hearth where he settled down to spend an uneasy rest of the night. Worried that her nightmare might return, Alex never completely surrendered himself to sleep. As the first rays of light began to peek across the horizon, he slipped back into the passageway. He quickly fell asleep and was able to capture a couple of hours of sleep before the keep began to stir. Alex rubbed his eyes and stood up to stretch. He opened the door a sliver and looked in on Brighde who was now sleeping peacefully. He closed the door as quietly as he opened it.

Chapter Five

The next sennight passed like a blur for Alexander but felt interminable for Brighde. Alexander woke stiff and somewhat sore each morning from sleeping on the floor. Most nights he continued to sleep just outside the door to his chamber, but three nights were spent lying next to his hearth after calming Brighde's night terrors. He was awake before most of the keep, so he would check on Brighde, who often slept through most of the morning, before making his way into the kitchens where he grabbed a couple of apples and one of the first bowls of porridge being prepared. He made his rounds to check on the guardsmen who stood duty that night before, and once assured that all was as it should be, he made his way out to the lists. He ran through some exercises and drills to loosen his tight muscles before any of the other men arrived. He then spent the entire morning training. Almost half the week was spent having his noon meal of bread and cheese out on the training field. He came into the Great Hall for his noon meal only three times. The afternoons were spent checking in on Brighde and then assisting his father with clan business. He wanted to take all his evening meals with Brighde, but he understood that would only fuel the gossip that had begun to circulate after his month of playing nursemaid. He allowed himself three evenings of having his supper with her during which she spoke little but encouraged him to talk. She still grew tired easily and retired early. Alex would return to the Great Hall to sit before the fire with his father and discuss the day and plan for the next. Alex felt like he spent most of his day in motion, and it was a welcome relief after so much time spent indoors and worrying.

Brighde thought she was going to go stir crazy. Each day she felt a bit better but could admit to herself that she was still weaker than she had ever been before. Despite a month of being in a deep sleep, she tired easily and needed more than one nap a day. However, it was the hours that she was awake and alone that nearly drove her mad. She was eager to get out of bed for as long as she could. Alex brought her various books from his father's solar which she appreciated immensely. Without the books, she would have had nothing to do but stare at the walls. Until her desperate flight from pursuers, she had been a deep and sound sleeper. The two weeks of traveling alone made her wake easily to the smallest disturbance. She heard Alex move around every morning but decided the less said the better. She would creep to the window embrasure and watch Alex as he made his way out to the lists. From the height of the window and its position in the keep, she could just make him out when he was alone on the field. She also listened for the men to return to the keep for the afternoon, and if she was alone, she would sneak a look out of the window hoping to catch a glance. She was often rewarded with a view of him shirtless. She was becoming more and more accustomed to his presence throughout the day, and while she did not want to admit it, she longed for his company. Hagatha and Aileen visited her regularly, but it was never quite the same as when Alex came to see her. She encouraged him to do most of the talking even though she knew he wanted to question why she did not want to speak more. He had even mentioned once that her voice would only grow stronger if she practiced. She agreed and then suggested that he continue the story that he had been in the middle of telling. She learned a great deal about his childhood with four siblings. By the end of that sennight, she felt like she knew them personally without ever having seen them. Knowing that Alex would not be satisfied without her sharing at least some information about her past, she settled on the most neutral facts that she could think of, and they were the most obvious. She had a mother, a father, and two brothers who were older than she was, and four siblings who were younger than her. She told him of her garden and her dog, but when he began to press for details about why she left those behind, she feigned fatigue. She kept her voice to barely above a whisper even though she knew that it grew stronger each day since she practiced when she was alone. She moved about the room and walked circles around the perimeter to help her regain her strength. It was during one of these tours, that Alex came for an unexpected midmorning visit. He knocked so softly that she did not hear it before the door opened. She was near the window and spun around to see him watching her. She knew it was him before she saw him or even caught the scent of his freshly washed hair and skin. She noticed that he always made a point of being clean before he visited her even when she thought he came straight from training.

"Lass, it is good to see ye up and aboot. Ye are looking better each day. Far less peaky than even a couple of days ago." Alex left the door ajar and moved further into the room. When Brighde only nodded her head and tried to turn back to look out of the window, he moved swiftly across the room.

"Lass, has the cat gotten yer tongue of a sudden? Ye arenae even speaking to me today. Usually, I get at least a few words from ye even if ye keep pretending that ye can only whisper."

With this veiled accusation, Brighde turned fully towards Alex, arms crossed, and an eyebrow raised. She cocked her head to one side.

"Dinna think that standing there trying to challenge me is going to distract me from the fact that ye arenae actually talking."

He inched slightly closer without infringing on her personal space. She seemed used to his presence, but he saw her shrink back the first time she met his father. He could tell there was a fear of imposing men, which his father was without trying. He did not want her to ever feel threatened by him.

"Lass, if ye arenae going to speak, then I will tell ye what I have been thinking since the first time ye awoke." When she did not stop him, he continued. "I dinna believe ye are a Sassenach. Ye forget that ye spoke before ye collapsed. I also ken what I heard when ye first came round after being unconscious for a moon. And what ye have muttered in yer sleep."

"You must have heard incorrectly. The wind was blowing a gale." *Bluidy hell, now what am I to do? He canna have heard me say that much. I ken I can do this. I can keep this going. I've practiced this accent plenty over the years.*

"I ken what I heard. What are ye hiding? Or better yet, from whom are ye hiding? Lass, I canna protect ye if I dinna ken who the threat is or where it might come from. Ye clearly were running from something or someone."

Brighde turned her head to look out of the window and refused to look at him. He watched as her shoulders slowly crept towards her ears, and she seemed to huddle into herself.

"Now I ken for sure ye are hiding something. Have we nae offered ye the safety of our home? Have I done ought to harm ye?" *Why is she being so stubborn? What is she hiding from me? Dammit, I only want to protect her.*

She only shook her head and continued to look out of the window. Alex came to stand behind her and put his hands on her arms. It was the first time he touched her while she was awake that was not to soothe her after a nightmare. He felt her tense under his hands and released her as he took a step back. She whirled around so quickly that she bumped into his chest.

"You have not done anything to harm me, and I appreciate your generosity and hospitality. I regret that my stay may have been an imposition."

"Ye ken I never said that. I never even hinted at that. Ye were looking for the Sinclairs that night, and ye found us. Why canna ye tell me the reason for coming to us?"

"I knew that I traveled north, and I heard from a village about a day away that yours was the next castle. With the storm, I was unsure that I hadn't lost my sense of direction. I was just glad that I finally knew where I was."

"That dinna ring true, and ye ken it. What are ye hiding? Who are ye hiding from?" *I dinna want to bully her, but I will get the truth sooner or later. I just want it to be sooner.*

"I am not hiding." *Like a dog with a bone, he is.* She had to tilt her head back all the way to look up at him when she stood this close. He towered over her, and she was considered fairly tall for a woman. She watched as his jaw set, and she saw his arms move as though he wanted to cross them. His feet had somehow spread slightly. She had seen this stance from both him and his father when they spoke to the men in the bailey or when she saw the men greeting Alex in the lists. She came to recognize it as his most comfortable way of standing. It just happened to be imposing and intimidating. She gave him a mutinous glare and moved to step around him. His hand shot out with lightning speed but grasped her arm with the force of a butterfly. She could have broken away easily, but something held her in place.

Both of them stood staring at the other while some type of invisible message passed between them. One that neither of them could see or hear, but they both sensed. Neither of them seemed willing to pull away, but neither was sure of what move to make next as the moment drew out. They were drawn together like a lodestone, leaning towards each other. Alex gently brushed the hair from Brighde's cheek and tucked it behind her ear. Her hand absentmindedly plucked at a loose thread on his leine. Neither could take their eyes off the other, and time stilled as Alex leaned forward. As his lips brushed hers, she spread her palms on his chest, and when she did not push him away, Alex pressed his mouth against hers a little more firmly. He did not want to scare her, but when her hands fisted into the front of his shirt, he pulled her more tightly into his embrace. With his feet parted, she fit perfectly in his arms. If asked who deepened the kiss first, neither would have been able to answer. The kiss began to take on a nature of its own, growing in heat and intensity. Alex brushed his thumb along her jaw and pressed lightly on her chin as his tongue slowly swept across the seal of her lips. Brighde was not sure what he wanted her to do, but what her mind did not know, her body seemed to. She opened her mouth and felt the velvety smoothness of his tongue move inside. It swept around her mouth and twirled with hers. Alex's hand slid back to cradle her head as his other arm pulled her in yet again. Brighde's arms crept up to wrap around Alex's neck, and she stood on her tiptoes to reach him better. Tentatively, she brushed her tongue against his and then slid it into his mouth where it was warm and tasted of mint. She did not recognize the mewling sound she heard as coming from her until she also heard a growl of pleasure come from Alex. She could feel the vibration from the back of his throat against her tongue. It was all she needed to hear to make her press her soft and malleable body against the hard and immovable planes of his. The arm wrapped around her waist slid down to her backside and rested there. When

Brighde moaned softly, Alex firmed his grip and walked them towards the wall. When Brighde's back brushed against it, he lifted her off her feet. Before either could think about it, her legs wrapped around his waist. Now even in height, their kiss became almost uncontrollable. Somewhere in the back of his mind, Alex knew he should stop. He knew from her initial kiss that she was inexperienced and that this was her first taste of passion. He knew he should be the responsible one since he clearly had far more experience, but no rational thought could have made him pull away. He drank up the sweet taste of her mouth as he gripped her backside tighter. He felt her press her core against his groin, and he thanked God that his sporran hid is rock hard cock. While all he wanted to do was plunge into her again and again until they both found their release, he knew that feeling such a turgid erection would probably terrify her.

Christ on the cross, I have never wanted a woman so damned much. I could spill maself now without her even touching ma cock. I want to taste every inch of her and drive ma cock into her until she's screaming ma bluidy name. Sweet Jesu, she feels so good. I dinna want to frighten her, but good God I want to stick ma hands under her skirts and feel her juices on ma fingers.

Brighde ran her hands through Alex's hair marveling at how soft it was. Her fingers played against the rough bristle on his cheeks and then slid to the sinews of his shoulders. Her fingers could not get enough of the sensation of touching him. She thought and wondered constantly about what he would feel like to touch. He held her after her nightmares more than once, and she felt a cocoon of warmth and security each time, but she had also been so exhausted that she had not been able to fully enjoy the feel of being pressed against him. Now she wanted to absorb every detail. She could feel her core aching as she tried to get even closer. It was almost as though she wanted to climb inside of him, frustrated that there was no way to get any closer. Her legs squeezed him, and she became aware of how her hips ground into his lower abdomen.

What has come over me? He will think me loose and wanton. I didna want him to think I'm a whore, but my goodness, what is he doing to me? I'm on fire, and I ache for him. I dinna ken what is happening to me, but I feel empty and like he is the only one who can make that feeling go away.

It was only when she moaned softly in frustration, that Alex was able to pull himself away. Their kiss escalated far faster than any other Alex had ever shared. He barely remembered moving her against the wall, nor did he notice when his own hips began to grind into hers. He slowly kissed a trail along her chin to her ear where he then trailed his tongue down the side of her neck. He nipped lightly where her neck met her shoulder. Her head fell back and to the side offering him greater access. He could feel the darts that were her nipples as they pressed through the flannel nightgown and his leine. Both of his hands gripped her buttocks now, and the desire to enter her was almost overwhelming. It was only when he felt his cock leak a drop of seed that he forced himself to stop. He rested his forehead against hers as they both tried to catch their breath.

"Lass, that was far and away the greatest thing I have ever experienced."

"Aye, ye have the right of it." As soon as the words left her mouth, Brighde's head snapped back, and she pressed against his shoulders urging him to release her. When Alex did not immediately respond, she pushed harder.

"Release me," she ground out.

Alex was shocked at how the mood so suddenly changed that he could not understand when she wanted him to put her down. Slowly, he gently placed her back on her feet.

"What have I done wrong? Just a moment ago ye agreed that this was---" Alex trailed off as what she said finally registered with him. There was no hiding the burr of her own accent.

"Now ye ken. Is that why ye kissed me? To distract me and trap me into giving ye the information ye wanted?" Brighde felt sick at the thought that the kiss had been a means to manipulate her.

Is he just as Grandmama warned? Does he want naught more than a tumble? Would he use me? Do I want more? What does that make me?

"What? Nay! How could ye even think that?" Brighde knew that Alex could not have pretended the level of hurt and insult that she could see in his eyes. He stepped away from her, and she keenly felt the loss of warmth both from his body and his mood. She immediately regretted her accusation.

"Nay, I suppose I dinna really believe that. But why else would ye kiss me if nae to get something from me?"

Alex looked down to see a genuinely perplexed face looking up at him.

"I kissed ye, mo leannan because I dinna think I could have nae." He said softly. He could not help but wonder what experiences she must have had to think that a man kissed a woman only when he expected something in return. "I kissed ye because I have thought of it so many times that it has made me feel wretchedly guilty for wanting ye while ye are still weakened. I kissed ye because ye are the bonniest woman I have ever seen, and I am drawn to ye." He noticed that he was now holding both of her hands.

"I didna kiss ye because I expected something from ye though I did hope ye would return ma kisses. I would never abuse yer trust that way nor take advantage of ye like that." He paused as he looked into her upturned face and shook his head slightly. "I feel guilty now for having done it since mayhap I did take advantage of ye since ye arenae fully healed, and ye are alone in here with me."

"Dinna think that. Ye didna take advantage of me at all. I wanted yer kisses as much as I wanted to give ye mine." She lowered her head and shook it before

37

looking back up at him. "We are a right pair. I have wondered what it would be like to kiss ye since I awoke. I thought ye were an angel at first, but once I realized ye were the brawest and most handsome man I have ever met, and ye treat me like gold, I couldnae help but wonder."

Alex brought her hands to his lips and pressed soft kisses on each knuckle. He then placed them over his heart with his hands covering hers. Alex's heart was still pounding, and Brighde could feel it. It was a strong and steady rhythm even if it was a little faster than usual. He smiled down to her and kissed her forehead.

"Mary, I do want to ken yer past, but I willna ask ye again. I dinna want to, but I can wait until ye're ready to tell me. If ye're ready to tell me."

"Brighde," she said with a sigh. *I canna keep lying to the mon. He doesnae deserve ma dishonesty. Nay, he is a mon with honor. I need to find some of ma own.*

"Pardon?"

"Brighde. Ma name is Brighde, nae Mary."

Alex forced himself not to step away. He was shocked to discover that not only had she been trying to deceive him with a false accent, but she lied to him about her name. *What else? What else hasnae she told me? Dear God, dinna let her be married. Please dinna let that be. I dinna dally with married women, and I dinna think I can let her go to some other mon.*

Bridge felt him tense under her hands and knew that he was withdrawing from her. She pulled her hands from his chest, and keeping hold of one of his, she pulled him towards the fireplace. As a bachelor, there was only one chair in the room, so she sat down on the floor. She looked up at him expectantly and said a silent prayer that he would sit with her. When he finally sat down, a small tear leaked from her eye. Alex reached out and wiped it away, and she could read the questions in his eyes.

"Why the tears, lass?"

"I thought mayhap ye wouldnae sit with me, so I am relieved that ye are. I ken ma dishonesty must seem ungrateful, but I do have a reason." She took a deep breath before looking up at him. "I canna tell ye the whole of it, but I will tell ye what I think is safe."

"Ye dinna have to protect me. That is ma job, to protect ye." Before he could continue, she pressed a slim finger to his lips. *Dinna suck it into yer mouth. This isnae the time. Pay attention with the right head. Dinna lick it either. Nay, dinna.* Alex settled for a small kiss against her index finger.

"It is nae just to protect ye, it is to protect yer clan and maself. I didna grow up in the Highlands, but ma mother did. She died when I was six summers, and I went to live with ma grandmother and grandfather for the next eight summers until they both passed away from an illness that swept through their clan. Ma grandmama was English and never lost her accent. My grandda was a Highlander. After so many years of living amongst them, my own voice developed a burr despite being born in the Lowlands. I used to entertain ma family by doing impressions of ma grandmama, so that is how I developed a believable Sassenach accent."

Alex waited for her to continue, but she seemed intent upon ending her story there. She explained only a small fraction of what he wanted to know, but he had promised not to push her into revealing anything she did not want to. He had always been the most patient member of his family, besides his father, but he found himself wanting to pull his hair out with frustration. He forced himself to sit silently in the hopes that she would continue, and he watched as she stared into the fire. The days were warm, but a fire was still being placed in the chamber because of her recent illness. Now it seemed sweltering to Alex who was trying to calm both his body that longed to return to kissing the soft warmth of the woman seated next to him and his mind which was jumping from one thought to another as he tried to puzzle out this mysterious woman. He forced himself to not fidget though he did lace his fingers back through hers and stroked his thumb along her palm. He heard her soft sigh as she turned to face him.

"I suppose ma story is nae too different from most women. Ma father arranged a marriage for me, and so I was being sent off to be wed." Again, she stopped, and again Alex wondered if she was going to tell him more. She leaned into his side, and he wrapped his arm around her as he interlaced his other hand with hers. He wanted to not only maintain the bond they seemed to have at that moment, but he desperately wanted to make it grow. Never in his life had he had any serious interest in getting to know a woman. The only women currently in his life were his sister, Mairghread, who was married and living with her new clan, and his new sister by marriage, Siùsan, who was traveling with his brothers to see her family. Other than that, it had been ages since he had enjoyed the physical company of any woman, and he could not think of a single woman outside of his family that he had ever wanted to talk to in any great length, let alone get to know emotionally. So he continued to stroke her palm with one hand and run his other hand up and down her arm.

Brighde had never sat so close to a man before who was not her grandfather or uncle. When her grandparents and uncle and aunt by marriage all died within days of each other, she had thought she would never receive or want affection again but being wrapped in Alex's arms seemed like the most natural place for her at that moment. She knew she would tell him more, but she also knew she would draw out this moment for as long as she could.

"Brighde, I amnae going anywhere." She knew that he was not talking about just that moment nor was it a threat to make her talk more. She felt his presence like a rock grounding her when she thought she might blow away with a strong wind. She leaned her head against his shoulder, constantly finding more and more comfort as more of her pressed against him.

"I ken," she whispered. She turned her cheek to press it against the side of his chest. "I just need this for a moment longer."

Alex lifted her from the ground and placed her gently on his lap. While he seemed to find himself often cradling her in his arms like a small child, there was nothing about this woman that reminded him of a child. He breathed in the familiar scent of lemongrass. While lemongrass usually reminded him immediately of his mother, it also gave him a sense of comfort and familiarity. He thought the first time he smelled it on Brighde would douse any physical interest he had in her, but his mind and body were more than willing to overlook the connection to his mother. He leaned his cheek against the crown of her head, and they sat like that for a long time. They were like that for so long that the fire began to die down, and Alex wondered if she was falling asleep. He was just about to move her to the bed when she spoke again.

"I dinna ken the mon that I am to marry." The use of the present tense was like a knife to Alex's heart. "When I first learned of it, I accepted the arrangement simply as a way to leave ma father. He was nae pleased to have me return home, so he arranged a marriage as quickly as he could. After ma mother died, he remarried before the year of mourning was even over. He married his mistress who had already given him three sons, two of whom are older than I am. The third is less than a moon younger than me. Since marrying they have had three more children, two daughters, and a son. There was nay place for me, and with the way his wife spoke of ma mother, I was more than willing to leave." Brighde had not noticed that she was wrapping and unwrapping the string on the front of Alex's leine around her finger until he stopped her by tilting her chin up and kissed her gently.

Alex already knew that his family was unusual in the amount of emotion and affection they shared. Their pledge of loyalty and love was unsurpassed and was what kept them bonded to one another even during times of trial and strife, but Brighde's story sounded all too familiar after what he learned of Siùsan's life before arriving at Castle Dunbeath. He was coming to realize just how fortunate he and his siblings, especially Mairghread, were to have been raised by two doting parents. While Mairghread was originally intended to enter an arranged marriage, their father had refused within days of meeting her intended. He would never sentence his daughter to a life of unhappiness or mistreatment. Alex remembered the bruising he had seen the first night Brighde arrived. He wanted to know who had done that to her. He remembered now that they had been varying shades of green, yellow, and purple which meant they were not all from the same incident. It had not registered until now.

"Brie, did ye father beat ye?" Alex did not want to hear the answer, but he also did not want to wonder any longer.

Taken aback by the use of a nickname only her grandmother and mother used, it took her a moment to register what he asked. *How could he possibly ken? He couldnae. It doesnae sound the same coming from him. When he calls me Brie, it makes ma insides feel wobbly and warm.* When his question finally permeated, she froze. *Wait! Why would he ask that? Did someone tell him about the marks? How bad were they when I arrived? He canna ken what ma father did or that wretched mon.*

"How did ye ken aboot that?" she asked rigidly.

Alex sighed before answering. He was going to have to share his own truths now.

"Please dinna fash at what I am aboot to say. That first night, ye had nae developed a fever yet. I brought ye up here, and the women came in to bathe ye in a hot bath. I came back once ye were settled into the bed. I sat in the chair next to the bed, and sometime in the middle of the night, I woke to ye shivering so hard that the bed shook. I kenned the only way to warm someone who is chilled to the bone is laying skin to skin. I ken I generate a lot of heat naturally, so I slipped into bed with ye."

"Ye slipped into bed *naked* with me, ye mean." Brighde interrupted.

"Aye, well, ye were unconscious at the time."

"So that makes it all right," she tried to shift out of his lap, but Alex held tight.

"I didna do it to take advantage of ye, and well ye ken that. I thought ye kenned better of me than that by now. I did it to save yer life. I did it because I kenned that I could call one of the women in to help ye, but they wouldnae generate nearly as much heat as I would nor, would they be able to cover as much of ye. I slid into the bed and gently gathered up yer nightgown as I rolled ye onto yer side. I kept ma hands on the outside of yer nightgown, but I did touch ye bare back. That is when I noticed the bandage around yer ribs. When I looked down, I could see yer back and sides were covered in bruises. I rolled ye over, and I did look at all of ye, but only to see the extent of yer injuries. I thought I was going to be sick. I have never seen a woman's body so beaten and battered. I wanted to kill whoever was responsible with ma bare hands and then run ma sword through him for good measure. I tucked ye back in and held ye while we slept. It was early the next morning that I woke to ye having a raging fever."

A surge of emotion swept through Brighde after hearing Alex's story. First, she was angry that he had seen her undressed without her consent. She wanted to rail at him for taking advantage of her, but she knew he had not. He could have, but he had not. Then, she felt embarrassed that he might not have liked what he had seen, with or without the bruises. After all, he did say he wanted to be sick. Finally, she felt overwhelming shame that he saw what had been done to her on more than one occasion. Taking a shaky breath, she nodded her head.

41

"Brie, I saw the bruises around ye breasts and neck. Did a mon rape ye?" Alex was nearly whispering.

There was heavy silence after Alex's quietly asked questions. He held his breath fearing what she might say. She turned into him and wrapped her arms around him, and he could feel her sobs. His heart broke at that moment, not because she was no longer a maiden, that mattered not a whit to him, but because someone had violated her, and he did not know if he would ever be able to avenge her.

He doesnae ken I was thrashed before this. He thinks it's just recently. But I've already admitted that Father did. Damn witch's tits. He's figured out too much. I willna lie though. I am done with that.

"Nay. I killed him. Alex, I killed that mon and more than one other. I had to." Brighde dissolved into body rattling sobs that she had been holding in since she was attacked. Alex let her cry until she had no tears left and was only able to shudder as she tried to calm her breathing. He found himself rocking her as he stroked her hair and whispered reassurances in her ear. When she was finally able to breathe easily, he cupped her cheek and looked into her watery eyes.

"I saw those bruises at least two weeks after they happened. I canna imagine what they must have looked like or the pain ye must have been in when they were fresh. Any mon who would hurt a woman deserves whatever death ye gave him."

"Ye dinna think me a criminal for killing someone?"

Alex shook his head as he reassured her. "Do ye think I have never been in battle before? Do ye really think that I made it to this age without having killed instead of being killed? *A 'chiad fhear agamsa*, ye didna do aught wrong."

His sweet one? How can he think of me as sweet when I've just told him that I killed more than one person? How sweet will he think me if he finds out the whole story? Bah, not if but when. He willna give up till he kens it all. He maynae push me today, but I ken it will come out soon enough. Then what?

"Ye are ma sweet one. I ken what I said, and I mean it. Dinna doubt that." He smiled at her surprised face. "I ken what ye are thinking. It is written across yer face. There is naught wrong with defending yerself especially when a mon, who is larger and stronger than ye, is trying to do ye harm. Ma sister, Mairghread, was kidnapped shortly after arriving at the Mackays. A potential betrothal went badly, but she married a mon who loves her more than aught. When her now-husband, my brothers, and I found her, she was strapped to a bed and aboot to be raped. I canna even tell ye exactly what happened next, but I ken that those two men didna live, and I had a bloody dirk that needed cleaning. Does that make me a criminal? Does any of that make me a criminal?"

She could only shake her head as she felt more tears leaking from her eyes. At this point, she was no longer sure what she cried about. It was a swirling mixture of her own guilt, a sadness for what he and his family experienced, respect and admiration for him and his protectiveness of his sister, and an overwhelming need to be closer to him again.

"Alex, I need ye." She could barely do more than murmur her request. She was shocked to hear herself speak, but she did not regret the need she felt. It was only seconds before his mouth crashed down on hers. They breathed life into one another as their mouths and hands explored one another. Alex laid her on the ground and moved his body halfway over hers. He did not want to crush her, but he needed to feel her against him. He pushed his sporran out of the way, this time allowing his cock to press against her belly.

What is that? Good God, how can it be that long? I want to see it and touch it, but I canna do that. He will think me a whore for sure, and I dinna want this to end. I just want him. I want him not only like this but argh, I dinna even ken what else I want. She moved restlessly against him as she tried to pull him more fully on top of him. She lifted her hips to try to press more firmly against him. She felt a pressure building that she did not know how to release.

I must stop her now. If I dinna put an end to this, I'm going to deflower her right here on the floor. That isnae how any woman should make love for the first time, and certainly nae here. Make love? Where the hell did that come from? Tup. Toss her skirts. Slake ma lust. Nae make love. Bah! Who am I kidding? I would kill any mon who thought to use her like that. I want more, so much more. Even as Alex chided himself for his runaway thoughts and for not stopping them, his hands pulled up the length of her nightgown. Somewhere it registered in the back of his mind that he needed to get her some real clothes. Once they found their way to her hips, he pulled one of her legs over his hip and angled them, so he could feel the heat coming from her through his plaid and against his swollen rod.

"Lass, do ye ken what happens between a mon and woman? I mean I ken what nearly happened to ye, but do ye ken how it works?"

"Aye. The men were sure to tell me in great detail."

"I doubt any of what they said is how it should be done. I willna bed ye here on the floor, but I can bring ye some relief if ye will let me." *Please let me. Please, please, please. I will stop but I dinna want to.*

Brighde looked at him intently and slowly nodded her head. It was all the invitation that Alex needed. He pressed his mouth against hers and rolled her on top of him. He grasped her bottom and was inordinately pleased to feel it fill his very large hands. He had never been overly enamored or attracted to small or thin women. He liked that Brighde was tall enough that he did not have to stoop too far over to kiss her, or that when they lay like this, their mouths lined up just as well as their hips. He began to rock her hips back and forth as his rose to meet hers. Once she picked up on the rhythm, he untied the strings at the neck of the nightgown and pushed it off one shoulder. He freed her breasts and began to feast on them. He licked, suckled, nipped, and suckled some more like a drowning man finding a sip of water. One hand still gripped her backside as the other hand slid around so that a finger could trace over the moist seam between her legs. He could not stop the groan of pure pleasure when he felt how wet she was. He knew she would be embarrassed if she realized that she was practically drenched down there, but his male pride and stiff erection could not have been happier to know she desired him just as much as he did her. He slid a finger into her and listened to her moan. He added another finger slowly since he knew this was all new to her. When her hips rocked harder and faster of their own volition, he pressed a third finger into her and moved them as far as he could reach. He angled his hand as best he could to reach the front of her where the curls hid the source of greater pleasure. He rubbed his forefinger over the slick hood and teased the tiny bud out, so he could bring her closer to completion. As his fingers felt the beginnings of small tremors, he rolled them over again. When he pulled out of her reach, she grunted her displeasure, but before she could ask any questions, she felt his warm, smooth tongue pressing against her nether lips. He parted them with his fingers and nuzzled her then breathed in the musky scent of her. While this was something he had done before, it was far from his favorite sexual act. However, he could not wait to taste Brighde, and as he breathed her in, he reached a hand under his plaid to fist himself. He ran his tongue up and down until she began to writhe, then he pressed his tongue flat against the little button that made her back arch off the ground. He pressed three fingers back into her as he sucked on the intensely sensitive flesh. His hand squeezed his own cock as he pumped it up and down. He had more than once gone down to the loch and taken himself in hand since she arrived. The past week had seen him slipping away to relieve his aching cods more than once. The more time he spent around her, the deeper his attraction grew.

I just need to last until she comes. I dinna want her to ken what I am doing. I dinna want to embarrass either of us, but ma bullocks will explode if I dinna find release too. Nay woman has ever tasted this good. I could feast on her morn, noon, and night. I will for a lifetime if she will let me. Where did that come from? Nay. I didna really mean that. I dinna ken her well enough to be considering a lifetime of anything with her even if this is the sweetest nectar I've ever tasted.

Alex's hand began to move faster as Brighde's hands ran through his hair. As he felt her release sweep through her, she pulled his hair almost painfully, but the sensation only aroused him more knowing that he was the only man to have ever pleasured her. Her body was still wracked by tremors when she pushed hard against him. Balancing on only one elbow and most of his weight on one knee, he toppled quite easily. Before he knew what was happening, he felt a small hand nudging his out of the way.

"Let me."

I want him to feel the pleasure he gave me, to satisfy him as much as he did me. I want him to want me again. Dear heavens, I've acted like a loose woman today, and I dinna even care. I just dinna want this to end, and I canna bear the idea that he would find his release elsewhere. I ken men have to be pleasured regularly to be kept interested by a woman. He so much bigger and harder than I ever imagined a mon would be. How does this even fit?

Alex could only stare up in disbelief and nod his head as she stretched over him and held him firmly in her hand while kissing him. He could feel the passion that he had released pass through her as her tongue dueled with his. Her small, inexperienced hand stroked him as he covered it with hers and guided her into a rhythm that had his eyes rolling back. It took next to no time before he was pulling her hand away and pressing his plaid down. She reached for his cock over his plaid and continued to rub up and down until they could both feel a little dampness seep through. He pulled her tightly against his chest, and they held each other as they basked in the euphoria that was a new sensation for both of them.

Chapter Six

Alexander held Brighde while she dozed lightly. Even though he could tell that she was not deeply asleep, she slept peacefully. He knew it was the most peaceful sleep she had since her arrival. He was glad that he was able to provide the sanctuary that she needed, but he worried that she would regret her impulsiveness once she awoke. The sun was high overhead when she began to stir. Alex felt her move against him and realized that he had dozed off too. He looked down to see two fathomless grey eyes peering up at him from where she had once again burrowed herself into his shoulder. He could not help but smile slightly as he realized he rather liked having her tucked next to him while he slept. It felt entirely natural. He always avoided falling asleep with any of the women he bedded. He did not want to suggest any type of commitment nor did he enjoy the awkwardness that he was sure would follow if he spent the night. He had never had a woman in his chambers other than servants sent in to clean. The Sinclair men generally reserved their chambers for their wives only. Bachelors sought their pleasures outside of the keep. The current laird and those past set strict rules against members of the laird's family dallying with the help, never wanting a woman to feel that her livelihood was dependent upon bedding the laird's relative. As Alex returned Brighde stare, he realized that there was a certain sense of rightness with her in his chamber. This went beyond just having her remain there because of illness. No, this was decidedly more.

I dinna ken why I feel that she belongs in here with me. We barely ken each other, or rather, I barely ken her. She kens a great deal aboot me after avoiding talking aboot herself. Even with that, I feel like I ken her or at least have learned quite a bit aboot her. There is a strength there that I cannot help but admire. Even her desire to protect us speaks to her character. She may have lied, but I can see clearly enough that she felt it was a necessity to stay alive. I wish she would open up to me more. I want to get to ken her, and I want to be the one who does the protecting. I dinna want her to feel that she is still alone.

When she did not immediately pull away, Alexander tested the waters by brushing a kiss against her forehead. The angelic smile that she gave him almost took his breath away. She ran feather-light fingertips over the stubble on his cheeks and jaw.

I canna believe what we did, or rather I did, this morn. He doesnae seem repulsed by me, nor does he seem to think he can take more liberties. Nay, just the opposite. I dinna understand why he's looking at me like this. It's almost tender, reverent even. It isnae the lust or passion I saw earlier. Why do I feel like I could stay just like this forever and never feel like I have missed aught? His body is always so warm, and while it's not soft anywhere, it's incredibly comfortable. How can that be?

Alex watched as her brow wrinkled while she was deep in thought. He could tell they were questions, but he had no idea about what. He began to worry that she was, in fact, doubting their time together.

"Penny for yer thoughts, lass." He lightly ran his hand up and down her back.

"Ye would be paying far too much." She smiled faintly.

"Ye have a keen ability to try to evade telling me what ye're thinking. Ye do ken that I have seen the ploy all along and have just gone along with it because it seemed so important to ye?"

She had the good graces to blush slightly and lower her gaze. He tilted her chin up and lightly brushed his lips against hers. He pulled away before it could become anything more.

"I was worried that ye would awaken to regret earlier." Alex tentatively broached the subject that was causing him a surprising amount of duress. His mind could not settle until he knew where things stood.

Brighde pushed herself up on one elbow, so she was eye level with Alex. She felt a disadvantage being so much lower than him.

"I worried the same thing. Or rather that ye would think less of me for it. I dinna regret it. I just hope ye dinna either."

This time when Alex pressed his mouth to hers, he swept his tongue against her lips and pressed his way into her mouth. Her jaw relaxed immediately, and her mouth invited him in. He pulled her back on top of him, and her legs instinctively opened to wrap the sides of his hips. He forced himself to keep his hands on her waist, though the temptation to move them lower or higher was nearly unresitable. She slanted her head to deepen the kiss even further. She drew his tongue back into her mouth and lightly sucked on it. He groaned and rolled them back over, holding his weight above her so as not to crush her.

I want to feel him closer. I dinna want any space between us. Does he really think he will hurt me if he lays upon me? Or does he nae want me to feel how hard his shaft is? Because if that's it, he's a mite late.

She opened her legs once again to allow him room to settle upon her. When he still held most of his weight on his elbows, she wrapped her legs around his waist and pressed her heels into him while wrapping her arms around the middle of his body and pulled. When that still did not work, she grumbled in frustration and used one hand to fist his leine and yank him towards her. Alex chuckled and lowered himself a little more onto her, but he still kept the majority of his weight off of her.

"Alex, dinna. Dinna hold back from me. Nae now. I want to feel all ye against me. I am made of sterner stuff than ye think. Ye willna break me, but I may bite ye if ye keep frustrating me." With that, she nipped his shoulder. Alex stared stunned at her before smiling widely and growling in response. He pressed his weight slowly onto her, still cautious, but when she did not push him away, he cradled her head in his hand and feasted upon her mouth, cheeks, neck, and earlobes. Anything that he could reach. His other hand found the loose neckline of her nightgown, and he palmed her breast, groaning as he felt its weight and how he had to spread his fingers as wide as he could to wrap them around the warm flesh. He kneaded it gently until he felt her hips lift against his. He ground his length against the crest of her thighs and pinched her nipple. She broke off their kiss as she sucked his earlobe into her mouth. She moaned softly near his ear, and he almost spilled himself again.

A loud clearing of the throat brought them to an instant halt. Brighde tried to shrink into the floor while Alex expanded his shoulder as best he could to shield her from whoever intruded.

"Ye ken the door isnae locked. It isnae even closed all the way. Ye're mighty luck it is me who found ye and not Hagatha. She'd turn ye over her knee. Both of ye." Liam Sinclair stood just inside the door which he had the common sense to close. He looked up at the ceiling as they scrambled to their feet. Alex helped right her flannel gown and then pushed her behind him as he spun his sporran around to cover his very obvious arousal.

"Da, I didna hear ye come in."

"Clearly," he said dryly.

"Da, it isnae what ye think," Alex tried but paused when he saw his father's raised eyebrow. "It may be what it looks like, but nae what ye think. I havenae, we havenae, I mean, dear God, this hasnae ever happened before today."

"I ken that, Alexander. I believe Mary to be a moral young lady, and besides, she's been too ill to learn of yer charms. Until now." He watched as Brighde sneaked a look around Alex's shoulder. She braced herself with a hand on each arm, and Alex wrapped his arm back and around her, drawing her flush with his back.

"Ye canna hide what I have already seen. It didna work when ye were a wean, and it isnae working now." The Sinclair leaned slightly to peer around Alex. "Lass, ye can come out now. Dinna fash. I amnae upset. I rather suspected as much when Alex disappeared hours ago, and nay one kenned where he was. Luckily, it wasnae during the time of his usual daily visit, so nay one seems to have figured it out."

Brighde stepped around Alex even when he continued to try to shield her. She gave him a pointed look and stepped in front of him.

"Brie." He placed his hands on her shoulders and squeezed softly. The pet name did not escape the Sinclair's notice, but he chose to not remark upon it.

"I am happy to see that ye are much improved, lass. Ye've given us all a right scare," as Laird Sinclair said the last bit, his gaze drifted purposefully up to Alex. "I think it is time that we found ye some proper clothes to wear and let ye escape these four walls. Ye must be bored stiff most of the day."

"Thank you, my lord. I would indeed appreciate it."

Alex's grip on her shoulders tightened to an almost painful pinch for a moment when he heard her false English accent again, but he said nothing. He would question her later. It was one thing for her to be evasive with him, but when she would not tell the truth to his father, the laird, he could not risk the safety of his clan. He knew the Sinclairs to be one of the strongest clans in the northern Highlands, and he rarely feared an attack, but he was also mature enough to understand that an unknown foe is the most dangerous type of foe. He was still resolved not to push her into telling him against her will, but he would ask later.

"Perhaps ye would care for a tour around the gardens. I'm sure Alex would be happy to accompany ye. I will send Hagatha up with some of the gowns that Mairghread left behind the last time she was here. She was expanding rapidly with the bairn and didna see the point in carrying them back. She is aboot the same size as ye."

He gave a pointed look to his son and stepped towards the door. He opened it and held it open for his son. Alex looked down at Brighde and only moved away when she gave him a slight nod.

He passed through the doorway and heard his father close the door behind them. He took a deep breath and anticipated his father's lecture. When nothing was forthcoming, he looked over at his father. He did not expect to see a broad grin on the man's face.

"Have ye gone daft in yer dotage?"

"Dotage is it, ye wee laddie? I grin because I kenned it was inevitable. I am only mildly surprised that it took ye so long. She's been up and pacing that chamber for days. Mayhap ye have been sneaking kisses these last few days, and today is just the day ye were caught with ye hand in the honey pot."

Alex's cheeks flamed from his father's analogy when he remembered what they had done the first time they had come together.

"Hmmm. So, ma guess isnae far off. Have ye compromised her in truth?"

"Nay! Da, I amnae like ma brothers, and ye ken that. I dinna have dalliances like them, and I would never take from a woman what is only meant for her husband."

"I ken that, but ye have been drawn to her since the night she arrived. Ye've been nearly obsessed with her from the start. Remember it wasnae so long ago that I suggested that ye travel with yer brothers, and I thought ye might mutiny."

"I amnae obsessed, but I am drawn to her in a way I canna explain. I can honestly say that it isnae just her looks. She is the most beautiful woman I have ever met, but there is so much more. So much more that she hasnae shared with me yet, but I see hints of. I want to get to ken her better, and mayhap we will find we suit. Mayhap we dinna, but I want to ken."

"Ye have the right of it all, son. She has much more to tell than what she has yet, but they may be her secrets to keep for a while longer. Dinna push or rush her, or ye may find her fleeing again. She trusts ye, and I dinna think that comes easily. If ye break her trust, ye willna regain it easily. Bare that in mind."

"Aye, Da. I will."

They had reached the bottom of the stairs and moved into the Great Hall. Laird Sinclair called Hagatha over and arranged for her to take Brighde some of Mairghread's kirtles.

Alex did not have long to wait before Brighde came down the stairs. She was dressed in a dark blue gown that contrasted with her flaxen hair which had been swept up into a braid that hung down her back to her waist. Alex realized he was holding his breath until she reached him. Taking a deep breath, he extended his arm to her and guided her down a passageway. He knew that he could have taken her out of the main doors of the keep, but he perversely did not want to share the sight of her with anyone else. He justified it to himself by arguing that he was helping her to reenter the land of the living slowly. He did not want her overwhelmed with too many curious stares the moment she showed herself for the first time in nearly six sennights. There were constant curiosity and speculation about the mystery woman who was healing in Alexander's chamber, but Laird Sinclair easily quelled most of the talk.

He navigated them down another passageway to a door that was tucked into a large brick wall. He pressed down on the handle and had to push his shoulder into the door to make it budge. The door had not been used much since his mother passed away, so it stuck in the jam. The door led them to the lady's garden where his mother had once tended a veritable jungle of flowers. Mairghread maintained most of it until she moved away. Now it faced a year of neglect. The women who tended the vegetable garden on the other side of the half wall came in somewhat regularly to prune and weed, but the garden was not nearly in the glory it had once been. Alex knew that they would not be disturbed in here, and it was late enough in the day that it was unlikely that anyone would be in the adjacent garden.

Brighde let go of his arm and moved across the garden as she took in the flowering lavender that his sister so favored. She moved to the lemongrass and bent over it to take in its refreshing scent. She looked back over her shoulder at Alex who was leaning against the garden wall watching her.

"This is what the soap I've been given is made from."

Alex pushed off the wall and walked towards her.

"Aye, it was ma mama's favorite. She used it in her soap and oils. She kept fresh sprigs of it in ma parents' chamber and in the rushes of the Great Hall. Do ye like the scent or would ye prefer something else? Mairghread tends towards lavender, and ma sister by marriage seems to like heather."

"I used to use violets to make ma soaps, but I have come to like the lemongrass. But if ye dinna like it because it reminds ye of yer mother, I would use something else."

Alex broke off a sprig of violets that he passed and then a sprig of lemongrass. He brought both to her, and when she reached for them, he kissed her palm before placing the flowers into her hands.

"I dinna mind either, lass, as long as ye let me stay near enough to catch a waft of yer perfume from time to time." He gave her a smoldering look, but his lips twitched.

"Cheeky devil, arenae ye? I can make ma own soaps if I may collect the flowers. I dinna want to use all of the lemongrasses as it is obviously made for someone other than me."

"Many of the women who work in the keep use the lemongrass soap, so it is never in short supply. But if ye would prefer violets, I will ensure that anything ye need is made available to ye." He lightly pulled the flowers from her hand and tucked the lemongrass behind her ear. He slid the violets into the crevice between her breasts. He let the back of his fingers graze over the top of the swells of her breasts and felt her draw in a shallow breath as he looked into her eyes. She swayed into him, and he leaned forward to softly kiss the sensitive flesh just behind her ear. She placed her hands on his chest to keep her balance. The fresh air, the smell of the flowers that swarmed the garden, and Alex's own unique scent flooded her senses and was almost too much for her after so much time spent cloistered indoors. At first, Alex thought that she simply liked their closeness, but he quickly realized that she was holding onto his chest for balance. He pulled back and saw that her face had gone deathly pale with only tiny pink spots in the center of each cheek. He swept her into his arms and moved them to the closest bench in the shade. He sat with her in his lap and rubbed her back until some of the color was restored to her cheeks.

"I dinna ken what came over me, but I suddenly felt faint and the smells of all the flowers were too much."

"It is midsummer, so the blooms are rather pungent. This might be a bit much for yer first time out of doors. Would ye like to go back inside."

"Nay," she rushed to say. "I dinna want to go inside again until the sun is ready to set. I have spent more time indoors over the last moon that I probably have in ma entire life. I generally spend most of ma day outside. I used to tend ma grandmama's garden, visit the crofters in need of assistance, or to help the healer.

If I wasna doing that, then I was usually on ma horse." At the mention of her horse, Alex heard her breath hitch.

"Lass, what happened to yer horse?" He asked quietly. He hoped this was the opening he needed to learn more about what had happened to her.

"He was killed when I was attacked. Shot out from under me by an arrow." Her voice came out as little more than the barest whisper. Alex had to turn her head towards him, so he could hear.

"Who would do such a thing?"

"Ma father. The mon I was to marry." She shrugged and stared off into the distance as though she was lost to a memory. After a moment, she looked up at Alex. "I dinna ken which one. I suspect they both had something to do with it."

She shook her head and pushed herself out of Alex's lap. She turned away from him and wrapped her arms around her middle.

"I ken ye deserve an explanation, and I want to give ye one, but I just canna bring maself to talk about it yet. If I do, I will have to relive it all."

There. I've said it. He kens I wasna wanted. I'm just convenient when money is involved, and inconvenient the rest of the time. Even here I'm inconvenient. I dinna fit anywhere.

Alex wrapped his arms around her from behind and covered her hands with his. He leaned forward and kissed her temple before answering.

"I willna press ye to talk about it, but ken that I will listen any time ye are ready. Brie, I would ken what befell ye because I dinna want aught else to happen to ye. I canna protect ye from a danger I dinna ken exists." He kissed her temple again before stepping around her to take her hand. He took her on a couple of tours around the garden before they returned to the bench in the shade. They simply sat together with Alex's arm around her and their hands entwined. Both were lost in deep thought, but they enjoyed each other's companionable silence.

Chapter Seven

For the next three days, Alexander and Brighde fell into an easy routine that centered upon Alex returning to the keep in time for the noon meal and then secreting Brighde out to the lady's garden for a picnic. They were keenly aware that they could have an audience at any time, so they kept to holding hands or sitting next to one another on a bench or plaid. Hagatha and Elspeth conveniently had a picnic meal ready for Alex as he returned to the keep. Hagatha would fetch Brighde by way of the back stairs and meet Alex in the passageway that led to the side door. They spent the afternoon together telling each other stories about their childhood. Alexander enjoyed getting to know Brighde and her past, but it still nettled that she refused to tell him which clans she was a part of or who attacked her. He asked small questions that he hoped would give him more insight, but she was adept at skirting the issue. After a few futile attempts, he would settle for whatever details she would give. He regaled her with stories of the antics that he and his brothers got into, and how his sister was almost never far behind. She told him tales of how her grandmother taught her to read and write, and about the healing arts. She told him of her grandfather teaching her to ride and taking her out to hunt when she was still young enough to sit in the saddle in front of him. By the third day though, Alex could tell that Brighde was becoming impatient for more freedom. She never said anything, but he had seen her looking longingly at the curtain wall and what lay beyond it. He found her looking out of his chamber window when he joined her for the evening meal, which he did every night since the morning they discovered their attraction for one another, and when he would check on her before she retired for the night. Sometimes he saw a look of apprehension as she stared out of the window, but mainly it was a strong desire to venture beyond his chamber or the walled in garden.

On the morning of the fourth day, Alexander tapped lightly on his door just as the sun was rising. He entered his chamber quietly and walked over to the bed. He was hesitant to wake Brighde since she was sleeping peacefully. She had another nightmare that night, and it had taken him over an hour to help her calm enough to fall back to sleep. She begged him to stay with her until she fell asleep. Once he wrapped her in the cocoon of his arms and stretched his body along her back, she drifted off to sleep quickly. He felt her body twitch a few times as she shifted into a deep sleep. Even when he knew she no longer needed or was aware of him, he stayed. He watched as she slept and imagined what it would be like to fall asleep to her every night and wake to her every morning. The need to make that happen was nearly bone jarring in its intensity.

What is she doing to me? She is a bushel of secrets and evasions, but yet, I canna keep away. I canna get enough of the crumbs she throws me. I come back for more each time, and I dinna really mind if I'm honest with maself. I pray that she will tell me the whole tale one day, but even if she didna, the woman that I ken now is the only woman I want.

It was with that resolve that Alexander gently shook her shoulder.

"Brie. Mo leannan, wake up. It's me, Alex. Wake up, leannan.

Sweetheart. Who keeps calling me his sweetheart? Alex? What is Alex doing here so early? Am I dreaming? Nay, I dinna want to wake up if this is a dream. I would listen to him call me sweetheart forever if I could. I am yer sweetheart. If only ye were mo dhuine.

Brighde tried to roll over, but she felt a decided dip in the bed that drew her closer to the edge, making her hit a solid barrier that wore wool.

"I would be yer mon any day ye will let me." The declaration was made so softly that Brighde was sure that he had not intended her to hear him. She certainly had not realized she spoke her thoughts aloud. She wanted a few moments before she opened her eyes. The sight that met her took away her breath. Alex was freshly shaved, and he was wearing a leine that looked freshly stitched. All in all, he was the most handsome man she had ever met, and on that morning, the most wonderful sight she could have awoken to.

"Alex, what are ye doing in here?" She turned her head toward the window and squinted as though she was searching for something. "Where is the sun? It isnae even up yet. Why canna I sleep a little longer?"

"It's time to get up, little one, because I have something planned for us, and it's best that we make a start before the entire keep is up to ask questions when ye venture beyond the curtain wall today."

The mention of leaving the keep and even leaving the bailey was enough to have her pushing Alex out of the way as she scrambled to get out of bed. She went to the armoire that held her borrowed gowns and turned towards Alex.

"Ye will need an arisaid for the morn, but it will certainly warm up once the sun is higher. Wear whichever gown is most comfortable, and dinna worry about looks.

It'll just be me, and I already ken how ye look." With that, he winked and stepped into the passageway. Alex felt like he had only just closed the door behind him when Brighde emerged with a freshly scrubbed face, hair pulled back into a braid that was pinned up, and a practical kirtle. As she stepped closer, he caught a whiff of violets.

She is using the soap I left for her. I didna think it mattered, but I do prefer that she doesnae smell like Mama anymore.

"I almost forgot to thank ye for the soap." She stood on her tiptoes and kissed his cheek. She ran her fingertip between his furrowed brows. "Who else kens that I prefer violets. I've only told ye, and then like magic, the soap shows up. Nay. I ken ye arranged it, and I thank ye."

Alex bent over and gave her a quick peck on the lips. Their time for intimacy had been limited by silent agreement. Both knew that too much time alone would result in things moving too far too fast. While they did share the evening meal together, it was always with the chamber door wide open. Even though no one other than Hagatha and Laird Sinclair would venture above stairs in the evenings, they used it as a reminder that they needed to tame their desire for one another. It did not stop them from sharing a few passionate kisses before Alex retreated to his spot outside the door. Brighde felt guilty that he had now spent almost a fortnight of sleeping in the doorjamb. She tried, albeit unsuccessfully, to convince him that she was well enough for him to sleep in one of his brothers' chambers or that she could be moved. It took only a single night terror for Alex to successfully defeat that suggestion. Instead, she began giving him an extra plaid and pillow. He had even tried to refuse that, but she stood firm on the matter. She refused to kiss him until he took the bedding. Once he had, she rewarded him with a kiss that made his cock and ballocks ache for hours after he stretched out in the passageway. With no way to relieve his pent-up frustration, he had groaned and decided it was easier to give in the next time.

"Are ye going to tell me why we're up before the cocks?" Alex stopped dead in his tracks and looked down at her. It was only when he covered his mouth to silence his laugh that she realized what she had said and what it implied.

"I amnae talking about yer cock. That seems to be up whether the sun is or nae." At her brash comment, he pulled her into the shadows of the dimly lit corridor and pressed her against the wall.

"I'm most definitely up before the sun today." He pushed his sporran out of the way and let her feel his arousal as he nibbled along her neck. Brighde ran her hands up and down his back and felt her own arousal build as his muscles rippled under her fingertips. Feeling rather brave, she let her hands travel down to cup his behind. She could not believe how tight his buttocks felt or how it fit perfectly within her hands. She squeezed gently and received a groan from Alex before he caught her in a searing kiss that made her toes curl. She pulled his hips tighter against hers and ground herself into him. Alex lifted her high, and she wrapped her legs around his waist.

"Lass, if we keep this up, the only place we will be going is back to ma chamber and claiming it as ours." He kissed her jaw before setting her down. He heard a soft growl come from her and looked down to see her none too pleased face. He cocked an eyebrow at her, she glowered at him.

"I'm nae the one starting something I didna want to finish."

"Nae much of a morning person, I see."

"Nae much of a morning person when I'm woken early only to be teased," she grumbled.

Alex pinched her backside and then took her hand as he guided her down the stairs. They quietly crept through the Great Hall to the massive double doors that led to the bailey. She had no recollection of passing through these doors or the Great Hall the night she arrived.

She took in the two large fireplaces that two adult men could easily stand shoulder to shoulder within. Only one was lit this early in the morning. The air was warm enough that the other was not needed. Soft snores and other bodily noises drifted through the air as she watched dust moats float by. As they approached the double doors, she took in their massive size and iron-studded reinforcements. She looked over her shoulder as Alex picked up a picnic basket that was waiting just outside the kitchen. As he approached, she realized that the massive doors were needed with men his size around. Laird Sinclair was the same size as his son, still lean and fit, and she knew from Alex's stories that his three brothers were all of a similar height. Having only seen a few people since her arrival, Brighde was beginning to wonder if she had woken up in a land of giants.

"Are ye ready, lass."

"I canna say since ye havenae told me aught."

"Hmmm," was his only response. He did not need to say any more for his point to register with Brighde. She felt a moment of chagrin before the fresh air distracted her. She looked out over the bailey, seeing it in its entirety for the first time. She was mesmerized by its size. She could see the stables, the smithy, the storage buildings, the laundry, the kirk, and even a few small crofts tucked away at the far end. Alex took her hand and drew her towards the stables where they entered quietly so as not to disturb the stable hands. Alex moved them swiftly down the length of stalls until he stopped in front of a large, entirely white, stallion.

"Good morning, *Naomh*. Are ye ready to stretch yer legs a bit? I ken it's been ages since ye've been for a run. Will ye be well behaved today?"

"Isnae he generally well behaved?" Brighde sized up the giant horse. She had spent most of her childhood on a horse and rode out from her father's keep any chance she had. As Alex moved into the stall to begin to saddle him, Brighde spotted a bucket of apples. She picked one up and went back to *Naomh* who whinnied softly as she blew into his nostrils. She rested her cheek just below his eyes and stroked his neck. With her other hand, she offered him the apple. When Alex heard him nicker and then chomp, he rushed back to the front of the stall. His heart nearly stopped as he watched *Naomh* lick Brighde's hand. He was sure that she would come away a few fingers less. When he heard her soft tinkle of laughter, he felt the blood rush back into his head as it pulsed up through his neck.

What is it about the women of this family taming warhorses? Family? Bluidy hell.

"What are ye doing? Are ye daft? He could have taken yer fingers off. Didna anyone teach ye nae to stick yer hand in a strange animal's face?" The stallion stomped his hoof at his owner's agitated tone.

"I amnae any dafter than a mon who would name an ill-tempered horse Saint."

This was the first flare of temper that Brighde had seen in Alex, and part of her wanted to avoid an argument, but another part of her wanted to see how he would treat her when angry. She needed to know now if he would ever raise his hand to her in anger.

I dinna think he would ever harm me. His honor wouldnae allow it, but I dinna want to be with a mon who will beat me or berate me. I've had enough of that, and I didna run the length of Scotland just to have history repeat itself. Nay. This stops now if he threatens me at all.

"Mayhap ye should learn to control yer horse better, or perhaps ye should try training it. Or more likely, he doesnae care for ye and has found me more appealing. I didna have a single bit of trouble feeding him an apple. He just doesnae like ye." She crossed her arms smugly.

"Lass, are ye trying to provoke me? I've had this horse since the day he was born, and he has been temperamental from the start. Dinna think that him accepting ye once means he'll accept ye every time. That's why Magnus suggested that I name *Naomh* since he's exactly the opposite. Deceptive as the day is long."

Alex walked over to Brighde and cupped her shoulders with his hands pulling her in for a long slow kiss. Brighde tried to stand like a stone, but she could not resist the lure of Alex's everything. Her hands crept from his chest down to his waist and then down to the side of his hips. Even through his plaid, she could feel the grooves on the outsides of his hips. They felt as if they had been made specifically for her hands. Their tongues dueled as Alex's hands cupped her breasts.

I havenae given these nearly enough attention. That pert little arse of hers has been distracting me. How could I ever forget how large and firm these are? I could feast on them like they were mana from heaven. What I wouldnae give for that taste now. This woman will be the death of me. I crave her like a drunkard craves his next pint. Bluidy hell, I want to be inside her, feeling her all around me, on me, over me. Och, but this torture of nae having her.

Alex kneaded the supple flesh through the outside of her kirtle, grumbling at the barrier that kept him from what he wanted. He at least still had the last shred of common sense to not undress her somewhere they could be easily caught.

Caught! Hell. I canna keep her here all day. That was the whole point of setting off so early. So nay one would catch us. I dinna want to share her yet, and I dinna want anyone to talk until I ken the whole of her story. I canna protect her if I dinna ken what I'm facing.

Alex slowly broke the kiss and stepped back. Brighde looked up at him with passion glazed eyes. She looked around and seemed to snap back to the present when she realized they were in a very public place.

"Ye never answered me, Brie. Were ye trying to provoke me? Were ye trying to avoid going for a ride with me, or were ye doing it to see how I act when angry? I would rather it was the latter than the former."

Brighde sighed deeply. *How does he ken? I barely even seemed to get under his skin. I would rather he end arguments with a kiss like that than the back of his hand across ma face. If every disagreement ends like this, I'd be the luckiest lass in Scotland. I dinna think they would. I still dinna ken what his temper is like. I prefer kisses though. I'd be a damned fool if I didna.*

"Brie, I willna ever hit ye or raise ma hand to ye in anger. Mayhap we will disagree or even argue, but I dinna ever want ye to fear me. Ye dinna have to test the waters with me."

"How did ye ken?"

"How could I nae? Ye have never intentionally insulted me before, and ye've never used that tone with me before. And I dinna think ye believe that about *Naomh* anyway." Alex finished with a smile that almost melted Brighde into a puddle right there in the hay.

"Ye did ken. I needed, nay, need to ken that I am safe with ye. I dinna want to find out that ye will play a pretty part in front of yer clan, but behind closed doors will beat me."

"Brie, I'd kill any mon who dared touch ye in anger. The men in ma family dinna beat our women. We maynae always agree, Callum and Siùsan are steady proof of that, but we dinna raise our hand against someone who doesnae have a fair chance to fight back. That doesnae make a mon. That only makes a coward. Women are to be respected, protected and cared for just as they do for their men. A wife is a partner, and a daughter is a treasure. A real mon doesnae abuse that or them." Alex cupped Brighde's cheek before pressing a gentle kiss to her temple.

Our. Our women. Our. Does that mean I am his? Nay. I may want him desperately, but I canna be his. I canna be any mon's as long as I am hiding or being chased. I dinna ken if I'll ever be free to be any other mon's wife. To be Alex's aught.

Brighde felt a moment of pure anguish. Alex watched as several emotions crossed over her face as she thought about what he had just said. He worried that he was frightening her away, but he wanted her to know that not only would he never intentionally harm her, but he also wanted her to be with him for more than a passing fancy.

"Brie, what is going on in that head of yours? Ye seem to have drifted away with worry. Didna I reassure ye that I will never lay a hand on ye in anger?"

"Alex, it isnae that. I was just lost in thought for a moment. Are we going to ride out soon? I can hear people in the bailey, and the stable boys will be awake soon. Do ye want to have to explain what we're doing here?"

"Nay, I dinna."

Alex hurried to finish saddling his horse and led him to the door of the stables. Before lifting her into the saddle, Alex pulled the extra material of Brighde's arisaid over her hair and tucked it close to her face. She clasped it closed under her chin.

"I think yer hair is like spun gold, but it will also be a beacon in the sun. I dinna want to draw any more attention to us than can be avoided."

He grasped her around the waist and lifted her into the saddle. She swung her leg wide and settled astride. She held the reins loosely as Alex mounted behind her. Once he was sure she was comfortable and tucked between his powerful thighs and arms, he nudged the horse towards the gate. He barely nodded to the men on duty as they passed through the portcullis. Once clear of the curtain wall, he veered sharply to the left and skirted the nearby village. He took them along a path that led to the loch. Brighde took in the rugged scenery all around her. The landscape was nearly the exact opposite of where her clan lived in the Lowlands but reminded her, almost painfully, of growing up in the Highlands with her grandparents. She looked out over the gleaming water of the loch as they sped towards it. She thought that perhaps that was their destination, but Alex spurred his horse past it and continued to ride toward a high ridge. As they approached, Brighde could just barely make out the sound of crashing waves. When they crested the ridge, Alex pulled his horse to a stop affording Brighde a breathtaking view of the North Sea. There were clouds on the horizon, and the water was a metallic shade of gray. It looked more like a sea of steel than anything else. The waves churned as they crashed against the shore. The swells were quite high and dotted with white foam.

Brighde rested her hands on Alex's arms for the ride, and now she squeezed them as she took in the scene in front of her. She watched as birds glided and swooped to catch fish. She smelled then saw seals on the far northern part of the beach below them. She pointed to them as though she were a little girl again. Alex's chest rumbled behind her as he laughed at her excitement.

"Can we go down there, Alex? To the water?"

"That was ma plan all along. I thought we could spend the day, or at least part of it, down there. There is plenty to explore, and I wasna sure if you'd ever seen the sea before." Alex slid the last part in with the hopes that it might clue him in at least a little about where she was from.

"Only a few times when I was much younger. I sometimes traveled with ma family to clan gatherings that were held along the coasts."

That gained Alex nothing. He almost groaned in frustration. Instead, he tugged on *Naomh*'s reins and guided them towards a steep slope.

"We must get off here. There isnae anywhere safe to tie *Naomh* down there, and there isnae any grass for him either. We walk the rest of the way."

Alex dismounted and lifted Brighde down. He handed her the picnic basket while he loosely tied *Naomh*'s reins to a nearby tree. There was plenty of grass for him to graze while they spent time on the beach below. Alex took the basket back and led them towards the steep slope that went down to the sand. Alex placed his hand on Brighde's lower back to guide her along the path. She was sure-footed and easily made the descent, but Alex was enjoying the feel of her next to him.

"I amnae going to fall, Alex. Ye dinna need to hover so." Brighde reached back and pulled his hand from her back. At Alex's look of surprise, she slid her hand into his and entwined their fingers. She glanced up at him briefly and then purposefully continued to stare straight ahead as they approached the sand. When they got to the beach, Brighde paused to pull off her boots and stockings. She scrunched her toes into the sand and marveled at the feel of it as it trailed off the top of her feet. It had been nearly a decade since she had last been on a beach, sandy or pebbly. She loved the sea when she was younger and would beg to be taken to any clan gathering where she might be able to play near the water's edge.

She used the sea to keep her bearings as she fled north but never came too close for fear of being spotted by a fisherman or accidentally passing too close to a fishing village. She took Alex's hand and pulled him towards the wet sand.

"Be forewarned. That water is still a wee chilly even in summer." Alex laughed at a little water lapped over her feet, and she yelped. "I told ye."

Alex was not prepared to see Brighde lift her skirts above her knees and wade into the water. He marveled at her as she tucked the extra material into the belt of her arisaid. He had only ever seen his sister and mother do that. No other woman, at least not one young enough to catch his eye, had ever waded in like that.

She has gumption. I will give her that. Alex shucked off his boots and laid his sword close at hand but out of reach of the tide. He waded in behind her, wrapping his arms around her waist as he rested his chin on her head. Brighde relaxed into his hold and closed her eyes. She let the early morning sunshine seep into her skin, and Alex's unique scent fill her nostrils. It was a heady sensation to feel his arms wrapped protectively around her and the strength of his body as a wall around her. His hands rested on her abdomen in an almost protective and possessive manner. With any other man, an act of possessiveness would have made her resist or even flee. With Alex, she never wanted it to end. Her head fell back to rest against his shoulder, and once again, she found herself completely cocooned by his body.

This is where I belong. If only it could stay this way forever. Nay where feels safer or righter than when I am with him and he is holding me. I dinna ken what to do. I never intended to stay here permanently, but now I canna imagine leaving. But I canna stay here forever. I came for their help and temporary protection nae to make a home here. Brighde swallowed down the lump that formed in the back of her throat. *Mayhap the rest of his clan and family arenae as wonderful as he and his father. Mayhap meeting them will make it easier to leave.* Brighde knew that for the lie that it was before she even finished the thought.

"I shall be a vera poor mon if I have to keep offering ye a penny for yer thoughts."

"I was just taking in how peaceful this is. I could spend a lifetime looking out over the water and still see something new every day."

I would offer ye a lifetime if only ye would let me in.

"I never grow tired of coming down here. This is a special spot for ma family. We used to picnic down here when ma mama was still alive. She taught us all to swim, and we would spend hours down here. When Magnus was a little over six summers, he was convinced that our mother was a selkie because she could swim out among the seals, and they never bothered her. Just the opposite, they seemed drawn to her and would swim protectively alongside her. That winter, Da gave Mama a seal skin lined cloak, and Magnus went positively berserk. He was convinced that meant she truly was a selkie and that she would be leaving us to return to the sea. He was inconsolable for days."

Alex laughed lightly at the memory. For years after his mother died, it was painful to remember such stories, but now they filled him with a sense of peace. He knew how fortunate he was to have two parents who loved all their children and enjoyed spending time with them. As he looked down at Brighde and felt his hands resting over her stomach, he suddenly had a longing to create such a life for himself. But only if it was with Brighde. He had never given much thought to marriage before meeting her. He assumed it would happen one day, and most likely by arrangement. Now he could not see himself ever being with another woman. He was man enough to admit that he was falling deeply and quickly in love with the woman whose surname he did not even know.

"Are ye hungry, mo leannan?"

"Aye, a little bit." As if on cue, her stomach rumbled.

"I had best feed ye before ye perish," Alex laughed.

Chapter Eight

hen Alex and Brighde returned to the basket, Alex spread a plaid down while Brighde investigated what had been packed. There was enough food to feed a small army, or at least enough to keep them going for a full day. She pulled out a couple of apples and pears, along with a wheel of cheese, and a fruit tart. She enjoyed Elspeth's tarts several times during her recovery, and they quickly became a favorite. The woman packed three, and Brighde had every intention of eating two of them. By herself.

Alex watched as she lifted the food out, pulling only two tarts out. She handed one to him and took a bite into the other.

"I ken there were three in there. Ye dinna need to hide the third. I willnae take it from ye."

Her eyes opened wide mid-bite. She covered her mouth with her fingers as she chewed, choking down a bite.

"How could ye ken? I havenae seen ye look inside."

"I ken since I asked Elspeth to pack an extra one because I ken they're yer favorite."

Brighde tried to think of things she noticed about Alex's preferences in food. She looked in the basket and pulled out an oil cloth-wrapped bundle that could only be one thing by its smell. She tossed it to him.

"Ye dinna need to worry about yer pickled herring. I will keep ma tarts while ye have yer little dead fish."

"So ye noticed that I favor those. I am glad to ken I dinna need to share them, but I dinna think I'll be breaking ma fast with them. Mayhap a midmorning treat, but most definitely nae this early in the morn."

He pulled the last tart from the basket and broke off a small piece. He watched as a look of dismay flashed across Brighde's face. He chuckled as he pretended to lift the bite towards his mouth. At the last moment, he reached over and brushed it against her bottom lip. She took the bite from him, her tongue skimming his finger as she licked a bit of fruit from her lips. Alex's cock had already been half awake while standing behind her. Now it was fully paying attention. He fed another bite to her. On the fourth bite, Brighde's tongue purposely licked the side and tip of his finger. Alex caught his breath as he paused with his finger against her lips before breaking off another piece. With the fifth and final bite, Brighde sucked the tip of his finger into her mouth. Alex held his breath as her smooth and slippery tongue slid up and down his finger. She slowly took more of it into her mouth until she had it entirely between her lips. She sucked gently on it, gliding her lips up and down. With a growl, Alex launched himself at her. He cradled her as they landed together on the plaid. He attacked her mouth with a savagery that he had never shown before, and she responded in equal measure. She took his tongue into her mouth and mimicked what she had just done with his finger. She reached down and pulled at his plaid until she found the hem, then pulled it up high enough for her hands to find his bare skin. She ran her hands over his backside, squeezing and pressing until her hands once again found the grooves on the side of his hips. She felt him tugging at her kirtle as he, too, raised the material until he could reach her. She felt three fingers press into her making her arch her back off the ground. This only served to present him with her breasts. He pulled the strings loose from the front of her kirtle and freed one of her breasts. He licked and laved until her nipple became a sharp dart then suckled on it as she moaned. His fingers danced in and out of her sheath as her hips moved to a rhythm she could not control. As he moved her closer and closer to completion, she tilted her head back and her eyes closed. The feelings that Alex elicited from her body were almost too much. With her neck now exposed, he shifted to kiss the sensitive skin behind her ear. Pleasure shot straight from her ear to her aching core.

"Alex. Alex, what are ye doing to me?"

She could feel the muscles low in her belly beginning to squeeze and quiver as spasms shook her entire body. Alex worked his fingers in and out as he used his thumb to rub the hidden bud that was the secret to her pleasure. He felt her go rigid for a moment before melting back into the plaid with a moan that made him leak. His engorged sword ached to find a home in her sheath.

Shite! My bullocks feel like they'll explode. Bluidy hell, a dip in the sea isnae going to make this cockstand go down anytime soon. What the hell am I going to do without scaring the lass? Jesus, Mary, and Joseph, this bluidy well hurts.

Alex did all that he could not to groan or wince as he rolled off Brighde. Her eyes were still closed and the rapid rise and fall of her chest told Alex that she was still very out of breath. The glow that exuded from her was enough, or at least nearly enough, to make Alex forget his discomfort. He found an inordinate amount of pride in knowing that he was the first and only man to bring her to completion, twice now, and to have ever touched her in such an intimate way. Along with that came an overwhelming need to claim her as his and only his. The idea of another man ever seeing the look that he saw now made him see red. He forced himself to take deep breaths to slow his own racing heart. He leaned forward and brushed the damp hair from her forehead and placed a gentle peck on the tip of her nose. Brighde's eyes fluttered open, and she looked into the smoky brown eyes that she was getting accustomed to waking to. She reached up and stroked his cheek, and Alex turned his face into her palm. She ran her thumb up and down to feel the smooth skin that was usually hidden by stubble. Her brow crinkled as she thought back on what had just happened.

"Alex, what about ye? I didna get to touch ye. I didna do what I did last time."

"Lass, that is fine. This was for ye, nae for me."

"Couldnae it have been for both? That's why I sucked on yer finger. Cause I wanted to feel ye in ma hand again. To bring ye pleasure."

"Brie, ye do bring me pleasure. Every time I see ye. Every time I'm near ye."

"Alex, that isnae what I mean, and ye ken it. Why didna ye let me help ye find yer release too?"

"Brie, if ye'd touched me, I wouldnae been able to last long enough to enjoy it or to make sure ye enjoyed it too. If I didna come right away, I would have been far too tempted to take yer maidenhead, and that is something nae mine to take."

"But, Alex—"

"Shh, lass. Let it be. It's fine."

Brighde pushed at his shoulder and sat upright. Alex watched the color rise in her cheeks, and he knew it had nothing to do with the pleasure he had just given her. This was anger, and he was about to weather his first storm. What he had seen in the stables was a mere blustery wind in comparison.

"Why dinna ye want me to do it? Is yer desire for release just going to magically dissolve? Or do ye have other plans for how to relieve that cockstand? Aye, I can see ye're still aroused. Who is going to take care of that?" Brighde pushed up to her feet, grabbed her stockings and shoes before moving toward the slope that would take her back up to the horses. She barely took five steps before she was lifted off her feet and tossed over a hard and unforgiving shoulder that bit into her stomach. A firm hand swatted her backside, but only playfully. Her hair came undone while they rolled about, and now it hung down Alex's back almost to his knees. She watched as water began to lap around his ankles and then to his knees. The tips of her hair were beginning to trail in the water.

"Alex, what are ye doing? Ye canna go any deeper. We'll both be soaked."

"I think that temper of yers could do with cooling off." She felt him slide her off his shoulder. He caught up the end of her kirtle but lowered her until she was knee deep.

"Alex, put me down. On the shore," she added as she felt the water rush up towards her thighs. She was surprised that the water was not nearly as cold as she had anticipated. Cold but not frigid. It was relatively bearable.

"I dinna have a temper!" she yelled as she tweaked his ear. "I will give ye an earful if I end up soaked."

"Nay temper, ye say. What do ye call this? A fit of calm?"

"Alex! I'm giving ye fair warning. If ye dinna take me to shore, I will nae give a flying fig about a soaked gown, and I will kick ye in yer swollen cods."

To this Alex only guffawed. Brighde tried to swing her legs, but he easily wrapped his around hers and pinned them between his thighs.

"Haud yer wheesht, Brie." Alex tapped her on the backside again. "What has ye behaving as though ye've sat in a bush of nettles? What did ye mean when ye asked who was going to take care of it?"

"If ye dinna want me to touch ye, then ye must have someone else ye would rather have do it."

Alex was so stunned that this time he did actually let her slip. She landed with a splash, but he was still too shocked to reach out and help her. He felt as though someone had, in fact, just kicked him in the cods. Brighde stood up and pushed her hair out of her face.

"How dare ye? Ye arse! I'm drenched now. Ye have ruined a kirtle that doesnae even belong to me!"

Alex could only look at her dumbfounded. He still could not work through what she had just implied.

"Are ye trying to catch flies or fish with yer gob hanging open?" If Brighde had not been hopping mad about being dropped into the sea, she might have considered Alex's expression humorous. That was until she looked more closely. She saw surprise, but she also saw hurt and confusion.

"Alex?" she asked quietly.

He shook his head as though to clear his thoughts.

"How could ye possibly think that I want any other woman? That I would leave ye and go to another woman?" he asked hoarsely.

"Everyone kens that men must be kept satisfied, or they will find somewhere else to find their pleasure."

"Who kens this?" Alex asked through gritted teeth.

"Well," she shrugged, "everyone. That's who."

"That is a pile of tripe. I dinna ken who's been filling yer head with such rubbish, but ye insult me. I dinna want anyone else! I only want ye, damn it. I canna stop wanting ye. I can barely think of aught other than ye. The thought of any other woman touching me makes me ill." He turned away and stalked out of the water.

Brighde lifted her skirts up as she tried to catch up to him.

"Alex, wait. Wait, damn it. I canna keep up with yer long legs and nae with these sopping skirts tangled aboot mine."

At the reminder of having dropped her into the water, Alex did pause. As shocked, hurt, and now angry as he was, he had not meant to drop her. Brighde caught up to him and stepped around him, so she was facing him.

"Alex, it's what I was told ever since I arrived back at ma father's clan. Ma stepmother, his former mistress, said that's why he didna want ma mother and why she was better than ma mother. Ma grandmama said that most men will go for the willing and easy catch and that I should prepare for ma future husband to have a mistress too. It's just the way of men."

"It isnae the way of the Sinclair men." Alex looked down at her as her teeth began to chatter. He took her wrist in his hand and tugged her back towards their abandoned picnic. He yanked another plaid from the basket and wrapped it around her. He lifted her hair from beneath the blanket before taking a deep breath. Her innocence and naivety hit him fully as she looked up at him with tears threatening.

Alex pulled her into his arms and rested his cheek on the crown of her head. He liked that she fit so perfectly, tucked under his chin. He stroked her back to warm and comfort her.

"I'm sorry I dropped ye, but ye shocked me. I wasna expecting such a question or accusation. I didna ken that's what ye'd been taught about men. Leannan, nae all men are like yer father. Is that how yer grandda treated yer grandmama?" He felt her shake her head. "See. Yer grandmama may have been wise to warn that *some* men behave that way. But nae all, leannan. I would never do that to ye or any woman. And if that doesnae reassure ye, ken that ma da would skelp me within an inch of ma life if I ever did something so dishonorable. I amnae a fickle mon. I would never lead a woman on like that, nor use any woman like that. I dinna ken what is worse. Ye thinking that I would toy with ye, or that I would seek out another woman and use her to slake a lust created by someone else."

Brighde leaned back and saw the concern in Alex's face. But she also saw the steadfastness that saved her life when she fought a fever that kept pulling her under, that took her to his mother's garden every day just so she could feel the sunshine on her face, that organized a picnic she now ruined.

"I'm sorry, Alex," she whispered, "I just didna ken. It hasnae been ma experience to see men so honorable. Other than ma grandfather and uncle, I havenae been around too many faithful or honorable men."

Alex scooped her up and sank down to the sand. He kept her bundled in the plaid.

"Brie, I think it is time that ye finally told me yer past. We canna continue like this. The secrets are only going to cause us trouble. I canna fight ghosts. I canna fight demons I dinna ken to look for."

"It isnae yer responsibility to fight ma demons."

"Canna I decide what responsibilities I take on? I chose to make ye ma responsibility the moment I brought ye inside the gates. Brie, who are ye?"

Brighde looked out to sea for so long Alexander doubted she would ever answer the question. He was about to give up when she finally spoke.

"Ma full name is Brighde Mairi Kerr. Ma father is the Kerr laird, and ma mother was a Campbell, but her mother was from Northumberland. Ma grandfather's mother was also English, but I dinna remember who her kin was."

"Ye are from the vera opposite end of Scotland from where we sit now. How did ye come to be so far away from home?"

"That isnae ma home," she said with bite. "I mean, that may be where I lived for the past several of years, and that may have been where I was born, but ma father and stepmother made it vera clear it wasna ma home. Ma home was with the Campbells until ma grandparents and uncle, along with his wife and ma wee cousin, all perished. There wasna aught left for me there. The new laird wasna a member of the old laird's immediate family. I was far too young to marry off, so I was just another mouth to feed in a clan that had just lost half its people to disease. I was more a burden than a blessing. Seems to be a common occurrence in ma life."

Brighde rested her head against Alex's chest while he took in all she told him. This story sounded all too familiar after what he knew of Siùsan's life before she came to Castle Dunbeath to marry his brother. Alex was not so sheltered that he could not understand that life was hard for a woman who had no protector or family, but he took that for granted when he thought about how his sister was a cherished member of his family and his clan. He could not imagine ever neglecting a daughter or sister, but he could see that it was all too frequent an occurrence. He held Brighde just a little tighter.

"Ma father decided about a year ago that I was too old to stay at home, and I was overdue to be married off. He began searching for someone who would be willing to pay a small fortune as a bride price and not expect a large dowry in return. Needless to say, such a mon is hard to come by. During the early part of this past spring, ma father finally found someone who would agree to marry me under ma father's conditions. The mon was the bastard son of Nicholas de Soules, Randolph de Soules."

Brighde knew she shocked Alexander without looking at his face or hearing a word. The tension radiated off him and practically pulsed through every nerve.

"Aye, that de Soules family."

"But how?"

"Sir Nicholas was willing to pay the bride price on behalf of his bastard because his legitimate sons were beginning to grow angry at Sir Randolph's privileges within their father's house. Even though Randolph is the oldest, William is the legitimate heir and wanted Randolph as far from him as possible. The talk is that William isnae right in the head. He is easily brought to a rage, and he has been kenned to kidnap and abuse local girls. Apparently, Randolph isnae any better. Randolph admitted to killing his first two wives who did not produce sons for him. I wasna willing to make him a widower thrice. I was not adverse to the idea of marriage until I found out who I was to marry. When ma father announced who he planned to marry me off to, I tried to run away. I made it almost two days before his men tracked me down. The bruises that ye saw that were closest to healed were from him beating me before locking me in ma chamber for two days. A day locked away for each day that I ran away. On the third day after I was returned, we rode out to meet the de Soules in Liddesdale. Ma father set a grueling pace and wouldnae stop each day until the horses were nearly dropping out from under us. We were about two days away from Liddesdale when we were attacked, but it wasna like any attack I could imagine. I mean I assume every battle is some form of chaos, but this was far too orchestrated. The men rode into the clearing where we just set up camp. It was dark, and half the men hadnae returned from hunting. Looking back, I ken that it was odd so many men went hunting when all we needed were a few hares and maybe some squirrels. I never saw ma father fight. He wasna even there. There were only about five men who attempted to defend me. The rest just melted into the woods. The men who attacked far outnumbered us, so most of them did not even engage. Three of these men found me hiding behind a tree and pulled me into the center of camp. One of them threw me to the ground, and" she took a breath to collect herself, "tried to rape me, but I kept a dirk in ma boot and stabbed him in the neck. When the other two tried to hold me down, I slashed at them as I scrambled to stand up. I think the others were too stunned to move at first. I dinna ken if I killed them, but I think I did. Nae mon came to help me. Instead, they and Randolph de Soules watched. When de Soules grabbed me, he threw me to the ground and landed on top of me. He started pawing me, pinching and squeezing. I truly thought he was going to be the one to succeed. I tried to fight him off, but he was so much larger than me, and all it did was anger him and made him more vicious. One of ma father's men who had been with me since I first went to ma grandparents was able to get me away from him and on ma horse. I rode as far and as fast as I could, but I was followed by Sir Randolph himself. One of his archers shot ma horse, and I was thrown. I rolled off a ledge into a ravine. It was too dark for them to see me, so I laid still until I hadnae seen anyone for at least an hour. I did hear the men talking aboot me just after I stopped falling.

"What I heard them say was enough to make me want to run, but I forced maself to wait. I could hear them say that they wouldnae risk their own necks by going down to retrieve me, that ma body would still be a tangle whether they dragged me out then or when the sun rose. Randolph laughed and said this was the easiest purse he ever earned. I strained to hear and understand what he was talking aboot. I could only catch snippets, but I heard enough to understand that he and ma father conspired to do away with me, so ma father could keep ma dowry, and Sir Randolph would make off with the bride price he carried that was supposedly for ma father.

"Ma father hadnae signed the betrothal papers yet, but I wouldnae doubt he has since then. Aught to make it legal for him to allegedly receive the bride price, but without a marriage, he wouldnae have to surrender the dowry if I was dead first.

"I waited that hour before I even checked to see if I could move. When I was sure that I hadnae broken any part of ma legs, I stood up. I nearly fell back over. The pain in ma ribs was so severe that I retched. I was terrified they would hear me and then find me. I forced maself to take one step at a time until I could orient maself. I kenned that Liddesdale was only miles from the border, but we were still at least a day and a half away. Ma father purposely aligned himself with a family that has nay loyalty to Scotland and enjoys the prosperity that comes from selling themselves to the Sassenachs. Anyway, I forced maself to find moss on the trees around me and headed in the opposite direction until I made ma way out of the ravine. I traveled south until I was sure I created a trail long enough to lead the men in that direction. I barely managed to pull maself up onto the opposite side of the ridge and doubled back, praying they wouldnae find ma second trail. When I was back to where I started and directly across from them, I was sure one of the men on guard spotted me. The sky was starting to lighten, and I worried he saw the motion, but he was only getting up to pish, which he blessedly did facing away from me. I forced maself to walk as quickly as I could while remaining silent. Once I was a mile or so past them, I forced maself to start running. I have never felt pain like I did that day. That first day of running with battered ribs nearly defeated me. I could barely see straight as there were stars dancing in front of ma eyes for hours, but I ran and ran, and when I thought I couldnae go any further, I remembered what I heard about Randolph's two previous wives, what Randolph said when he thought I was already dead, and that ma father disappeared when we were attacked. I ran because I didna ever want to see either of them again, and I ran because I kenned that if I ever did, I really would be dead.

"After that first day, I slept most of the next when I found a cave tucked into a small hill a mile or so from the road. I'd spent the time traveling through woods with the road just barely visible to help me keep ma bearings. I was terrified that I would find a snake or rodent in there. I kenned it wasna large enough for a mountain lion or wolf because I could barely move once I was inside. It was all I needed. I awoke just before dusk the next day. From then on, I slept during the day and traveled at night. I constantly feared running across lawless men, but by traveling in the dark, I kenned I was far less likely to be spotted or tracked by anyone. The quiet of the night made it easier for me to avoid people whether there were campfires or villages. I did this for the two weeks that it took me to travel north."

"Good God, what did ye eat? How did ye manage the mountain passes? How could ye travel that far in only two weeks if ye were on foot?" Alex was struggling to make heads or tails of what Brighde was telling him. He did not have any trouble believing that a de Soules would be deceitful or dangerous. The family was known to play both sides of the field when it came to their loyalties. They were also well known for having a cruel and mad streak that ran wide. Alex simply could not imagine this woman traveling alone so far and for so long. He would not want to undertake such a dangerous journey on his own let alone without a horse and supplies. He knew she could not have known her way, so he was rightly impressed by her navigation and survival skills.

"I hunted when I could, and cooked ma catches just as the sun came up or before it set, so ma campfires couldnae be seen. I kept them small and only burned them long enough to cook the rabbit or squirrel or fish. When I made it to Douglas territory, I found an inn I stayed in several times with ma grandparents when we traveled. Blessedly, the innkeeper remembered me. One look at me and she didna ask any questions. She arranged for me to ride in a hay wagon with a farmer to Campbell territory where I knew I wouldnae be turned over. I walked for a day until I found a village where I was recognized. I tried to stay hidden, but I collapsed in a pasture I tried to sneak through. A farmer who had been a warrior when he and ma grandfather were young took me in. His wife fed me and packed food for me. I told them only what I had to. That I wasna safe with ma father, and I had to get away. They could see from the state I was in that I wasna exaggerating. The farmer's wife bound ma ribs, and the next day, the farmer put me in his wagon and took me to Loch Lochy where I hid aboard a fishing boat that was headed further north toward Loch Oich. I met the young son of the boat's owner and convinced him to hide me. He was barely older than I was when I left the Campbells. I managed to stay hidden under a large tarp behind several barrels for nearly three days. I only moved the smallest bit at night when the crew slept, and the boy brought me food or shielded me when I needed to relieve maself. It was calm at night, so there often wasna anyone awake but the boy and me. When they docked just before Loch Oich, I scrambled over the side and then walked until I was able to find another boat to take me most of the way up Loch Ness. I traded ma mother's ruby necklace I stitched into a hidden pocket in ma gown before I left Clan Kerr for passage to Inverness. Before I left Kerr land, I had an overwhelming feeling that I would need something of value if I was to survive. I just hadnae imagined it would be to flee ma own father. I was able to travel all the way to Inverness. I then walked from Inverness to here. I dinna even remember when I lost ma shoes, but they fell apart at some point. The innkeeper and the farmer's wife both offered me clothes, but neither could afford to spare them. They were already doing so much including risking their lives to help me. I just couldnae take more. Being able to travel along the lochs saved me weeks of walking and hiding. I dinna think I would have survived if I hadnae been able to sail most of the way. Nae only did it keep me moving quickly, it gave me time to rest and kept me out of the rain for several days. But it rained almost every single minute that I walked from Inverness to here. I would be happy if I never saw another raindrop in ma life." She finished with a weak laugh. "I'm sorry I didna trust ye and questioned yer honor when ye keep proving to me ye're the most honorable mon I ken."

"Nae every mon is a cad. Aye, some are, mayhap even many, but nae all. To be unfaithful would be disloyal and dishonorable. I am a Highlander, and I live by ma honor, but as a second son, if I dinna have that, I wouldnae have aught."

Alex pulled back to see how Brighde received his declaration. She appeared thoughtful before her face relaxed, and she nodded her head. Alex was relieved that she so easily accepted his explanation.

"Lass, I am grateful that ye trust me enough to tell me yer tale. I have been wondering and picturing any number of things, but none comes close to the story ye have just told me. I thank the blessed Lord that ye survived after all ye endured."

Alex pulled her into his embrace and rested his cheek on her crown. This position was becoming as familiar and natural as his broad stance with arms crossed.

"I'm sorry I dropped ye. Ye're wet and cold now, and it's ma fault. If ye'd like to return to the keep, I'll pack everything back into the basket."

Brighde bit her bottom lip and pulled at it with her teeth. Heat shot through Alex and settled in his already aching groin.

This isnae the time to be feeling randy, but she is the most sensual and attractive woman I've ever met. It should be ma teeth pulling on that plump lip.

"Do we have to go back because I really dinna want to. I'd rather stay here with ye." She could feel herself blushing at the end. "Mayhap we could go for a walk and ma gown will dry." She tilted her head up towards the sun.

"Ye ken there isnae much likelihood that will happen. Ye're more likely to catch the ague and be feverish again before nightfall."

Brighde looked around and spotted a larger boulder a little further down the beach. She looked over her shoulder as she began to walk purposefully towards it.

"Dinna follow. Just wait here a moment."

She dashed over to the rock and threw the plaid over it. She began to tug at her laces. Her plan had been to take off her gown, wrap herself back in the plaid, and lay her kirtle out to dry, but she quickly realized she was stuck. The saltwater and sand had already started to harden the laces, and the more she yanked, the worse they knotted. Frustrated, she blew the hair off her eyes and tried to calm herself with a deep breath.

Zounds! Now, what am I going to do? The whole point of coming behind the rock was to avoid Alex seeing any more of me than he already has. Granted he has basically seen it all. Why, dammit? I just need to get these laces untied, but I dinna even have a dirk to cut them, and kenning me, I'd probably cut ma finger off while trying to slice laces up ma back. There's no helping it. If I want to stay, then he must help me. Argh!

"Alex." Brighde poked her head around the rock, but Alex was too far for him to hear her if she did not call louder. *Wonderful. Now, nae only do I have to ask him to undress me, but I have to caterwaul to get his attention. How vera ladylike. As if swearing werenae enough for me to have to confess. Now I'll be saying a baker's dozen of the Lord's prayer and another dozen Hail Mary.*

"Alex!" she tried a little louder as she kept peering around the wall.

"Aye?" Alex had been watching her, but he could see very little thanks to the boulder blocking his view, a view he very much wished he could enjoy.

"Alex, I need help. Please." Brighde wanted to sink into the sand and disappear. It was one thing when they were in the throes of passion. She had not even thought twice about what he might have seen, but now, like this, she was embarrassed to the point where she reconsidered his offer to return to the keep.

"Aye, lass. What's wrong?"

Brighde had not heard him approach and yelped. She covered her heart with her hand and looked up. The sun was behind his head and cast gold threads through his hair. She had to screen her eyes to see him otherwise his head looked like it glowed with a halo. What she was about to ask of him would make him either a sinner or a saint.

"I canna untie the laces. They're stuck because of the salt and sand. I dinna have a dirk with me, and even if I did, I dinna think I could cut upwards behind me without taking off a finger or two. Can ye help, please?"

Alex looked down at her for a moment and could only nod his head. She turned and presented her back to him while pulling her hair over her shoulder. He waited so long that she looked back at him with an eyebrow raised.

"Right, aye. The laces." Alex lifted his hands and watched as his fingers trembled.

I amnae some green lad with his first lass. I have undressed enough women to ken what I am doing, but I never really cared before. It was just a necessary step to get to what I wanted. Now? I care just a wee bit too much.

Alex lifted the end of the laces and examined the tangled mess that they were and tried to start pulling them apart with his fingers. He knew he could not cut through them because even though that would solve their immediate problem, it would cause nothing short of a calamity if Brighde returned to the keep with her dress cut open. As harmless as they might know it was, the rest of the clan would be shooing them to the kirk before the moon rose and the stars came out. *Mayhap that wouldnae be so bad after all. Where the hell did that come from? I dinna want to marry. Dinna lie to yerself, mon. Dinna lie.* The realization that he would not mind marrying Brighde was a strong one, but at the same time, it seemed like the most natural thing for him to do next. As though marriage was the only logical and inevitable next step. However, he was quite sure that she would not see it that way.

"Brie, ye're going to have to be a bit patient. These laces are a right mess. I canna cut the laces unless ye want the whole clan to gossip, so it'll take just a moment."

Brighde shifted her weight from foot to foot as Alex worked to free the tangled web. He tried prying them apart with his fingers and even considered using his teeth. He finally settled for using his dirk but only to give him some leverage, so he could loosen the knots. It took almost five minutes for him to work everything free, but once the last knot was untied, the kirtle slid down her shoulders. Alex saw the creamy skin that the kirtle and nightgown always hid. The chemise she wore had been a snowy white but was now translucent as it clung to her. Brighde looked over her shoulder again to thank Alex but froze when she saw the hunger in his eyes. The gnawing need to be closer to him made her core ache. She turned to look forwards again as she let the gown puddle about her feet. She felt the softest feathering touch as Alex ran his fingers up her arm, and along the top of her shoulder until he reached her neck. He lifted her hair and pressed soft kisses to her nape. He wrapped his other arm around her middle and pulled her back against his hard body. The warmth that he radiated against her made her think that she was standing too close to a fire that would soon burn her. She knew that they were entering even more dangerous territory with her practically naked in front of him, but she was willing to get a little singed.

Alex licked and nipped and kissed along her shoulder and nape as the hand that had been resting across her belly splayed and moved down over her mound. He grasped the material of Brighde's chemise and pulled it up until he found the hem. Brighde reached down to take the material from him as she held it above her waist. She pressed her bottom back against his hips and reached her other arm back over her shoulder to run her fingers into his hair. This forced her to arch her back, and Alex reached around to cup her heavy breast. He feasted on her neck, chin, and shoulder while kneading her breast, and massaging the tender folds of her nether lips. As he dipped two fingers into the moist seam, Brighde ground her buttocks into him. Frustrated by his sporran, she released his hair and pushed the offending accessory out of the way. She ground her backside into his rock-hard cock. She reached back with both hands to grip his hips and pulled them towards her as she pressed into him. She moaned, and he groaned at the same time. Alex turned them, so they were facing the bolder. He gently pressed Brighde to lean forward against it and lifted her left leg to place her foot on the rock. He covered her body with his own, and she luxuriated in the feeling of his sheer size against her smaller body. He completely encompassed her as he ground his cock into her bottom.

"Do ye ken how badly I want to be inside ye right now? Do ye ken how much I want to feel ye squeeze me dry as I watch ye ride me? I want to plunge maself into ye over and over until I canna see straight. I have never desired *anyone* the way I do ye. What are ye doing to me, lass?" Alex whispered in her ear before he dropped down to his knees.

He grasped her buttocks and spread the cheeks apart. He had the most glorious view of everything he wanted to claim as his. He palmed the junction between her legs and could feel the heat emanating from her. He slid his hand back and forth using his middle finger to unveil and release the sensitive flesh that was hidden within her curls. Slowly, he slid two then three fingers into her and began to stroke her from the inside.

"Alex, what are ye doing to me? How do ye make me feel hot and cold at the same time? Ye make me ache and burn, and I dinna ken how to make it stop. I dinna understand what I need, but I feel so empty right now. I ache, Alex."

"Sshh, mo ghràidh. I will ease yer ache, but I willna rush us."

My darling. God, how I want to hear him call me that every day for the rest of our lives.

Brighde's thoughts were cut short as she felt him blow cool air against her most sacred of spaces. She tried to clench her bottom, but he gently pressed his free hand against her. Then she felt his cool tongue against he, and it felt like ice melting on her scorched skin. He used the flat of his tongue to run from stem to stern and back again. He left not an inch free from his tongue's inspection. When Brighde began to writhe, he used the tip of his tongue to play around with the button at her apex. She nearly screamed when she felt the tip of his tongue press into her, and her knees gave out as he sucked on the button that opened the flood of sensation rushing through her. As Alex felt the spasms begin within her, he drove his three fingers back into her and worked her as he came to his feet. As quickly as it had started, the tremors passed. Alex barely lifted his plaid to take himself in hand when Brighde spun around and pushed him back a step. She fell to her knees, and looking up at him, pushed his plaid out of the way, so she could lean forward to lick the drop of seed glistening on the tip.

"Mmmm. A bit salty but better than seawater." She gave him a saucy smile before looking down at his engorged length. She wrapped her hand around him and swirled her tongue around the head of his shaft. Alex watched in amazement as she opened her palm, so she could lick him from top to bottom and all around.

"Does what ye did to me feel that good for ye?"

Alex could only nod his head.

"Can I put it in ma mouth?" Alex nodded again.

"And suck on it." Alex made a strangled sound, and breathed out, "please."

Brighde looked down and had a moment of doubt as she considered just how endowed he was. Alex realized what he thought was also what he said aloud.

"Ye dinna have to. I dinna expect ye to do this. Ever." He tried to step back and lower his plaid.

"I ken. Even more reason why I want to." She licked him again and found a ridge that ran along his length. When she flicked her tongue against it, he twitched. The groan that escaped Alex let her know she had done something he enjoyed. She swirled her tongue around the head of his cock again and then sunk her mouth onto him. It took every single ounce of any control Alex could still muster not to find his release right then and there. The sight in front of him was the most purely erotic thing he had ever seen or experienced. Brighde wrapped her hand around the part of him that was too much for her to take in and began to stroke him. Her head moved in time with her hand. When her hair fell forward and created a curtain that kept him from enjoying his view, Alex scooped her hair back and held it out of the way. Alex knew that if he kept watching her, he would not be able to stop himself from climaxing. He tilted his head back and closed his eyes. Without the sense of sight, his senses of touch and sound only heightened. The feel of her warm, soft mouth gliding over him as her hand stroked him and the soft slurping noises were more than he could take. He looked back down and released her hair. He tried to gently push her away from him, to get her to release him, but she batted his hand away.

"Brie, ye must stop. I canna come in yer mouth. If ye dinna stop now, I will explode. Brie!" It was too late. As he tried to convince her to stop, she only sucked and stroked harder and faster. Before he could stop himself, he felt jets of his seed spray into her. She swallowed as much as she could as it trickled down the back of her throat. When she felt the last drop dribble onto her cheek, she pulled back. She felt quite proud of herself and slowly licked her lips. She looked up at Alex, and had it been anyone else, his look of shock and awe might have made her smile. Instead, it only made her feel self-conscious. She pushed back off her heels and tried to take a step away, but the bolder blocked her retreat. She looked around and then down at her feet.

Gentle fingers lifted her chin, and she looked up into the nut-brown eyes she was growing to adore. Alex's lips descended onto hers in a gentle kiss. She reached up on her tiptoes, so she could wrap her arms around his neck. Alex lifted her off her feet and propped her against the rock as he settled between her legs. He wrapped his arms around her as his hands ran up and down her sides. He kissed her cheek and tilted his forehead against hers.

"I dinna ken what to say. I havenae ever experienced aught like that before."

"Ye mean nae woman has ever done that for ye?" Brighde scoffed, "I dinna believe that."

"I dinna mean that. Aye, there have been others who have done that, but none have ever done it like that. It hasnae ever felt like that."   ·

"If I wasna doing it properly, ye should have told me how ye wanted it."

Alex almost choked on his tongue as he looked down at her. *Will this woman never cease to say the last thing I ever expect to hear. Is she a bampot? How could she possibly think I didna like that or that she did it wrong? Alex, ye daft bugger. She's never done it before. I should be counting this as a blessing both that I am the only mon she's ever touched and she's a bluidy natural.*

"Brie, I dinna ken how ye could think ye didna do it right. It was the most pleasurable thing I have ever felt. But, Brie, a mon doesnae ask a lady to do that. That's nae even something many men ask a whore to do. Ye didna have to do it."

"I ken, but I wanted to. What ye did for me was—was---well, I dinna even ken how to describe how good it all felt and how much I wanted to do the same for ye. It was like ma mouth suddenly ached too and watered at the idea of tasting ye. I just felt this overwhelming need to take ye into ma mouth." Brighde shrugged, "And ye didna let me touch ye earlier. I wanted to then, and it was like a need now. Nae only because I felt like I should reciprocate but because it gives me pleasure to touch ye. To hopefully give ye the pleasure ye gave me."

Brighde fisted his leine and tugged none too gently.

"Come here," she breathed out.

Alex leaned forward, and she pulled him in for a scorching kiss that lit the fire all over again. Alex laid her back on the rock and stretched her arms above her head. He pulled the ribbons loose from the neckline of her chemise. He pulled apart the collar and freed both her breasts. He simply took a moment to look down and appreciate their size and dusky rose tips. His stare and the cool breeze made them harden into little points. He grasped one of them and lifted it to his mouth. He had no patience to toy with it, and instead took as much of the generous mound of smooth flesh into his mouth as he could. He suckled like a starving bairn. He simply could not get enough, and Brighde's moans only spurred him on. Switching hands on her wrists, he used the other to gently pinch her free nipple. When her knees clenched his hips, and hers lifted off the rock, he bit lightly onto the nipple in his mouth and pinched the one between his fingers.

"Alex!"

Brighde could feel the pressure growing between her legs again. It started as a slow ache and restlessness that eventually began to burn almost to a level of pain.

"Alex, *please. Please.* Do something. I dinna ken what's happening again, but dear merciful God, I ache for ye."

Alex lifted his plaid and fisted his fully erect rod, bringing it to her entrance. He allowed the head to slide through the juices pooled within her again. He slowly rocked his hips back and forth as he coated the head of his shaft. He was seconds away from finally finding relief for them both when a seagull squawked, and a seal barked. The noise somehow permeated the sound of his heartbeat pulsing in his ears. He jumped back and looked down at his cock in his hand and Brighde's legs spread wide. He looked around at the beach as if in a trance. It was only as Brighde scrambled up the rock, tugging her chemise down, that he fully understood exactly how close he came to claiming her innocence. His honor rebuked him for being so reckless and selfish while his desire screamed that he should have made her his.

Brighde watched Alex through lowered lashes. She watched the confusion, the shock, and then the shame wash over him. He pulled his sporran back in front of him and pushed his hands through his hair before scrubbing his face with his palms. She slid down from the rock and grasped his wrists. She tried to pull his hands away from his face, but he was too strong and too stubborn, so instead, she wiggled her way into his embrace by sliding up between his elbows. She wrapped her arms around his waist.

"Alex," she whispered. "Alex, look at me. Please dinna shut me out and dinna ignore me."

When he lowered his arms to his side but would not look at her, she pinched his backside. Hard.

"Brie," he warned.

"Nay. Dinna 'Brie' me. Ye dinna do aught wrong. I was as much a part of what happened, and I enjoyed it just as much as ye. Dinna retreat from me. If I wanted to end things, I would have."

"Ye dinna ken what I was planning to do. Ye dinna ken how close ye came to losing yer maidenhead. Yer virtue is nae mine to take."

"True, but it is mine to give. Mayhap it wouldnae been the best choice either of us could make, but I dinna think I would regret it."

"Ye canna say that. Ye canna ken for sure it wouldnae been the greatest mistake of yer life."

"Because it would have been yers? My greatest mistake because it would have been yers too?" Brighde released him and spun away. She ripped her gown off the ground and moved away from the rock.

"Brie, dinna walk away. Please. I'm only trying to protect ye."

Brighde halted and when she spun around, Alex braced himself. She marched back to him and threw her kirtle back down. She stood to her fullest height and pointed an angry finger at him.

"Dinna! Dinna think that ye ken what's best for me all the time. Dinna think ye have the right to take ma choices away from me. Ye'll never have that right. And dinna feel like ye must protect me all the time. I dinna need it. I certainly dinna need ye protecting me from yerself. I'm a woman full grown, and I ken ma own mind. I ran to the Sinclairs to escape men who would control me nae to find more." She was fully yelling by the time she was finished.

Alex spread his feet wide and crossed his arms then leaned forward from the hips. Even like this, and even though she was not that much shorter than him, he still managed to tower over her.

"Dinna need to protect ye? From me? Ye really are naïve then. Do ye ken what I was aboot to do? I was aboot to fuck ye. Aye, fuck. I was going to take ye against a rock as hard and fast as I could. I was going to stick ma cock in ye, and pound into ye until ye were screaming ma name. I wanted to fill ye with ma seed until I couldnae see straight and then probably try it again in five minutes. Ye make me lose all sense of self-control, and ye ken the only person that would harm? That would be ye. What if I planted a bairn in yer belly? What if people learned that I'd compromised ye? Ye want to talk about nae taking choices away from ye, well what kind of choices do ye think ye would have then?" Alex bellowed. He was shaking with anger that was as equally directed at her as at himself. "I dinna want to force ye into aught, and that includes staying here. If I had taken yer maidenhead, that choice would have gone away because I can tell ye that I wouldnae let ye walk away once we'd been together. Ye can be bluidy certain of that."

Alex stood up and stared out to sea. He was still shaking with anger and guilt. It was an overwhelming sensation that left him feeling like he had just been in battle. His chest heaved as he took deep lungfuls of air. He looked down when he felt two small hands gently rest on his forearm. He tried not to scowl, but he was not sure he was successful.

"Alex, ye are right. I dinna think I'm wrong either, but I can admit that ye are right. Either way, I dinna want to keep arguing today. We have argued more in this morning than I would have ever imagined. The daftest part of it is that I think we are arguing the same side but against one another. I dinna think this is us. Nae really. Our frustration comes from us both wanting something we ken we canna have. Ye are temptation incarnate for me, and I ken that. If I can just keep a little distance from ye and nae let maself get carried away by yer muscles and whisky colored eyes, then we would both be better off. I still dinna want to give up on the day ye planned."

Alex looked down at her and uncrossed his arms. As he did so, he purposely flexed his chest, so it would strain against his leine, and he batted his eyelashes at her. She could not help but giggle.

"Ma braw muscles, ye say. And what was that again? Ma whisky colored eyes. Lass, ye're going to make me blush."

Brighde swatted at his arm and leaned down to yet again pick up her clothes.

"I didna mean it as a compliment. I was just stating a fact." She turned to once again walk towards their abandoned picnic. She felt a swat on her backside that made her jump forward a step or two.

"If I'm temptation incarnate, then ye are the devil in disguise. I canna help but want to spend ma day staring at and touching yer petal soft skin and silky skeins of hair. I have never seen hair like yers before. It and all the rest of ye mesmerizes me."

"See, now. Ye can be quite the charmer when ye want to be," Brighde said as Alex walked alongside her. She leaned back slightly to get a good look at his backside as his plaid swished about his legs. She once again caught Alex off guard when she gave him a firm swat on his backside. At his look of surprise, she responded smugly, "what's good for the gander is good for the goose."

The rest of the day passed nicely for them. Alex had the foresight to pack up their picnic while Brighde had been walking to and then hiding behind the rock. It has saved it from the seagulls that were dancing around the basket in search of a way to claim the booty. They ate and talked for a while, and once the tide began to go out, Alex took Brighde over to a sea cave that he and his siblings explored often as children. With the water low, they were easily able to wade and climb into the cave entrance. The sun was angled to let light into the dark recesses, and Brighde could see where the Sinclair children had carved their names and pictures into the walls. There was still a pile of driftwood stored in the back, but it was old and rotten after too much exposure to the water and damp air.

Alex led Brighde to the back of the cave where she found a deep pool that looked like it was naturally lit from below. Alex explained that it was actually light refracted through a hole in the ceiling. When the tide came in and the water was rough, the opening served as a blowhole. The water spout could be viewed from the ridge above where they had tied up his horse.

"The water is actually warmer in this pool than ye would expect. We think there is a natural spring that helps to fill this because even with all the seawater that washes into the cave when the tide is high, the pool never gets that cold."

"Can I swim in it?"

"Do ye ken how to swim?"

"Aye. Like a fish."

"Then ye can, but we canna dally once the tide begins to shift. If we dinna leave the cave right away, we'll be trapped. Neither of us would fit through the blowhole, so there is nae escape once the water rises, and the waves will only push us back in rather than letting us out."

Brighde nodded her head as she peered over the side of the pool. She could see the bottom, and it was far too deep for her to ever dive all the way down. She moved along until she inched her way up a cluster of rocks to the ledge that jutted out over the water. Alex watched as she climbed, only mildly surprised at her agility and strength. He reminded himself of all she survived to make it to his clan. He was just about to warn her about the rocks being slippery with algae when she stepped to the edge and dove into a flip. She did two somersaults before diving perfectly into the water, leaving nearly no splash at all. Alex watched as she traveled further and further into the pool's depths like an arrow shot from a Welsh bow. He began to worry when she did not turn to come back up to the surface. He unfastened his sporran and let his plaid drift to the ground. He pulled his leine over his head and gripped the handle of his dirk between his teeth. He and his brothers and sister had often seen menacing fish when they dove too deeply. He was kicking himself for forgetting to warn her about them. He scaled the ledge from which Brighde dove, knowing that he needed the added height to give him enough force to follow her down. He plunged into the water and looked around for her. Between the light that glowed in the water and her luminescent blonde hair, she was easy to spot. She was no longer moving deeper but was simply floating. He kicked his legs to reach her but was careful not to startle her. The last thing he needed was for her to expel all her air or suck in water when they were so far below the surface. He carefully came around her and approached slowly. He swam into her line of sight, and she waved. Then she pointed down to where a group of fish was swimming. Alex nodded his head but pointed upwards. She nodded, looking once more down at the school, and then began to kick her way to the surface. Alex watched as her hair flowed around her back, and her strong legs moved her higher and higher. If he had been a sailor, he would have sworn he was watching a mermaid or a selkie.

When they both reached the surface, they pulled themselves out and laid on their backs to catch their breath. When Alex finally felt like his lungs were not going to explode, he rolled onto his side to look at her. She smiled up at him and then rolled to face him. They lay on their sides looking at each other for what felt like an eternity, but they were both content. Brighde shivered once and found herself being pulled into Alex's embrace. She burrowed her way into his chest to find the spot on his shoulder where her head fit perfectly.

"Alex, thank ye for bringing me here. I ken this is a special place for yer family. I dinna think ye've brought anyone else down here, so sharing this means a great deal to me."

"I havenae brought anyone else here. I dinna think any of ma brothers or ma sister have ever brought someone else here either. Mama and Da taught us to explore the cave, and once they were sure we wouldnae easily get ourselves killed, they let us come down here as long as there were at least three of us."

"Three?"

"That way if something happened to one of us, there would be one to go for help and one to stay with the injured."

"So, who was usually left out? Mairghread?"

"Nay. She was usually the first one to make it in here. Ye say ye swim like a fish, but ma sister was born with gills, I swear. For the longest time, it was all four of us who came together, but as Callum got older and started being trained to one day be the laird, he wasna able to slip away as easily." Brighde watched as Alex stared over her shoulder lost to memories. Memories that Brighde would never have. She had been raised like an only child when she was with her grandparents because her uncle did not marry until just a year before her family died of sickness. When she returned to her father's keep, her half-brothers were not only disinterested in her, they were often cruel. Her half-sisters thought themselves better than her and snubbed her at every opportunity. She spent much of her time in the gardens or riding her horse alone. A pang of emotion that she realized was jealousy washed over her. It was brief but intense. She knew she would never have what Alex had, and that was more than just siblings. She would never have a warm and loving family, a place where she felt like she belonged, or a home where she longed to stay. These had all been out of her reach her entire life, and they did not appear to be getting any more attainable.

Alex brushed the backs of his fingers against her cheek and then stroked the back of her head.

"I ken ye didna have a similar upbringing, but ye are home here for as long as ye would like."

She smiled up at him and nodded. She closed her eyes and rested her head against him. They laid like that until Alex felt himself starting to drift off.

"Brie, we canna stay much longer. I nearly fell asleep. It must be getting close to when the tide changes. We need to go before it's too late." Alex stood and reached out a hand to help her up. He quickly pleated and wrapped his plaid around him securing it with the double belt that held his sporran and kept his plaid in place.

After gathering up the remnants of their picnic, Alex helped Brighde back into her now dry but very stiff and crunchy gown. She tried not to let Alex see just how itchy it was as she climbed the slope back up to the horse. Brighde had not noticed when they arrived, but there was the tiniest of streams on the other side of the tree from where Alex had tied *Naomh*. The horse had grazed down all the surrounding grass and been able to drink as he wanted. They mounted up and returned to the keep.

Chapter Nine

Alexander and Brighde returned to a bailey full of horses and men. Not recognizing anyone, Brighde immediately froze out of fear. Alex could feel the tension pouring forth but did not understand her sudden change. He watched as her head swung on a pendulum, and she took in all the activity. She did not even realize her nails were biting into his forearm until he covered her hands with his.

"Dinna fash. It's just ma brothers returned. Though I dinna ken why they are back so soon. We expected them to be away with Siùsan's kin for quite a while longer. I can see Tavish and Magnus, but I dinna see Callum or Siùsan." Alex rode them over to the stable entrance and helped Brighde dismount.

Brighde kept looking around with her head on a swivel. It had been nearly a decade since she had been in a Highland keep filled with warriors. It was a little overwhelming and intimidating for someone who was in hiding.

"Alex, what aboot all these men? They arenae all in Sinclair plaids. Who are they?"

Alex noticed the same thing, but it did not trouble him since he recognized the pattern right away.

"MacLeods. They are Siùsan's mother's clan. But I dinna ken why they are here. She, Callum, Magnus, and Tavish went to visit them. Come, I'll introduce ye."

Alex reached to take her hand, but she shied away. She ducked behind him as a group of men passed by. Alex felt her quiver as he reached back to take her hand. He silently guided her to the lady's garden and let them through the gate.

"Brie, I dinna ever want ye to be afraid here. Ye are safe nay matter who comes to visit. Ma da doesnae tolerate anyone mistreating women, and he will never turn a blind eye to a badly-behaved guest. Ye dinna have to fear them."

"Alex, I'm a runaway. A runaway bride at that. I fear any and every one I dinna ken. Anyone of them could tell the wrong person that they saw me, and de Soules or ma father could come beating down yer gate. Or worse, lay siege to the castle. What then? That would harm everyone who has been kind to me. I dinna think ye should introduce me to anyone. The fewer people who ken I am here, the better for all of us. I dinna want anyone to come to any harm for hiding me."

"Mo ghràidh, first of all, this is ma family that ye're talking about. Ma brothers learned of ye when they were here last. Ye were still ill, so there wasna much to tell, but they ken of ye. Secondly, the MacLeod chief seems to ken ma da vera well from the looks of how they were getting on. Thirdly, anyone foolish enough to lay siege to this castle will starve long before we would need to surrender. We are well provisioned and well-armed. I amnae afraid of that, and I dinna want ye to be afraid either."

"Ye keep saying that, Alex, but it wasna ye who had a father and future husband try to kill ye. It wasna ye who traveled the length of Scotland to escape those two bastards. It isnae ye who must make her way alone. It's easy for ye to tell me nae to be afraid when ye have naught to fear yerself." Bridge shook her head as Alex reached for her. Instead, she laced her fingers with his. "Alex, I just need to go slowly until I ken for sure who I can trust. Right now, I dinna want to meet anyone in the state I'm in. Please let me get cleaned up, and then I will return. I just need to gather maself a bit before I'm launched into socializing with more people than I have seen in nearly two moons."

"Fair enough," Alex kissed her hands and opened the side door to let her in. He followed her in and made sure she made it up the stairs safely before searching for Hagatha. He had a bath sent up for her while he went to the back of the kitchens for his own chance to sluice down.

~~~

Alex had just finished bathing and was drying off when he heard two of his brothers enter the kitchens.

"There he is. The mon lives! He isnae just a memory or a trick of our imaginations," boomed Tavish.

"Aye. I thought he'd scampered off and left us for good," laughed Magnus.

"Haud yer wheesht. I havenae ever 'scampered off' anywhere. I dinna even ken how to scamper," he playfully growled as the three hulking men hugged and shoved one another like a pack of puppies.

"How was yer journey? Ye are back far sooner than we expected."

Magnus and Tavish exchanged a look before Tavish nodded his head.

"We had a bit of trouble. Siùsan was kidnapped one night after most of us ate a drugged supper. We tracked her down, but we had to stop at the MacLeod's first to get help and men from her grandfather. Alex, it was bad. Vera bad. As bad as with Mairghread," Magnus explained.

The mere mention of their own sister's abduction just before she married was enough to make Alex blanche and then feel the blood pulsing through his scalp. He, his brothers, and his now brother by marriage arrived just in time to keep Mairghread from being raped. It had been and still was the worse day of his life. The memory of what he saw was enough to make the bile rise in his throat. He could only imagine what his brothers must have gone through to experience something so similar all over again.

"Is she well? I mean did they--?"

"Nay. We arrived in time, but it was vera close. I dinna ken if Callum will ever forgive himself for how badly his courtship and marriage started. He has been doting on Siùsan every minute of every day. But I can hardly blame him," Tavish shook his head slightly.

"What about ye, big brother? How fairs yer mystery woman? She must be back in the land of the living because we heard ye've been away from the keep with her all day."

"Aye, she is hail again. I took her down to the beach. She hasnae had much chance to get out and aboot since being ill. I wanted her to be able to get some fresh air and sunshine."

"And to be alone with her for a while, I'm sure. Is she really that bonnie?" Magnus asked. He elbowed Tavish and grinned.

"Aye." Alex had no intention of telling his brothers any more than he must. He did not want to give them any ammunition to taunt him for fear they would embarrass Brighde later or humiliate him in front of her.

"If that's all ye have to say, then mayhap I'll have a go since ye dinna seem too interested. Have ye sampled her honey yet? Is it sweet?"

Tavish found himself face down on one of the giant kitchen tables. Alex pulled his head back by the hair and slammed his head down.

"Watch what ye say, little brother. I dinna want to thrash ye, but I will. Dinna ever speak of her like that again." There was no mistaking the threat that Alex issued, and the term "little brother" rankled Tavish since he was not only younger than Alex, but he was the shortest of all the brothers, if even by barely a hair.

Tavish slapped his hand on the table as he said, "I yield."

Alex immediately let go, and Tavish stood up, pulling at the collar of his leine and turning his head from side to side. He put his hand out to Magnus.

"See. I told ye."

"Aye, so ye did." Magnus handed over his favorite dagger. It was a favorite among all the siblings, so it was what they wagered with. The dagger passed back and forth countless times over the years. Mairghread was the one to hold onto it for the longest.

"Told him what?"

"I wagered that ye would be chasing her skirts by the time we got back, but that ye would be like a rutting stag in heat when ye couldnae get anywhere within yards of whomever this mystery woman is."

"Ye may be half right. I do feel randy as a buck, but I amnae entirely failing. I do think she is fond of me, but I dinna seem to be making any progress. Two steps forward and one step back."

"And in the meantime, she has yer cods in a vice. Find a willing woman to scratch yer itch."

"I canna seem to win her over nay matter how I try. Besides I dinna want any other woman, and that certainly wouldnae win her over. Oh, I can see it now, 'I wanted ye, but since ye wouldnae have me, I figured any quim will do.' She'd geld me in a heartbeat, and I would just prove her fears right. Ye dinna ken aught aboot women, Tavish."

"I ken plenty of women."

"Nae what I said, and ye ken it."

"Geld ye, would she? Sounds like she can be as testy as Mairghread or Siùsan," Magnus snorted, "she'll fit right in. But what do ye mean about proving her fears right."

"Her father is a right piece of work. Took up with some woman before he married her mother, sired three bastards, married her mother and was unfaithful, and when his wife died, he married his mistress. He went on to have three more children with her. Four sons in all."

Magnus and Tavish scowled. The Sinclair men had no tolerance for men who mistreated women in any way. Ingrained from a very young age, all Sinclairs value loyalty and honor, but it was drilled into the boys that they were to never abuse their size or power over a woman. Only cowards prey on those who are unable to defend themselves.

"Sod."

"Piece of shite."

"Both," Alex looked at his brothers. "Ye will have a chance to meet her tonight. Be polite. She hasnae really met anyone other than Da, Hagatha, and Aileen. A few other women have been in to assist her, but she was too ill to remember Siùsan or Elizabeth." At the mention of their oldest brother's former lover, Magnus and Tavish paused.

Alex looked back at them and tilted his head.

"There is quite a tale to tell about that, but there isnae time now. We all need to be ready for the evening meal. If we're late, Da will have our hides since we have more than one guest here tonight," Magnus said. "It'll all come out soon enough, I'm sure. But I wouldnae be in a rush to hear this sordid tale."

The men climbed the back stairs and moved down the passageway to their respective chambers.

Chapter Ten

Alex knocked lightly on his door and waited for Brighde. When she opened it, he could not believe what he saw. The sun had lightened her hair even more, and she had a smattering of freckles across the bridge of her nose and the tops of her cheeks. Her skin glowed from being sun-kissed, and the lavender kirtle she wore made her grey eyes look translucent silver. She had scooped the sides of her hair into a braid that hung down the center of her back. A lavender ribbon was woven through the braid, and a fawn green ribbon framed her face. The rest of her hair hung loosely down her back.

Alex tried, but could not stop staring at her.

I dinna think I will ever get used to how beautiful she is. She is lovelier every time I see her. Even when I was blazing mad at her this afternoon, I still couldnae ignore how fine she is. There isnae another woman in any land that can hold a candle to her. And, aye, she has the bonniest face I have ever seen, but I still think most of her beauty comes from within. There is something that draws me and willnae let me go. I dinna ken what I'm going to do if she really does decide to leave one day. I dinna even want to think aboot it.

"Alex? Alex? Can ye hear me?"

"Aye, what's that?"

"I've said yer name five times already. Ye seem leagues away. Is aught wrong?"

"Nay. Naught at all. I was just thinking to maself."

"I think it's ma turn to ask a penny for yer thoughts. Ye seemed so far away. Were ye remembering something?" Brighde took a breath before she could finish her thought. "Or someone?"

Alex looked down at her as he lifted her hands to his lips. He swept his lips over them, back and forth. He kissed each knuckle and then turned her wrists over before pressing his lips to the pulse points inside each wrist. He rubbed his thumbs in small circles on her palms. Just when she thought he decided not to answer, he looked into her eyes and smiled.

"I was thinking aboot the only thing that matters. Ye. There isnae anyone else, and there never has been, and I dinna want there to be."

Brighde's heart began to beat harder and faster. She could not tell if it was excitement at what Alex hinted at, or fear that he would want more from her than she could give. She knew what she wanted, and it was him, but she also knew that she was not free to give herself to him. Not beyond the physical anyway. She stood on her tiptoes and did the only thing she could think of to keep him from saying any more. She kissed him. It was quick but passionate; however, the memory of their arguments from earlier in the day that was the result of shared frustration had them pulling apart. Brighde stepped out of the doorway and pulled the door shut behind her. They descended the stairs together, but before they could enter the Great Hall, she stopped. She looked around and spotted an alcove just behind the stairs. She pointed to it. Alex let her lead the way, and when they were safely tucked away, she leaned forward to whisper to him.

"I dinna think we should use ma real name. I think I should be Mary again."

"Why? And why are ye whispering? We are alone."

"First of all, ye are never truly alone in a castle this size. The walls have ears. The whole reason for not using ma real name was to protect maself but also ye. Now ye ken it was Randolph. Dinna ye see why I didna want to say aught. He's a dangerous mon. When ma father and de Soules discovered there wasna a dead body at the bottom of the ravine, they would have searched for me. I told ye I did the best I could to make the trail look like I headed south towards England. They'll be looking for a Scottish woman in England, nae an English woman in the vera northern part of Scotland. Ma hair alone is enough to give me away, so I dinna want to use ma real name too."

"And ye dinna think that stories of a blonde English woman living with the Sinclair clan wouldnae sound suspicious to anyone?"

"It might be, but I dinna think they would believe I could make it this far alone so that coupled with any story being about an English woman, means I stand a fairer chance of being safe."

"Ye never did tell me why ye came to us. Why Sinclairs? Why nae the Sutherlands. Ye would have gotten to them sooner. Even if ye were trying to get as far away as ye could, they are still one of the furthest clans from the border."

Brighde peaked around Alex to look outside the alcove. When she was sure that no one was nearby, she continued.

"The Sinclairs and Sutherlands may be getting along now because yer mother was a Sutherland, but that hasnae always been the case. I dinna trust the Gunns after the tales I've heard, and the Mackays are allies of yers now, but ye were feuding with them nae long ago."

"I ken ma clan's history. That still doesnae explain why ye came all the way to here."

"I needed somewhere to stop and rest before continuing on."

"Continuing on? There isnae any 'on.' There isnae any more of Scotland short of the Orkneys and Shetlands." When he saw Brighde's face, he shook his head vigorously. "Nay. Ye canna be serious that ye would go to either of those isles. Do ye wish to be even more mistreated than ye would be with de Soules? I canna believe that."

"There is at least one monastery and nunnery on the Orkneys where I could retire."

"If ye dinna get captured and sold by the Danes. If ye think yer hair will help ye blend in, ye arenae right in the head. Some jarl will take one look at ye and either make ye his own bed slave or sell ye off to the Holy Lands for a fortune. Nay. I willna allow it."

"Allow it," she hissed. "Ye dinna get to decide that for me."

"I do when ye show that ye canna make sound decisions for yerself. Ye're jumping out of the pan and into the fire. And little one, ye willnae just get burned. Ye'll go up in flames."

"I amnae asking yer opinion or yer permission. I dinna have to do as ye say."

Alex decided to take another tac.

"Brighde, it's so dangerous. I canna stomach the idea that someone could buy and sell ye or trap ye into being a concubine. It makes ma stomach churn, ma heart skip, and ma head pound. Please dinna go. Ye can stay here for as long as ye like, but ye dinna have to put yerself in more danger. If ye want yer space and privacy, Da could give ye a croft within the walls or even in the village. If ye dinna want to be around anyone, ye dinna have to. Aught but going to the Danes. I couldnae live with that kind of risk to ye."

The air seemed to go out of her sail when she saw that Alex was not exaggerating his feelings but telling her the truth. There was genuine concern and fear as he talked. She knew he was right, and she did not really want to go to either place, but the Orkneys and Shetlands were as far as she could go to escape her past.

"Brighde, ye still havenae really told me why ye were coming here. Ye told me why ye werenae going anywhere else, but nae why ye were trying to get here."

Brighde blew out a small puff of air and looked up at the ceiling before looking at Alex.

"The Campbell and Sinclair territories maynae be vera close, but we are connected by marriage. A distant cousin of yer father married a second or third cousin of ma grandfather. I ken the clans arenae very closely allied now, but they were at one point. When ma grandparents got sick, they warned me that returning to ma father would be dangerous. They feared what he might do, but they kenned they could do naught at that point. Ma grandmother told me that if ever I should fear for ma life, I should run as far and as fast as I could, and that meant coming to ye. Ma grandparents both spoke highly of yer father and assured me that if I could make it this far, then I would have a good chance of surviving. Ye and yer father have proven them right. Ye took me in and cared for me even when ye dinna ken who I was. Ye allowed me to stay even after ye kenned I deceived ye. Ye have befriended me, and—"

Alex cut her off by pressing a finger to her lips.

"Yer grandparents were right. We wouldnae turn ye away, and I will thank God every day for the rest of ma life that ye made it here, so we could care for ye. But I didna hear anywhere in that story that yer grandmother or grandfather told ye to risk yer life further by going up to the isles. They wanted ye to come here. And I want ye to stay."

Brighde looked up at Alex. His meaning was clear, and she was not in the mood to argue with him any further. They could discuss her coming and going later. Right now, she just wanted to make it through dinner with his family, so she nodded.

"Alex, naught is decided, and it willna be tonight. Can we talk about this later? I need to ken whether ye will agree to carry on the ruse a little longer. I ken lying to yer family willna sit well with ye, but I'm just nae ready to risk being found."

Alex gave her a long look before nodding his head.

"Come along, Mary. We dinna want to keep anyone waiting." Alex placed her hand on his arm and moved the curtain aside just enough to look around. When he was confident no one would see them coming out of a small enclosed space together, he led her to the Great Hall.

Lairds Sinclair and MacLeod sat chatting by the fire, but the rest of his family had not yet come back down. Alex steered Brighde over to a window in the corner. He could sense without seeing all the eyes that followed them. When he did look around, he saw far too many appreciative looks on the men's faces. He scowled and placed his other hand on top of Brighde's. He would make it clear from the very beginning that she was not available.

Just a few minutes after he and Brighde walked to the window embrasure, Magnus and Tavish entered the Great Hall freshly washed and shaven. Alex nodded to them but turned back to Brighde who was talking softly to him about how she hoped he could take her back to the sea cave soon. His brothers settled in for a game of knucklebones, and Alex turned his full attention back to Brighde. They talked about what times of day the cave was safe to explore and made plans to go riding the next day. Alex would have preferred for them to share a horse again simply because it was as good an excuse as any he could think of to have her in his arms and practically on his lap. He knew she longed for the freedom and excitement of riding her own horse, so he already had one in mind for her. It was not very long after they began discussing Brighde starting to tend the lady's garden that Callum and Siùsan entered the Great Hall. Tavish called them over, and Alex seated Brighde and stood behind her chair.

"Dinna hover," she whispered to him.

"I amnae," he whispered back.

She just shook her head. They both knew exactly what he was doing, and that was standing guard. While Brighde thought it was to make her feel safe with so many strangers around her, Alex knew he did it to keep any other man from ogling her which meant it kept him from killing any of his own clansmen.

The family, along with Brighde and Laird McLeod, listened as the story unraveled about what had befallen Siùsan while they traveled. Brighde's eyes watered as she heard what Siùsan endured. Her tears were mainly from sympathy, but a small part knew how easily that could have been her if de Soules caught her. She also had to admit that Siùsan's experiences would probably be hers too if she tried to travel among the Danes. Except there would be no one to come to her rescue. She was lost in thought when she heard her chair groan, and she realized Alex was gripping the back so tightly, that he was beginning to crush it.

As discreetly as she could, she reached her hand back and tapped his shin. Immediately, she felt the chair settle back into position. Alex's hands brushed against her shoulders as he shifted them lower on the chair back.

The entire family was about to move to the dais when Siùsan suddenly bolted from the Great Hall with Callum not far behind her.

"She's been doing a lot of that of late," Tavish mused.

"Aye. Every time she smells food. Is it wrong of me to say that it leaves more for me to eat?" Magnus joked.

Tavish and Magnus were already walking towards the table with Alex and Brighde close behind.

"Uncle Alex," she said with a chuckle.

Alex, Tavish, and Magnus froze, then as a one, they turned to look at her. Brighde tried not to laugh, but their expressions were truly hysterical. Alex stared at her in shock, but Brighde heard Tavish mutter, "bluidy Sassenach," under his breath.

It was Brighde's turn to smile. *Aye. Ye keep believing that, and we'll all get on like a croft on fire. Ye can call me that all day and all night as long as ye keep believing it.*

Chapter Eleven

*A*lex was still taking in Brighde's revelation from the night before as he went to the lists to join his brothers, who were still taking in the fact that their brother had developed an overly strong attraction to an English woman.

"Have ye learned aught about where she comes from?" Tavish asked as they swung their swords in sweeping arcs to warm up.

"Aye," Alex's noncommittal answer caused Magnus to stop mid-swing.

"That's all ye're going to say? Shouldnae we ken who we harbor under our roof?"

"Her story is hers to tell, and she is a guest here."

"Guest?" asked Callum who was just joining them. "When we left, ye were calling her yer ward. Now she's a guest. I amnae sure that's an improvement. Guests leave, so, when does she?" Callum sounded lighthearted, but there was some bite to his question.

"Late start, brother? Nursemaid seems to be yer new calling. Are ye sure ye have time to be in the lists? Ye might be needed to hold Siùsan's hair back or onto her apron strings."

Alex was not going to let his brothers bait him into giving anything away. He would simply deflect.

"Dinna speak about ma wife like that. *Uncle Alex.* Just wait. Ye'll get yer turn, and mayhap sooner rather than later." Callum jerked his chin in the direction of the keep. Alex looked over and saw Brighde and Siùsan walking towards the gardens, each with a large basket tucked under her arm. They seemed to be carrying on a lively conversation. Alex smiled to himself before he noticed that his brothers were watching him and grinning.

Alex put a hand on his hip since he was still holding his sword and broadened his stance.

"Doesnae work with us," Tavish laughed as they all stood the same way. It was the most natural position for them short of having their arms crossed.

Alex shook his head, "Are we going to train or stand around clishmaclavering like a set of fishwives?"

Alex joined the other men who were lined up to begin sparring. Like a well-choreographed dance, Callum stood across from him. After several turns, strikes, and parries, the brothers smoothly switched partners as if there were invisible cues. They continued sparring throughout the morning, offering Alex an outlet for all his frustrations, both physical and emotional. He was almost nicked more than once when he let his mind wander to Brighde. Luckily, he had not been partnered with Callum, Tavish, or Magnus. He would never hear the end of it if he had been.

~ ~ ~

Brighde emerged into the sunlight with Siùsan. They had been talking together ever since they came below stairs to break their fast, or rather, Brighde came to break her fast, and Siùsan tried not to turn an off shade of puce green. Now they were headed to the vegetable and herb garden to weed and pick any ripe vegetables.

"Callum was trying to convince me to stay abed today. The mon is going to drive me batty if he's going to hover like a mother hen. As long as I dinna smell any food, eat only bannocks, and get a nap in the morn and after the nooning, I am right as rain."

The women laughed together as they settled side by side to weed a patch of leeks.

"Callum canna stand them." Siùsan nodded her head toward the shoots. "Apparently, he was once quite ill as a child. The healer at the time insisted that he eat them to the point where he'd be happy to never see another one."

Brighde smiled as Siùsan chattered on about her husband, but she thought about what she had observed about Alex's preferences. She felt a wave of discouragement flow through her when she could not think of anything he particularly liked, other than pickled herring, or disliked. Then she was discomfited to realize how much not knowing bothered her.

He maynae think I should go to the Orkneys or Shetlands, but I canna stay her forever. He maynae take the threat seriously, but I do. I dinna ken if ma father or de Soules are searching for me, but if they lost any of their money because I didna marry the beast or worse didna die, then they will search for me. They might vera well do it just out of vengeance for me thwarting their plans. I canna hide within the keep, or even the walls, forever. If I venture out, someone is bound to see me. If it werenae for ma hair, I might blend in. I can cover ma head, but I canna always be sure someone willnae say aught to the wrong person. Mayhap I should go to Iona. Mayhap I could convince Alex to take me there.

At the thought of leaving, Brighde felt her heart pinch. She caught herself just before she began to shake her head. The idea of leaving here, leaving Alex, was becoming harder and harder to accept. She could feel tears prickling behind her eyes.

"Ye didna hear a word I just said, did ye?"

Brighde looked blankly at Siùsan before coming back to the present. She looked sheepishly at Siùsan and shook her head.

"I ken where yer mind is. It seems to me that the men of this family have that effect on women. I dinna ken Alex as well as I do Magnus and Tavish, but if he's aught like the other three, which I canna see how he wouldnae be since they're four peas in a pod, ye have found yerself a good mon."

"It does not matter. I know he is a good man, but it cannot lead to anything."

"Why ever nae?"

"I'm here for only a short while before I continue on."

"Continue on? There isnae anywhere else to go before ye drop in the sea."

"This was always meant to just be a stop on my way. I'm going to Iona to join the convent."

Siùsan looked at her sideways. It made no sense to her that an English woman would retire to a Scottish convent on an isolated island. No sense, unless she was running from something or someone. However, Siùsan chose not to press the issue and resolved to talk to Callum to find out what he knew.

"I think we have done a fine job with the weeding and picking this morn. I dinna ken about ye, but ma knees are ready to be straightened."

Brighde looked at her basket and Siùsan's. She had not realized how much they had worked while her mind wandered. They both picked up their baskets and turned back towards the keep. The clang of metal on metal was almost deafening as they moved towards the lists.

"Nae too hard on the eyes, if ye ken ma meaning." Siùsan tilted her head towards the training men. Brighde leaned forward slightly to see around Siùsan and nearly tripped when her toe hit a rock. She pitched forward and would have fallen with her basket flying if Siùsan had not reached out to grasp her arm.

"I see ye are duly impressed," Siùsan laughed loudly enough to receive some looks from the men.

"Sshh! You are drawing attention to us!"

"It's their fault for drawing attention to themselves first. I canna help it if I enjoy watching ma husband without his leine on." Siùsan unabashedly shrugged her shoulders.

"Do ye watch Callum practice often?"

A shadow passed over Siùsan's face before she answered.

"Nay. I havenae seen him practice, but I have seen him fight. More than once."

"I am sorry. I did not mean--"

"Haud yer wheesht. Ye couldnae ken, and it is fine. I like kenning that ma braw mon can and will protect me. Even if the first time, it was I who protected him." At Brighde's curious look, she laughed and added, "that's a tale for another time. What aboot ye? Have ye watched Alex practice in the lists?"

Brighde had to clear her throat before she could respond. She had been watching Alex while Siùsan spoke, and she was having a hard time concentrating on anything other than Alex's body as his muscles clenched and bunched while he fought against one of his men. Every muscle sinew was on show for her from his calves up through his thighs, and then from his waist up through his shoulders. She watched them ripple and glisten with sweat under the bright sun. Brighde tried to answer, but nothing came out, so she shook her head.

"Come then." Siùsan grasped her arm and pulled her towards the lists.

"No. We can't go over there," she hissed. "We can't disturb them. I don't think they would appreciate us interrupting their training. I don't want to cause a fuss."

"Ye maynae, but I dinna care. I will talk to Callum since I'm sure he's been thrashing the men because he canna thrash me. He truly didna want me to move beyond the chamber pot today. We can say that I just wanted to reassure him that I hadnae expired from walking down the stairs."

Siùsan practically dragged Brighde to the rail that enclosed a large field where at least a hundred men were in various stages of the mock battle. Callum was already standing off to the side as he oversaw a group of men who were training with dirks and sgian dubh, a type of very small and very sharp dagger.

Out of the corner of his eye, Alex saw Callum push away from the rail and heard a feminine voice and then a laugh that he would recognize anywhere. He took his eyes off his opponent just long enough to receive an elbow to the eye and almost have his head lopped off with a battle ax. He staggered back a step or two as the man he was fighting dropped the ax and put his hands into the air.

"Ma lord, I didna mean—"

"Thomas, it wasna yer fault. I shouldnae have lost ma focus. That is a lesson to remember in battle. It takes but a moment to lose yer head, in every manner."

Alex turned towards the group that had gathered. Magnus and Tavish had already joined Callum and Siùsan. He saw Brighde standing with her hands covering her mouth and eyes as wide as saucers. He looked around to see what was wrong, but nothing seemed out of the ordinary. He could feel the sweat trickling from his forehead, and as he wiped it away, he saw blood on his fingers. When he looked back up, Brighde was clenching the wooden slat in front of her and straining to lean over it. As he came closer, he saw her face go an unhealthy shade of white that nearly resembled what she looked like the night she collapsed in his arms.

"Lass, what's troubling ye?" He asked quietly as he met her at the fence.

She shook her head slightly and pointed to his face. She pulled up the corner of her arisaid and gently blotted the sweat and blood from his eye. He could already feel it swelling shut. Her touch was feather soft as she cleaned his face.

"Does it pain you much?" she finally found her voice but sounded rather strangled.

"Ma eye? Nay, mo chaileag. Just a little sting, but naught I havenae felt before."

Before he could say any more, Magnus clapped him on the back and squeezed his shoulder mercilessly.

"A little pain to go with the pleasure? Dinna lose sight of what ye want."

Alex drove his elbow back and caught an unsuspecting Tavish in the gut. Magnus had accurately anticipated retaliation and moved aside in time.

"What the bluidy hell?" Tavish shoved Alex who in turn boxed his ears in.

"Dinna speak that way in front of the ladies."

"Siùsan's used to ma language. She doesnae care."

"Aye, but Mary isnae." Alex shoved Tavish again. Before Brighde understood what was happening, they were both rolling around. She looked around at Callum and Magnus. Callum and Siùsan were stealing a kiss, and Magnus was encouraging his brothers' tussle, calling out wagers.

"Isn't anyone going to stop them?" Brighde could not believe that no one else was bothered by the two massive men pounding each other into the ground.

"Stop!" she tried yelling, but there was too much noise and neither Alex nor Tavish were paying attention anyway. Looking around, she spotted a bucket and dashed over to grab it. She hauled it back to the railing and heaved it over the top slat. Stepping onto the bottom rung, she lifted the bucket as high as she could and doused the two men. They rolled apart like scalded cats.

"Christ on the cross! That was bluidy cold." Tavish barked, and Alex lunged for him again.

"Alex! Stop!"

Hearing Brighde's plea was the only thing that kept him from launching himself at Tavish again.

"Dinna swear in front of her anymore," he growled.

"Are her English ears that sensitive? She willnae last long here." Tavish thought he had said it only loud enough for Alex to hear, but when a dirk landed between his feet, he swiveled around in time to see another one coming at him. He leaped out of the way and barely missed having his toes nailed to the ground.

"My ears are sensitive enough to hear what you said. You're louder than a bear with a burr in its backside. I'm not the one upset by your swearing anyway. You haven't said anything I haven't heard before, but you did insult me by thinking that I am some weak English rose who can't manage the wilds of the Highlands or your clan," By now, Brighde had climbed down from the fence and was looking back and forth between Alex and Tavish. Alex had a cut lip that was swelling to match his eye. Tavish had a bruise forming on his cheek and dirt smeared all over his face along with a ripped sleeve. Brighde shook her head, planted her feet, and crossed her arms. She gave them both her most menacing look, which surprisingly was quite stern. Both men suddenly looked like shamefaced boys who had been caught doing something they knew they should not. She raised one eyebrow as she gave Alex a pointed look. Grimacing, he turned to face Tavish.

"I wasnae aiming for ye with ma elbow. That was for Magnus, but I shouldnae fought ye."

Brighde nodded her head and then gave the same pointed glare to Tavish.

"And I shouldnae antagonized ye nor used the lass as bait."

Now Brighde looked at them with both of her eyebrows raised. Alex and Tavish stared at her in disbelief, but she only tilted her head to one side and drummed the fingers of one hand against the other arm.

The brothers stuck out their hands and gripped each other's forearm before pulling in for an embrace with bone-cracking back pounding.

"Better."

Alex ducked between the rails and came over to her. Once again, she pulled out the corner of her arisaid and wiped his face. Alex bent forward to let her. When he was close enough, she whispered in his ear.

"Ye dinna need to protect me from yer brothers. They're harmless, and all ye're doing is drawing too much attention to me. I just want to blend in. Please, Alex. I dinna want to be the cause of any more scenes. People will start to talk and talk spreads quicker than a Highland snow storm. For ma sake, just leave be."

"Vera well, but only because ye ask it of me. I dinna take well to anyone insulting ye, even ma brothers. Though ye are far bonnier than any of ma brothers when ye stand like us." He tried to wink but winced instead.

"But ye ken they werenae really talking aboot me as much as they were trying to get yer goat, which ye let them. Ye've only given them more to tease ye aboot. Dinna rescue me if I'm nae in danger. Save it for if I really need it."

Brighde cleaned off Alex's face as best she could without soap and water. She could see where a couple of cuts would easily become infected if they were not seen to sooner rather than later.

"Alex, I need to —or ye need to clean these cuts," she stuttered. She felt her cheeks flush pink at her presumptuousness.

"I would prefer ye to do it, mo chaileag. Ye have a gentler hand and can see where I need it."

"I dinna think ye'll be calling me sweet after I've had to scrub the dirt and grit out of them."

Alex tucked hair behind her ear and leaned so close that his nose brushed her temple.

"I've tasted ye and ken just how sweet ye are."

Brighde's face went from a pretty shade of pink to a shade of scarlet that left her feeling like flames were licking her cheeks.

"Sshh! Dinna do that. Someone will hear ye."

Alex simply placed his hand on the small of her back and led her towards the keep.

Neither of them noticed as Callum, Siùsan, Magnus, and Tavish stood together making wagers on how long it would take before Alex was the next Sinclair headed to the kirk. Tavish had to relinquish the wagering dagger to Magnus who already accurately predicted Alex would react like a shaken hornets' nest if he thought Brighde was being mistreated.

"I give it a fortnight at most," said Callum.

"Nay. She will hold out for at least another moon." Siùsan spit into her palm and thrust it towards her husband for him to shake. The wager was on.

Chapter Twelve

*A*fter the nooning, the men and women went their separate directions. Brighde and Siùsan sat sewing for a while, but when Siùsan began falling asleep over her embroidery, she retired to her chamber to nap. Brighde went into the kitchens where she helped Elspeth bake tarts. She used the time to covertly learn about Alex's likes and dislikes. By the time they were finished, she had flour up to her elbows and sticky apple and pear filling on her hands and even her cheeks. She went back to her chamber to prepare for the evening meal.

Alex followed Callum and Laird Sinclair into the laird's solar. For the next several hours, the men discussed clan business ranging from crofters' disputes to planning for the fall harvest to trades they wanted to arrange with neighboring clans. As Callum's second, Alex was usually privy to these conversations, and his strategic mind was welcome. Callum had chosen Alex for the role of his second not only because Alex was the second son, but because they were virtually inseparable for most of their lives. Less than a year apart in age, they grew up with Alex always in a rush to catch up to Callum. They valued each other's company and each other's opinions. They had grown distant over the past few months when Callum became involved with a woman prior to meeting Siùsan. It had created a rift between them that both men were glad to mend. As their meeting began to draw to an end, Laird Sinclair looked Alex over. He had been none too pleased to hear about his sons' brawl or to see the damage they had done to each other. Not because he worried about either of them, but because it never looked good for the laird's two grown sons to have a spat, in public no less.

"Ye canna have such a thin skin where the lass is concerned. Ye will feed the gossip mills, and the only one who will be hurt is the lass. Dinna let yer brothers goad ye like that. She doesnae strike me as the type who appreciates men fighting over her. Ye willna win her over when she has memories of ye making an arse of yerself."

"I dinna think it'll matter much how big of an arse he is once she's on Iona," Callum said as he rolled up several parchments.

"What? Iona?"

Callum looked up then and saw the look of disbelief on Alex's face that was quickly dissolving into anger.

"Aye, well, that's just what I heard."

"From whom? Her?" Alex bit his tongue before he used the wrong name. She was not Brighde to his family, and he could not get used to calling her Mary.

"Nae exactly. Siùsan may have mentioned it as we finished negotiating our wager." Callum could have kicked himself. When was he going to learn to think before he spoke when it came to members of his family. He was a gifted tactician but almost hopeless when it came to tact and the people he cared about most.

"What bluidy wager?" Alex came to stand toe to toe with Callum. "Dinna try to hold back. Ye've gone too far to take any of it back. Why the hell is she going to Iona? And when exactly does she think she's going? Who the bluidy hell does she think is going to take her?" Alex's voice was getting progressively louder with each question.

Callum looked to his father who only shrugged. As the future leader of the clan, Callum needed to learn to solve his problems, especially when they were of his own making.

"I said that it would only take a fortnight to get ye both to the kirk, and Siùsan said a moon. I was so sure I was right that to make me stop gloating, she shared with me that Mary told her this morning that she plans to move on to Iona and retire to the convent there."

Alex did not wait to hear another word. He spun around on his heel and marched to the door. He flung it open so hard that is slammed shut after him. He did not even notice. He took the stairs to his chamber two and three at a time, and when he got to the door of the chamber that had been his for his entire life, he knocked once before barging in.

Brighde was not expecting anyone, least of whom Alex, to burst into the chamber. She held one foot poised in the air as she reached for a drying cloth while her other foot was still in the tub. She squeaked as she looked over at Alex whose face was a shade of enraged scarlet. As he took in Brighde's naked form, his cock came to attention. His anger was suddenly mixed with an overpowering lust that made his pulse pound in his ears. Part of him wanted to rail at her for wanting to leave and the other part wanted to beg her to stay, but all of him wanted to be inside her. To feel her warmth envelop him as he brought them both bliss.

Brighde's small movement to grab the drying cloth was enough to snap him out of his stupor. He was across the room in less than five steps. He snatched up the drying cloth and wrapped it around her before lifting her out of the tub. Brighde could feel the power and frustration pouring out of him, but she had no idea what had caused him to storm into the chamber.

"Alex, ye canna be in here. What if someone saw ye? The maids ken I'm bathing. They'll ken that ye've seen me in the altogether."

"Iona."

Alex said the single word between clenched teeth. He glared down at her even though his hands were ever gentle on her arms after he set her down. Brighde was shocked that he would know to ask about it, but she realized she should have figured that in this family, nothing would remain secret for long.

"Siùsan."

"Iona and dinna change the subject. Just when were ye planning to tell me? When ye rode out, or when ye led me on a merry chase after ye?"

"Chase? I was going to ask ye to escort me there." She had the good graces to look down at her bare toes after making that declaration.

"Aye, chase because there isnae any way that I would have let ye leave alone, and I bluidy well dinna want to take ye there." He pulled her in for a kiss that branded her with his passion and begged for her acceptance.

Brighde could not help herself as she was no better than a moth to a flame. She wrapped her arms around his neck and held on. The towel fell away from her when Alex lifted her up, and she wrapped her legs around his waist. He walked to the door and turned the lock. He grasped her backside and kneaded the damp flesh. He took her to the bed and climbed on with her still wrapped around him. Slowly he lowered them to the mattress while he did his best not to squash her with his weight. She tugged at him until he finally gave in and allowed most of his body to settle on her. Her moan of pleasure made his rod twitch. He was so very close to the edge. All he had to do was move his plaid aside a little, and he would be able to enter her with one quick thrust. The temptation to make her his by taking her maidenhead and spilling his seed was nearly more than he could resist, but he still had just enough honor left in his little finger to keep from doing that. He wanted Brighde to stay because she reciprocated his feelings, not because he trapped her.

"I dinna want ye to leave here. To leave me." Alex admitted hoarsely. His voice felt as though it was coming from somewhere other than him. He stroked her damp hair away from her forehead and chin. He nuzzled the sensitive flesh behind her ear. He brushed soft kisses along her jaw and down her neck to her shoulder where he nipped the skin lightly.

"I dinna want to go." Brighde sighed out her response.

Alex needed no further reassurances. He pulled her bottom lip with his teeth and used his tongue to press her mouth open. Their tongues dueled as their hands roamed all over each other. Neither seemed to be able to get close enough to the other. Brighde tugged at his leine until Alex kneeled back and pulled it over his head. She sat up to reach for him, and he laid back down once again covering her with his chiseled body. She ran her hands up and down his arms as he continued to kiss her. She slid her hands around to grasps his buttocks as she felt his fingers enter her. Her inner muscles clenched around him as she rocked her hips into his. He groaned and thrust forward. She pressed her hands against his backside to keep him tightly against him. She reached between them and pushed his sporran out of the way, frustrated that she could not fully feel his length against her. Once she could feel the turgid rod rubbing against her cleft through his wool plaid, she began to rock her hips again. Alex's fingers moved faster as she moaned. The pressure she felt from both the inside and the outside had her crashing over the top into the strongest release she had experienced yet. Alex had not even slid his fingers out before her hand reached beneath his plaid. Her warm hand wrapped around his cock and stroked him. He thrust his hips into her again and again until they were both finding their release.

Alex rolled onto his back and brought Brighde with him. She laid her head against his chest and felt more than listened to his heart pounding. She placed her hand over it and could not help the sigh of happiness that escaped her. Alex heard it and placed his own palm on her heart.

"I kenned Callum couldnae have the right of it." He murmured.

Brighde froze.

"Alex, I didna intend for ye to hear ma plans third hand, but Callum wasna wrong. I am going to Iona and the convent there."

Alex rolled her onto the bed and reared back to kneel between her feet. He took in her hair splayed across what had always been his pillow as he saw her lying on a bed he only ever imagined sharing with his wife. He watched her lick her swollen lips, and he gazed up and down a body that he was coming to know as well as his own.

"Ye want to leave." Alex could only shake his head. "After this, ye still plan to leave here, me." He backed off the bed and looked around quickly for his leine. He pulled it over his head and picked up his sword which he never even noticed he pulled off his back. He walked to the door and paused before unlocking it. Brighde watched his shoulder lift and fall as he took a breath and pulled the door open. He walked out without looking back. He quietly closed the door behind him, and then he was gone.

Brighde sat up and looked at the door for what felt like forever. The lump in her throat made it hard to breathe. She thought she would cry, but she could not even do that. She was numb.

What have I done? Is this really what I want? I love him. I ken that I do, and I dinna want to leave him. Ever. But how can I stay? What will I do if de Soules finds me? If he argues we were precontracted, the church and king could overturn ma marriage to anyone else. Alex doesnae believe de Soules is a threat, but I ken he would love nothing more than to lay siege to a clan that is as closely allied to the king as the Sinclairs. To weaken any clan, especially such a large one, in the Highlands would only endear him more to the English king. He plays both sides of the border and would sell his soul to the English king if he hadnae already sold it to the devil.

Brighde sat on the bed until she became so cold that she could no longer ignore her state of undress. She slowly climbed off the bed and found a fresh kirtle to wear. She brushed her hair and slid her feet into a pair of slippers. She forced herself to put one foot in front of the other as she made her way below stairs.

A crowd gathered in the Great Hall, and she could barely make out who was there, but she was able to find Alex in an instant. He was standing near the hearth speaking to a man who was equally as massive as he and nearly as handsome. The man's hair was darker than Alex's, and even from a distance, she could see his brilliant green eyes. She heard a baby crying and looked towards the dais. The face she spotted had her stop dead in her tracks.

"Brighde?"

"Mair?"

"Brighde!"

"Mair!"

The two women ran into each other's embrace and clung to one another. Neither noticed the entire Great Hall go deathly silent. They laughed until they both had tears rolling down their cheeks.

"What are ye doing here?"

"This is ma clan." Mairghread Mackay looked over her shoulder to look at her father and brothers, all of whom but Alex, stood with their mouths agape. Mairghread did not understand why Alex was scowling as if he had just eaten an entire lemon. She looked back to Brighde. "We never did exchange clan names. I assumed ye kenned from ma plaid. How long has it been since we last saw each other at a gathering?"

"Just over three summers ago."

"What are ye doing here?"

Mairghread's question brought Brighde to a halt. She suddenly became intensely aware that every eye in the room was fastened to the two of them. She looked around to see a combination of surprise and shock mixed with skepticism. Then there was Alex. He was seething. He did not need to say a word or even look at her. He was beyond even the rage he had been in only a short while ago when he found her naked and stepping from the tub. She looked back at Mairghread and took her hand before drawing her into the alcove behind the stairs.

"Brighde, what is it? Ye're worrying me. I havenae seen ye in years, and ye just went from being happy to suddenly looking terrified all in a matter of moments."

"Only Alex kenned ma real name until a moment ago. I showed up during a horrible storm and spent a moon with a raging fever. I've only been up and aboot for a short while. I tried to lie to Alex and tell him I was English, but he had already heard me speak. I did convince him to continue the charade, so I could hide. Ye havenae seen me in nearly ten summers because ma grandparents died shortly after the last gathering we were at together, and I was sent back to ma father. He wouldnae take me anywhere and wouldnae allow me to go anywhere. Ma father recently agreed to betroth me to Randolph de Soules."

Mairghread gasped. This only confirmed to Brighde that everyone on either side of the border knew of Randolph de Soules's perfidy. His father had been a loyal Scot, but the son was anything but. He had already sworn his allegiance to the English and was known for being a cruel man. Betrothing his daughter to such as man was the same as Laird Kerr signing his own daughter's death warrant.

"Aye. When I recovered, I convinced Alex to let me pretend to be Mary, an English lady. Ye remember ma grandmother was English and how I could impersonate her accent. I was doing just fine until just now. Between ye using ma name and me speaking, there isnae anyone left who will believe I'm English. Now I just have a great deal of explaining to do."

"But that doesnae explain why Alex has such a black cloud hanging over his head. I havenae seen him in such a mood in, well ever, really. Did ye two argue?"

"Nae argue so much as I disappointed him. I canna stay here, Mairghread. There isnae aught good that can come from yer clan harboring me for much longer. I told Siùsan that I plan to go to Iona and join the convent there. She must have told Callum because he told Alex. He came storming in his chamber, which I have been staying in—alone—and confronted me aboot it. We, um, became sidetracked, and I suppose he thought that I had changed ma mind. But I havenae. Mair, I must leave soon, and it's breaking ma heart too."

Mairghread pulled her long-lost friend in for a tight hug. They had been inseparable every summer for several years when both of their families traveled to the Highland gatherings for the games. They would sneak off to explore the area while their families visited with other clans. They often went swimming together or practiced archery when they were not too busy eating or telling each other wild and made up stories. Seeing each other had been the highlight of their annual journey. It had all come to an unexpected end when one year, Brighde just stopped showing up. Mairghread had heard that the Campbell laird's family had died of a sickness, and she worried that Brighde had been among those who did not make it. To see her alive and well, and very clearly attached to her brother, was a stunning surprise.

"We canna stay back here forever. I'm glad ye told me what has happened. Alex will come around eventually, but I wouldnae expect it to be tonight. Or tomorrow. Now come to meet ma son, Wee Liam, and ma husband, Tristan. We call him Wee so as not to confuse him with Da. Though I dinna think there'll be much confusion for a while."

Mairghread wrapped her arm around Brighde's waist as a reassurance and sign of solidarity as they rejoined everyone else in the Great Hall.

Brighde felt like there was a magnet that drew her to wherever Alex was in the room. She spotted him standing near the fire gazing into the flames. He was alone and everything about the way he stood screamed that no one should approach. He had a pint of ale in his hand he sipped from slowly. When Mairghread tugged on her hand, she was forced to return her attention to the people around her. She was introduced to Tristan Mackay and told the abbreviated version of how they came to be married. Mairghread skirted disaster when her father called off the betrothal to Tristan's stepbrother before anything was signed. The boorish lout failed to show any redeeming qualities, and it came home to roost for him later. Tristan and Mairghread had been married now just over a year and had a son that was the spitting image of Tristan but named after his grandfather, Liam Sinclair.

She could not help but laugh when Wee Liam reached as far past his father's broad frame as he could to get to his mother. He would have very nearly managed to fall out of his father's arms had they not been the size of tree trunks. Seeing the power that was constrained in Laird Mackay made her eyes wander over to Alex yet again. It was only when she felt a small, sticky hand grasp a hank of her hair that she came back to the present once again. She gently released her hair from Wee Liam's chubby fingers and giggled when he clapped his hands. Amused by his own antics, Wee Liam burbled and chattered as he reached for Brighde next. She looked to Mairghread who nodded before she took the baby from Tristan's arms. She cooed at him and made faces all while trying to ignore all the faces that continued to stare at her. She finally managed to distract herself enough that when she next looked up, she no longer saw Alex standing by the fireplace. In fact, she could not see him standing anywhere.

"He left, lass." She heard the deep timber of Laird Sinclair's voice just behind her shoulder. "Dinna fash. He hasnae gone far, I'm sure. But I dinna think he felt like being vera good company tonight."

Brighde turned to look at Laird Sinclair and was immensely relieved to see no blame or accusations written on his face. Just the opposite, he seemed incredibly understanding and forgiving.

"He'll come around, just give him a bit of time to stew and even sulk. He doesnae do it often, so it willnae hurt to indulge him and give him some space. In the meantime, the evening meal is about to be served. Shall we be seated?"

Brighde nodded her head and handed Wee Liam back to his mother. Laird Sinclair offered her his arm as he led her to the dais. This was not meant to be a courtly gesture or even a practical one, it was meant to show everyone in the clan that Brighde Kerr had the support of the laird.

The meal progressed uneventfully, and attention settled away from Brighde. She was able to focus on her meal without feeling like everyone was staring at her. She was not very hungry after everything that happened with Alex, but she was able to force a few bites down before just moving food around in her trencher. Part of her wanted to hide from Alex and wait until he was in a better mood and approached her. Another part of her wanted to face him and have it out with him about their unresolved situation, but a driving part of her just wanted to leave. She was feeling better every day, and with a plan somewhat formed in her mind, she wanted to leave before she became any more attached to the Sinclairs and before trouble could catch up with her.

"The Gunns are up to their old tricks as usual. They havenae slowed down, nae even in the past sennight since everything that happened with Siùsan. They are raiding ma lands again, and ma mon I placed there has heard rumblings about the Gunns wanting compensation for losing the laird's brother to ye son's sword. Even if they werenae close, the clan expects the laird to seek retribution." Tristan nodded his head towards Callum who had, in turn, pulled Siùsan into his lap. Brighde had learned what happened to Siùsan at the hands of one of the Gunns, and it made her feel ill to think about it. She tried to focus on something else, anything else. Just as her mind started to wonder, and she began to plan how to get to Iona if Alex would not take her, Tristan's comments permeated.

"Apparently de Soules is crying foul to anyone and everyone who will listen. His bride canna be found, and he's been tearing the Lowlands apart to find her. There's a pretty penny on her head. He has even gone so far as to petition the king to help him recover her. Ma mon at court has been busy. Fortunately, both Beatris and Sorcha love to be in the middle of everything, so ma mon who is conveniently one of their guardsmen for the MacDonnells, hear it all."

At the mention of Tristan's former stepmother and former mistress, Mairghread growled softly. Brighde looked over and raised an eyebrow as she continued to listen. For Mairghread, it was not the fact that her husband had a former leman, it was what had befallen her at the hands of the woman and his stepmother. Her irritation did not go unnoticed by her husband either. Tristan pulled her into his lap and wrapped his arms around her. She settled against him, and he continued talking. Brighde had an all-consuming wave of jealousy that flared as she looked at the two loving, married couples. She suddenly very much wanted what they had, and she did not. She tried to refocus on what Tristan was saying.

"The king agreed to support de Soules's search for his bride as long as he declares his fealty before the entire court. Which he did, but nay body believes for a moment that he means it. He's been traveling north for the past moon and questioning all the clans he comes across." Tristan looked pointedly at Brighde, and she felt herself squirm. "De Soules seems to have developed a friendship with Laird

Gunn a number of years ago when they were at court together. He is now staying with them before he continues his search for his bonnie bride with the flaxen hair that glows like a halo in the moonlight, or so it's said. That is why we are here. We came to warn ye." When Tristan saw Brighde's ash white face, he added, "and Mairghread wanted to show off Wee Liam to everyone."

Brighde thought she was going to be ill. The little food she had in her stomach churned, she felt bile rise in her throat, and she saw black dots dance before her eyes.

This is it. This is exactly what I didna want to have happen. He's practically on the doorstep, and I have brought him here. I canna stay. I have to go. Tonight. I dinna want to be anywhere near the mon, but I would rather he catch me than any harm come to the Sinclairs. They have harbored me for long enough. I need to get to ma chamber. The sooner they believe I have retired for the night, the easier it will be for me to slip out. I can go out through the lady's garden and slip out the postern gate. I never see many guardsmen there at night, and I have a clear view from ma chamber. Nay. Alex's chamber. Alex. Dear God above. I amnae ever going to see him again. I canna even say goodbye. Mayhap I can find some vellum in his chamber. I ken there is a quill with ink, but I dinna ken where aught to write on is stored. A final insult. I write him a note after digging through his belongings all so that I can say that I'm leaving him.

Brighde felt even more lightheaded than she did a moment ago. It would not be hard for her to pretend that she needed to retire for the evening.

"Please excuse me. I amnae feeling well of a sudden." She pushed back her chair and swayed slightly on her feet.

"Would ye like help up the stairs, Brighde?" Mairghread and Siùsan both began to stand.

"Nay. I am alright but thank ye. I just think I need to lie down. That was quite a lot to take in, and I need to think about what I am going to do next." She had no intention of letting anyone know that she had already made up her mind about what she was going to do.

She turned to face Laird Sinclair and gave him a weak smile.

"Can we talk in the morn aboot what will happen with de Soules so nearby?"

Laird Sinclair was an astute man. He looked at her sagely before saying, "Sleep well, lass. It'll all come right soon enough."

Chapter Thirteen

righde quietly entered the chamber that she had begun to consider her own. She could still smell a faint trace of Alexander from his visit earlier that evening. The fire had burned low, but she saw no point in stoking it. She could not allow herself to fall asleep, or she would never make it out in time. She moved quietly to the armoire that housed all the borrowed gowns she had been wearing. She moved them aside and looked for her own plaid. She had no intention of ever wearing the Clan Kerr plaid again. Instead, she would burn it. She would be better off wearing a Sinclair plaid, but she knew that would not work. The only way to do that was to steal the one she had been lent, and she would have to cross part of Gunn territory anyway. It was going to be dangerous enough without having any of the Gunns think she was one of the Sinclairs they sought vengeance against. She lifted the Sinclair plaid that she had worn since she awoke from her fever and held it to her nose. She knew from the start it was one of Alex's. His scent faded and been replaced by her own, but if she held it to her face long enough, it almost felt like Alex's touch. A slow, fat teardrop fell from her eye. She quickly wiped it away before folding the plaid and laying it aside. She then pulled out a cloak that had no clear clan markings but was lined with sealskin. It reminded her of the story Alex had told her about Magnus fearing their mother was a selkie. The weather during the day was still warm, but it could be like a January day in the middle of July this far north. She would be wise to have it not only to keep her warm but to hide within because it had a large cowl that would cover her head completely. She moved over to the window and pushed aside the cover, so she could look out over the bailey. There were still some people moving about, but for the most part, people had settled into their homes for the night. Brighde knew she needed to wait at least another hour before she could risk sneaking out. Sighing, she turned around. And screamed.

She did not expect to see anyone sitting in the chair by the fire, least of whom Alex. Alex sat mostly hidden in the shadows with his legs stretched out before him and crossed at the ankles. He had a cup of whisky resting in his hand. When he spoke, there was a note of warning.

"Going for a stroll tonight? Perhaps to Iona. A bit of a stretch of the legs, dinna ye think?"

"Alex, I didna expect to find ye in here. What are ye doing sitting in the dark?" She moved over to the fire and stooped to toss another brick of peat into the fire.

"Dinna," Alex's softly stated word forced shivers up and down Brighde's back. It was far more menacing than if he yelled at her.

"After all, what is the point? Ye arenae planning to stay here long enough to need to warm the room. And we both already ken what each other looks like." His meaning was not lost on her. She straightened to her full height and clasped her hands before her. She refused to speak, so they stared at one another in silence. The longer they stared, the more she wanted to shift back and forth on her feet, but she forced herself to be still.

Finally, Alex took another sip of whisky and let it roll around his mouth before he spoke.

"Dinna ye think it's a bit risky to leave the protection of this clan to go traipsing across the Highlands again, except this time, with yer pursuer only a day away. In the direction ye're traveling. Or have ye convinced some other poor sod to do yer bidding? Are ye leading him around by the cods too?" There was no imagining the bitterness in his voice. It was far too evident, and he made no attempt to hide it.

"So ye ken that too. Ye family does like to talk." Brighde looked towards the fire as her words came out barely more than a whisper. "Ye ken there isnae anyone else."

"Else? That implies there was ever someone, to begin with. But ye never wanted anyone, right? Ye dinna want anyone now."

Brighde's head whipped around.

"Ye think ye are the only one hurting right now. Ye think this is easy for me. If ye were in ma place, ye would really stay here and bring trouble upon the heads of people who were so kind to ye? Nay and ye ken it. Ye would do exactly what I must do."

"Nae at all. I wouldnae run from someone who wants to and can protect me. Ye just dinna want the help. Ye believe ye can do better on yer own than an entire trained army of battle-seasoned warriors. Oh aye, that makes plenty of sense."

"I did do well enough for maself when I had to. I dinna remember hearing aboot ye traveling the length of Scotland on yer own without a horse. I believe ye have always traveled with yer passel of brothers to protect ye."

Alex shot out of the chair, his cup forgotten as it rolled across the floor.

"Ye think insulting me will deflect attention from ye. It hasnae worked yet, and ye canna use ma own tricks against me. I see through them," he grasped her arms and almost lifted her off her feet, so they were nearly eye level. Brighde could smell the whisky on his breath, but it was faint enough for her to tell that he had not had much. No, his anger and frustration and hurt all came from a place of sobriety, and that almost scared her more than if he had been drunk.

"And how did that last flight across Scotland work for ye? Perhaps ye dinna remember. Because ye were unconscious for a moon. But I remember all too well because I was the one trying to keep ye alive. I was the one who sat with ye every bluidy day and night. More fool was I to admire the tenacity and fearlessness that I thought was what got ye here. Nay. Now I ken it was stubbornness and recklessness."

"Ye make me out to sound so selfish when all I want is to protect ye."

"That is selfish! Who are ye to think that ye could single-handedly protect this entire clan? Ye arenae a martyr. Ye're a fool. There isnae a warrior in this clan who would have the ballocks to believe that his actions alone would be all that is needed to save nearly ten score people. Nay. Yer actions are more likely to see members of ma clan dead if ye insist on running away. Even if I were willing to let ye go, which I amnae, Da would never allow us to let ye wander alone through the Highlands. There arenae so many lochs and rivers for ye to use this far north. Ye would truly be on foot the entire way. Highlanders arenae trusting either. Nay one will offer a single woman a ride on their wagon. Just the opposite, they'll ken straight away that something isnae right and will keep their distance. Then talk aboot it to any passing ear willing to listen. I'm sure de Soules's ear would be willing to listen. The weather will be changing soon, and there is always the chance that it could snow in the middle of summer. Then what? Ye freeze to death? Starve to death? Be eaten alive by a wildcat or wolf, or gored by an angry boar? Those sound like terrific ways to find yer path to heaven. And what happens to the men who are sent out to find ye? What happens when they must travel through foul weather to look for ye God only kens where? Or when they run into a Gunn scouting or raiding party?

"Or mayhap ye hope to wait somewhere until Mairghread and Tristan travel back to Mackay land and tag along with them. That way ye can put them and ma wee nephew in danger. Ye would rather do all of that than stay within the safe confines of this keep with a clan that has its own water source within the walls and enough food stored to carry us through a full year from now. Ye are exactly what the word selfish means."

Brighde listened to Alex's tirade with vacillating emotions that went from anger to remorse, to frustration, to self-pity and indignation, to anger again, and finally settled on guilt.

She placed her fists against his chest but did not have it in her to do anything with them. She felt herself deflating in the face of his biting but truthful words.

"Alex, I just canna bear the thought of ye being hurt because of me." Tears flowed down her cheeks. "I dinna want a single Sinclair to be harmed because of me, but if aught happened to ye because of me, I couldnae go on. I just want to be far enough away that if I am found, they willna come after ye. I ken ye wouldnae back down, and I willna, I canna, stand the risk ye might be killed."

She gripped his face in her hands and lifted her mouth to his. It was a hungry kiss, but not from lust. It was a need to find salvation and comfort in one another. It was a need to share the emotions that neither was ready to put into words. They both hungered for the connection they developed and that neither wanted to end, but both feared would. When they needed to come up for air, they smattered kisses over each other's faces. Alex slowly lowered her to the ground and rubbed her arms. He had not paid attention to how firmly he gripped them and now worried that he hurt her.

"I'm fine, Alex." She stroked his cheek as he leaned his forehead against hers.

"Dinna leave. Dinna run when all I will do is chase ye. Tomorrow, the next day, the day after that. Always. I ken we can keep ye safe, and I give ye ma word that we willna let harm come to ye."

Brighde looked into the eyes of a man that she had come to depend upon in so many ways. She knew he understood her in ways that were unnerving and yet comforting all at once. She knew she did not want to leave, and she knew he would come after her. She knew exactly where she belonged. She just had to accept it. But she also knew she was not there yet.

Slowly she nodded her head.

"I'll stay." *For now.*

Alex pulled her into his embrace and kissed her with all the longing and love that he could infuse into a kiss. She returned it in equal measure.

Chapter Fourteen

he next three days were busy ones for all of the Sinclairs. The men, including Laird Sinclair, trained during most of the morning and afternoon. While the laird did not make it out to the lists every day, he was still a fierce opponent to anyone who paired with him. It was clear where his sons gained their strength and finesse. Unlike many Scottish noble families, the Sinclairs had not sent their sons, or daughter, off to foster. Before Lady Sinclair passed away, she believed her children were too young to be sent far from home to only be seen a couple of times a year. She died when her sons were just coming to an age where the laird and lady were arranging for them to foster. After she was gone, the laird refused to even consider allowing any of his children to be sent away. He had been a loving and doting father from the beginning and understood that losing their mother meant they needed him all the more. The Sinclair brothers clearly benefited from their father's instruction, and the clan did not hurt for allies even without the connections that fostering made.

After the men bathed, they convened in the laird's solar. They received daily reports from their scouts and border patrols. The Sinclairs, along with Tristan, discussed various scenarios and how they would handle them. Their greatest concern was for the people who lived outside of the curtain wall. There was a large and prosperous village beyond the gates. The fields were full of crops that would need harvesting soon. The danger that the village or the fields might be set on fire was what worried the men most. They could neither afford to lose their people or their crops. It was clear that if the people could make it within the walls, there would be no worries of a food or supply shortage. The larders and storage rooms were well stocked and could last them a year. But if that many people needed to seek shelter here, the crops in the field were a necessity for the following year when all that was stored was already eaten. That first day, they set about creating a plan in case of attack.

"It has been unseasonably warm this summer, and several of the fields could be harvested early. It might even be better than waiting for them to wilt from the heat and sun. We could bring the crops in early that are ready and begin storing them. There is still room in a few of the storage buildings, and the men can move last year's stored food into the larders and buttery when Elspeth decides what she most wants."

"Aye, Callum, we can do all of that, but that will only draw attention to our concern about a siege. The clan members will want to ken why we're harvesting early, and if Gunn does have any scouts in the area, they will report back that we are preparing for a siege. With the men and women all working out in the field when de Soules is so close makes them an easier target. We want them all gathered together, but inside the curtain wall not out in the open of a field."

Alex ran his hand through his hair as he thought about the various factors that were at play. His natural disposition was to be wary of most things. He had a keen sense of observation, and he thought through things, albeit faster than most, before acting. He was the family's strongest tactician.

"It might be an inconvenience, but what if we harvest all that we can while doing it in the early morn and early evening. We need the light to see, but it would prevent it from being as obvious as having a field full of people working all day. We maynae have as much time to gather everything if an attack comes soon, but it would allow for people to stay closer to the keep during the day. Since this harvest would be earlier this year than most people have planned for, rotations would make it easier on families to spare their men. The women would also have time to prepare their family's storage spaces. It might confuse any spies or scouts just long enough to buy us a few days of work."

"I'm in agreement with Alex. Much of the wheat that we saw as we arrived is golden already. It can be brought in to be threshed within the walls. The cooler temperatures of early morn and early evening would make the men more productive too. What isnae ready for harvest can remain in the field. If an attack comes, then we open the water troughs and let the fields flood. It isnae ideal for the plants to get that much water that fast, but it will make them harder to burn. The vegetables in the gardens inside the wall will be safe, so there is that. Crofters will need to draw more water to keep on hand, so they can douse their roofs if we have enough warning. Let the village elders and Aileen ken that there is a threat of possible attack. This will keep them prepared for when the bells ring. They can get the women to the keep while the men tend their homes," Mairghread reasoned.

Mairghread had always been involved in the clan's business as much as her brothers. She sat at the table next to her husband who slung his arm loosely over the back of her chair and smiled like the cat that got into the cream. He was happy to listen to his wife's suggestions. In their year and a half of marriage, he learned quickly that Mairghread was the best partner he could hope for. She was astute, cunning, and always put the members of her clan before herself. Listening to her now made him even prouder. He was more than willing to offer his opinion if it was asked of him, but for now, he was content to let Mairghread represent clan Mackay.

"Mairghread is right. We need to make sure that there is time for families to prepare their crofts for an attack, and we canna bring everything else to a halt. I will speak to the smithy today about forging more arrow tips and have his sons come to check swords and shields that might need repair." Magnus was the member of the laird's family who oversaw the running of the clan's armory, so he was best informed about what needed to be done to keep their warriors' weapons ready.

"I will speak to Malcolm in the village and warn him that he and the other elders should be vigilant about keeping an eye open for raiders and to have the men prepare for an early harvest," added Tavish.

"Dinna get lost on yer way back," Magnus elbowed him. It was no secret Tavish flirted with Malcolm's oldest daughter, Isabella, for years. Tavish knew better than to touch her, but he liked the attention.

When the meeting ended, Alex sought out Brighde and found her with the other women in the garden. He noticed they were doing more than just weeding that day. His curious look had Brighde walking over to him.

"If an attack may come with de Soules so close and Gunn as an ally, we need to bring in as much food as we can, so it can be stored, and some of it can begin to be pickled."

Alex looked around but did not see his sister. There was no way that Brighde or any of the other women could know yet what was discussed in the solar.

"How did ye ken?"

"Ken what? To bring in the vegetables? Isnae it obvious? The warm weather ripened much of the fruit and vegetables, so there is nay harm in gathering them. The only harm would be nae being prepared for an attack. I came out to work, and Siùsan agreed to help. When we told Elspeth and Hagatha where we were going, they sent some of the other women with us. We've been here since just after the nooning."

Alex pulled her in for a quick kiss. Brighde looked up at him and then over her shoulder to see who was watching. None of the ladies were conspicuous, but she knew they watched. She tried to step out of his embrace, but it was like pushing against a steel wall.

"Alex," she hissed.

"I'm proud of ye, that's all. Ye are helping ma people, and ye've shown ye understand how a lady of the keep leads."

"Alex, I amnae the lady of the keep, and never will be one."

"I ken that, but as the wife of a nobleman, even a second son, ye will have responsibilities in any household. Leading the women is always one of them. I'm happy to see ye blend in so easily with them."

Brighde froze.

As the wife of a nobleman, even a second son...Was that a proposal? Does he just assume that because I agreed to stay that we are going to be married? Does he think ma agreement to stay began our betrothal? That wasna what I meant at all when I agreed to stay. But— would marriage to Alex be all that bad? Of course nae, ye goose. It's exactly what I want. Why canna I accept that marrying him is what I want? I ken I love him. I just feel so unsettled by this whole situation with de Soules. If only I could ken whether I am pre- contracted with him or nae, then I wouldnae have to worry aboot a marriage to Alex being set aside. That would be worse than never marrying him at all. To have him and lose him is more than I can bear. Who are ye kidding, ye dolt? I have him now. The mon is practically declaring himself. He did as much last night, and yet I keep running away. What is wrong with me?

"Mo ghràidh," Alex he stroked her arm gently. "Brighde, ye're somewhere far, far away. Where did ye just run off to? Ye arenae listening to me."

"Oh? I'm sorry. I was just lost in thought about what needs to be done with the vegetables." She knew it was a weak answer, but it was all that she could come up with.

Alex knew pressing her would do him no good.

~~~

The fourth day after the Mackays arrived brought heavy rains and thunder with lightning. Brighde awoke to the glass in the window frame rattling. The fire had burned low, and the chamber was freezing despite it being the height of summer. She eased from the bed and quickly padded across the room to pull on a fresh pair of stockings before completing her morning ablutions. She dressed and pulled the Sinclair plaid that she continued to wear around her as an arisaid. The night that Alex had waited for her in the chamber was the last time she had held it. She knew what everyone had been thinking since she had been wearing the laird's son's plaid for weeks. It just had not dawned on her just how significant that was. Alex had been offering for her since the beginning. He could have made sure that she received a plaid. The fact that it was his meant that he was staking a claim early on. She was not entirely sure how she felt about that. Part of her rebelled at any note of possessiveness. It rankled and quite frankly scared her. The other part of her relished in knowing that Alex wanted her as much as she wanted him and that he was not shy or embarrassed to let everyone know.

She walked over to the window and pulled back the cover. There were only a few people dashing about the bailey, and the lists were empty. Very few were braving the weather. She suddenly had flashes of memory from the night she arrived. She remembered praying that she would make it to the faint light that seemed to never come any closer. She remembered falling to her knees as she tried to call up to the gate, and she remembered the giant man who came out to meet her. She had thought she was on her way to heaven because an angel came to claim her. She smiled at that memory. *Aye, he's an angel but the devil in disguise too.*

When she heard a quiet knock at the door, she called out, "Come."

She did not need to turn around to know it was Alex. The shiver that raced up her spine had nothing to do with the weather or the lack of fire in the room. Alex stopped sleeping outside the chamber door shortly after his brothers returned. He began sharing a room with Tavish, and while he never complained and put up with Tavish's teasing, Brighde felt guilty that he had been displaced for so long.

She sighed as she felt his arms slip around her waist. It felt so natural to have him nearby. If she did not allow herself to think about the future, she was able to enjoy the closeness she shared with Alex.

"This weather reminded me of when I first arrived. I remembered a little more just now. I can recall praying that I would reach the lights that I saw coming from the wall walk and that I thought ye were an angel sent to take me to heaven."

Alex chuckled softly beside her ear.

"Funnily enough, I thought ye looked like an angel with the way yer hair shone in the lightning cracks." He placed a soft kiss on her crown and squeezed gently. "Are ye ready to go below stairs to break yer fast?"

"Aye."

As they left the chamber, Alex entwined their fingers together. They could see Tavish was reaching the bottom of the stairs as they approached him.

"Alex, I feel badly ye have to share a chamber with Tavish. It really is time for me to move up to a guest chamber. I canna keep occupying yer chamber forever." The moment those last words left her mouth, she wished she could swallow them. She was not in the mood for a discussion. She cringed at Alex's next words.

"I dinna see why ye canna occupy it forever." Brighde was surprised when that was all he said. She expected him to press the issue again, even if only subtly.

Alex knew Brighde became uncomfortable when he hinted at a future together. He felt her freeze the day before when he mentioned being the wife of a second son. He had been hurt that she still was not willing to consider a future for them. He was not ready to give up, but he also did not want her to agree simply because she relented and gave in to him. Badgering her into marriage was the last thing he wanted. He wanted her to desire a life with him just as much as he desired one with her. He wanted an equal partnership like he saw with his parents and as he saw now for his brother and his sister.

They arrived in the Great Hall, and he escorted her to a seat. He had begun to sit across from her when she started taking meals with the family. That morning, though, he needed some space. Being near her flooded his mind and his senses, and he needed time to breathe after yet another rejection. He moved down to sit between Magnus and Tavish. He saw the question spark in her eyes, so he gave her a small smile. He knew she saw it was half-hearted, but he could not dredge up more to give.

After the meal ended, he retreated to his father's solar. They had not planned to meet that day as most of the possible plans that could be made had been. He knew it was too early in the day to drink, but he poured himself a dram of whisky and found a book. It was not often that he felt reclusive, but he enjoyed time to himself more than any of his brothers. Mairghread was the only one who was like him in that. He had been in the solar for about two hours when the door quietly opened. He smelled the lavender his sister preferred before she joined him by the fire.

"I thought I might escape for a while too." She pulled a book from the shelf and quietly sat in the chair next to him. They both faced the fire and watched the flames dance. She opened the book and would have been quite content to begin reading.

"What are ye escaping from?"

"Wee Liam is napping, and Tristan is driving me slightly mad. The mon can find just aboot aught to talk about just to fill the silence. Normally, I dinna mind. I enjoy talking to him, but Liam didna sleep well with the storm, and I just need some quiet." She looked at him from the corner of her eye. "Why are ye hiding from her?"

"I didna say that I was hiding, and ye're the one who said we were both trying to escape. I wanted to catch up on a book I started ages ago and havenae had a chance to finish."

Mairghread looked at him and simply waited. He looked back and was prepared to wait it out too. While Mairghread had always been closest to Magnus because there was such a small age difference, her personality often tended to be most similar to Alex. They were both introspective and could sort out the finer details from within the grander scheme of events.

"Ye didna have to. Ye may want to finish that book, but ye want to hide more. What has happened between ye two? She looks lost and isnae sure what to do with herself, and ye're being a recluse in here."

Alex had a momentary pang of guilt and responsibility for Brighde, but in a keep full of people, she was bound to find something to do.

"I think ye are hiding because ye arenae satisfied with how things stand between ye two, and she isnae willing to commit yet. Ye're frustrated and disappointed."

"Ye think all that, do ye? And how did ye get to be so wise, little sister?"

"By listening to ye, of course, big brother." They looked at each other for a long minute before both began to laugh. They had the same color of chestnut hair and similar features, but where all the brothers had inherited Laird Sinclair's brown eyes, Mairghread had inherited Lady Sinclair's blue-grey ones. She strongly resembled their mother, and Alex found it reassuring to spend time with Mairghread. She had also inherited their mother's fire and feistiness. It made her a fun sparring partner in a war of words. She kept him on his toes.

"In all seriousness, is that what troubles ye?"

"Aye. She doesnae believe me that she can stay here and that everything will be alright. She agreed to stay. For now. But I think that once the immediate threat from de Soules is gone, she will still try to go to Iona. She worries that she is a danger to the clan. Once the danger is gone, she will probably argue that she has been a burden to the clan. I ken she cares about me. She even claims that is the reason why she must leave, and I believe she believes that wholeheartedly. I just dinna ken why she cannot see that her fears may be reasonable but dinna have to dictate her future." Alex tilted his head back and closed his eyes.

"What was her life like before she ran away from a mon who would sell her to a beast like de Soules? She must have had a terrific model of what married life is like. I'm sure that is why she is so excited to enter into it."

"Yer sarcasm is noted and nae at all needed, though ye do have the right of it. Her father was involved with a mistress who bore him two sons before he married Brighde's mother. He continued the relationship with this woman even after his marriage, and she bore him another son. When her mother died, he married his mistress and shipped Brighde off to her mother's parents. She lived there for nearly ten years while her father went on to have three more children with his new wife. I dinna ken how much of this she told ye when ye were children. When her grandparents, uncle and his family died of an illness that ravaged their clan, she was forced to return to the Kerrs. Her father mistreated her and beat her. When she found out who he planned to betroth her too, she tried to run away. She managed to evade him for a few days but was caught. He locked her in her chamber until they left to meet de Soules. While on the way there, their party was ambushed. Brighde watched her father run off and leave her behind. She saw de Soules and knew that he and her father planned this. They were prepared to leave her for dead, so her father could keep the bride price and de Soules kept the dowry. I suppose her father needed the coin to pay off debts, and de Soules wanted the land that must have been a part of the dowry. De Soules is known far and wide to be dishonorable. He's already had more than one wife, and his fealty is with the king of England nay matter what he might swear to now. Kerr sounds like a piece of shite from the way he treated her even before this betrothal business came up."

"Hmm. Can ye blame her for fearing marriage? Her father mistreated her mother and flaunted his affair by marrying the woman and making her his daughter's stepmother. He packed her off as a wean to her grandparents with whom she had less than ten summers. She then returned to a household that didna want her and saw constant reminders that marriage isnae a sacred bond to everyone. She hasnae exactly had the best examples of how to trust men and to believe in marriage. Mayhap she doesnae want to risk the same fate."

"How can she believe I'm anything like her father!" Alex stormed as he rose from his chair. He tossed the book onto the chair behind him and went to lean his elbow on the mantel.

"I dinna think she does. I think that is why she is so conflicted. She kens ye are naught like her father, and that's why she wants so desperately to protect ye. At the same time, she isnae sure that marriage is for her. Whether she admits it or nae, I would imagine she fears history repeating itself. And what if de Soules shows up with proof of a betrothal. She would be considered pre-contracted, and any other marriage could be set aside by the church. Could ye imagine being married to her and then having her ripped from ye? I dinna ken if she's strong enough to go through that. I ken I couldnae do it if someone tried to keep me from Tristan."

Mairghread came to rest a hand on his shoulder. She pulled gently until he looked up.

"It isnae that she doesnae care. Just the opposite. I think she loves ye vera much. But she's scared."

"I ken that. What I dinna ken is how to convince her or to allay her fears. I dinna ken what to do."

"Patience." Mairghread stretched to give her brother a kiss on the cheek and then quietly slipped from the room.

Chapter Fifteen

righde felt at a loss for what to do. Siùsan had not been feeling well that morning, so she retired to her chamber with Callum. Tavish and Magnus were sitting together playing knucklebones and basically entertaining themselves by telling one outlandish tale after another. She definitely did not feel like she belonged joining them. Laird Sinclair had braved the weather to go out with his second, an older man named Kenneth, to check on various crofters' homes to make sure their roofs were in a fair condition to not only weather this storm but the coming winter. Tristan was in his chamber with a sleeping Liam while Mairghread had sought out a book. She had no idea where Alex was. Feeling adrift, she made her way into the kitchens. The other women were accustomed to both Siùsan and her coming to work there. Mairghread and her mother before her had always helped with various tasks in and around the keep. Not all the clan had been prepared for outside women to do the same. It took a while for them to become used to Siùsan working alongside them. By the time Brighde was well enough to move about, the idea of a lady helping in the kitchens, buttery, or with the laundry did not seem so outlandish.

Elspeth was in the midst of directing her crew of women as they prepared for the noon meal. In a clan so large and a keep so big, one meal was prepared immediately after the previous one was served. There was little respite for those who worked for the head cook. Brighde looked around and found a pile of potatoes that needed peeling and chopping. She picked up a knife and began to work. She had been at it for a number of hours before she realized that time had actually flown by. She finished the last turnip that she was peeling, having finished the potatoes and carrots already. She put down the knife and stretched out her back. It felt good to stand upright after hours of leaning over the chopping table.

Brighde heard Elspeth speaking to one of the older girls about going out to the chicken coops just beyond the kitchens. It was still pouring, and the girl was not wearing an arisaid since it was usually far too warm in the kitchens to wear the extra layer of wool.

"Elspeth, I can go. I dinna want her to get drenched. I already have a plaid on." Before anyone could object, she snatched a basket from beside the door and went outside. The air smelled crisp and clean even though the rain was still coming down in droves. She lifted her skirts above her ankles and carefully picked her way around puddles until she got to the coops. With such a large clan, it was more like a small shed than just stands for the chickens to roost. She opened the door and stepped into the dimly lit space. As she went from nest to nest, she heard voices approaching. She did not recognize them, but she was able to hear every word they said.

"If she hadnae come here, we wouldnae be in danger. First, she lies about being English. As though that didna make us dislike her. Then, she's going to bring the Gunns down upon us. She maynae be an English bitch, but she is still a bitch."

"Aye, a right dog in heat. Have ye seen the way Lord Alexander is sniffing after her? Ye'd think she was the king's gold. Everyone in the clan kens where she sleeps each night. In his bed. And they arenae even handfasted. At least Lord Callum didna try to hide Lady Elizabeth. We all kenned what she was and why she was there. As though pretending to sleep outside the door or now in Lord Tavish's chamber is fooling anyone. She isnae aught more than a whore, but she traipses around in Lady Mairghread's gowns as though she is part of the laird's family."

"And if ye ask me, there must have been a reason that her father was willing to trade her to a mon like de Soules. He must really hate her to marry her off to that bastard. Do ye ken that he's killed off his three wives?"

"I heard it was the last four."

"Either way, it would be a small price to pay, so we dinna have to worry. And ma Andrew says that he's going to work in the fields in the morn and the evening to help harvest food that's needed for when the Gunns attack. As though he doesnae already have enough to do working in the armory. Now, this. She never should have come here. We would be a far sight better off if she'd made it to the Sutherlands or fallen off one of the cliffs than to darken our doorstep."

Brighde could not hear anymore since the women continued on and a loud crack of thunder blotted out any other sounds. She did need to hear any more. Every one of her fears had just been confirmed. The members of the Sinclair clan resented her being there. She was a danger to them, and everyone not only knew it but talked about it. She had already made up her mind before she entered the kitchens with her basket of eggs. She quietly put them into the larder where she pulled two loaves of bread, some dried meat, and oilcloth wrapped cheese from the shelves. She pulled a length of her arisaid out to make room to tuck the food within. She looked around and found a barrel of apples, so she grabbed several of them to add to her stash. She found a waterskin hanging from a hook near the door. She shook it and found it was

121

empty. With the amount of rain that was coming down, she was not worried about finding water.

She slipped back out of the kitchen and made her way to the postern gate. She looked around to see if anyone was watching her, and then she looked up to see which way the guardsmen were looking. She watched for a moment and could not believe her luck.

They are just changing shifts! They dinna seem to be looking out towards the loch. If I can get there without being seen, then I should be able to slip out to the woods. I dinna dare try to take a horse. I canna steal something so valuable, and I definitely willnae make it far without someone noticing a woman riding away from the keep. I arrived in a gale, and I leave in one. Fitting.

She ducked through the door in the wall and looked quickly over her shoulder. When she moved forward, and when no one sounded the alarm, she dashed towards the path that led to the loch. She reached the water's edge and hugged the shore as she skirted around the lake. When she was lined up even with a break in the trees, she looked back at the wall again. The men on the wall walk were little more than dots with the rain limiting anyone's visibility. She ran as hard and as fast as she could to make it to the woods. When she entered the woods, she slowed but only slightly. She had developed a dislike of the dark ever since she had traveled through the nights to escape her father. She forced herself to take a deep breath and slow her heartbeat. The woods were unusually dark for this time of day, and while she was thankful for the storm that allowed her to slip away from the keep so easily, she now cursed it for leaving her feeling disoriented among the trees. As she moved further into the trees, she made sure that she kept the castle within her sights to her right. She was having to double back slightly, but the distance from the postern gate to the tree line had been too far to try to cross without being spotted. She was grateful that she had put on boots this morning instead of slippers. Something in the back of her mind had said they were a better choice even if she had not planned to go outdoors. She pulled the cowl of her arisaid tighter. She wished she had the cloak that still hung in the armoire, but the plaid would have to do. The muted colors helped her to blend in. She thanked God over and over that the Sinclairs favored greens and blues over yellows, reds, and blacks like many of the Lowland clans. When she came even with the farthest end of the castle, she paused to look at it.

I am doing the right thing. I ken I am. I just wish it wasna the right thing to do. I dinna want to leave. I dinna want to lose Alex, but I canna stay. I am a danger to his people, and they hate me for it. They ken I am the reason why they're being forced to prepare for an attack that willnae happen if I canna be found there. I dinna want to marry de Soules, but I will if it's what it takes to keep Alex and the rest of his family safe and to keep his clan from growing angry at them. Goodbye, Alex. I love ye.

Brighde looked one last time at the castle before she began running again.

Chapter Sixteen

*A*lex!"

The banging on the door pulled Alex from his dark thoughts. He looked towards the window and realized that several hours had passed since Mairghread had left. He had spent the time reading but often lapsing in dark thoughts about a certain blonde who was inordinately stubborn. One moment he wanted to shake her and the next, he wanted to carry her away and spend every waking moment making love to her.

The door swung open, and Magnus rushed in.

"Alex, there's a problem. Neither Mairghread nor Siùsan can find Brighde. The last anyone saw of her was when she returned from gathering eggs. She went into the larder to put them away, but no one saw her slip out. Elspeth went to look for her thinking that she may have gone out to fetch more, but she found Morag and Bethea gossiping about her. They were saying vicious things aboot Brighde being the cause of the clan's troubles. When Elspeth confronted them, she asked if they walked past the chicken coop recently. They said they had, having nay idea that they just admitted that Brighde probably heard them. We think she's run, Alex."

Magnus had barely finished before Alex was tearing from the room. He bolted through the Great Hall not even bothering to look within the keep. If his sister and sister by marriage had not found her inside the castle, she was not there. He ran to the gardens and checked there. He looked around the bailey. There was barely a dry spot to be seen with mud and puddles covering all visible ground. He tried to see if there were any footprints that he could make out.

Alex pushed his sopping hair from his eyes and looked back at the gate which was lowered halfway. With few people coming and going in the storm, the gate did not need to be open all the way. He knew the guards would not have let her leave alone, and had she tried to leave with anyone, he would have been summoned. That left only the postern gate. He ran to the back wall caring little for the muddy water that was splashing up his legs. When he got to the door in the curtain wall, he could see a pair of footprints that had not been disturbed by the rain. He pushed open the door and found a matching pair. He scanned the land ahead of him and could not see a single soul out in the rain. He pulled the door shut and spun on his heels to head to the stables. He saddled *Naomh* and yelled for the gate to be opened wide enough for him to pass. He gave no thought to inform his family of his intentions, instead, he was singularly focused on finding the woman who drove him to the brink of madness and despair all while making him fall further and further in love with her every day.

Alex followed the path to the loch, but there was nothing to see. There were no footprints, and nothing looked like it had been disturbed by anything other than the weather. He rode up the ridge to look out over the beach below. There was nothing there. Not even the seals were on the sand. He looked to the sea cave but knew immediately that she would not have gone there. The waves were angry and churning against the rocks. She never would have survived, and he knew she wished to escape not to perish.

If she isnae found soon, she may vera well perish anyway. What could those auld biddies have said that would be enough to drive her away in yet another storm? Just how desperate does she feel that she had to leave and take naught with her. She doesnae even have that cloak. I dinna even ken if she has an arisaid. Where are you going, mo ghaol? Mayhap if I had actually told her she's ma love instead of hoping she understood, she would believe me when I said I would protect her, and I would come after her. She canna have been gone too long, so she canna be that far ahead of me especially since she's on foot. I just canna tell which direction she headed with nothing to track.

Alex pulled his horse around and scanned the landscape in front of him. He decided she must have made for the forest as a shelter from being seen and from the weather. He spurred *Naomh* into a gallop until he reached the woods. He had to slow his horse as he wound through the trees and avoided being knocked out of the saddle by low hanging branches. He headed west but allowed his path to take him south before heading north and then back south again. He rode in a huge "w" to try and cover as much of the forest as he could. He knew she must have some sense of direction if she had made it all the way to the Sinclairs but being in the woods made it easy to get disoriented.

He spent nearly two hours searching before seeing something white flash in the distance. At first, he was not sure what he saw, but when it moved again, he knew he would recognize her hair anywhere. It was the beacon he needed to find his way home.

~~~

Brighde was out of breath and tiring. She had rolled her ankle badly over an hour ago but did not dare slow down. Each step shot shards of pain up her leg all the way to her hip. She was to the point of hobbling rather than running when she heard trees rustling behind her. She peaked back and could only make the faint outline of a man on horseback. She had no way of knowing if he was friend or foe.

Dinna kid yerself. Ye've run from him. Ye dinna have any friends left.

She forced herself to run again as she tried to hide behind trees and branches. She could not afford to slow down even though she could barely catch her breath, and it felt like a dirk was being sliced through her chest.

Suddenly, there was a rustling up ahead. She pushed her dripping hair from her eyes and tried to see where the noise had come from. She did not see any other horses or anyone on foot, but she still heard the rustling. She took another step and froze with a scream dying on her lips. Less than a hundred yards in front of her was a very large and very angry boar.

Didna Alex warn me aboot this? He tempted fate. I am going to be gored to death, and when—nay—if I'm ever found, he will only have 'I told ye so' to say over ma grave.

Brighde could not move. She was petrified that if she tried to escape, it would only make her appear to be a more interesting and appetizing find for the animal. She tried to quieten her breathing, but she had been running so hard that she could not completely silence her wheezing breath.

The boar stamped its hoof and pawed the ground. It shook its head, and the tusks shone even though it was dark within the forest. She could see the steam coming from its snout each time it snorted.

She began to slowly inch backward but had barely taken three steps when the boar squealed and began to charge. She did not want to turn her back, but she also knew she would not stand a chance of escape if she tried to take any more steps going backward. She began to pivot when an arm shot out and wrapped around her waist. She was yanked from the ground and tossed across strong thighs as a very real and very sharp sword swung over her head. She felt the impact as it reverberated through Alex's body and heard the scream before Alex pulled back. She looked to her right and saw the bloody sword being lifted over her.

Without a word, Alex kicked his horse into a canter and moved them far enough away from the dead animal that he did not worry about wolves or other boars finding them. When he finally drew to a stop, he pulled Brighde upright and sat her across his lap. All he could do was look at her because he did not know what else to do. He felt anger, relief, fear, and loss all churned through him like the tempest that had been blowing all day. When Brighde threw her arms around his waist and collapsed forwards in tears, he did not immediately return her embrace. He was too stunned, but when he felt her pull away, he wrapped her in his arms and pressed his mouth to hers. He could not stop. He could not tell if she was breathing life into him, or if it was the other way around. He wanted to taste every single inch of her while berating her for risking her life. He wanted to thrust deep inside of her to claim her once and for all as his while shaking her for scaring him so badly. Since he could not do any of those, he poured everything into his kiss which she returned with equal fervor.

Brighde squirmed in Alex's lap because she could not get close enough. She wanted to crawl inside his clothes to be skin to skin with him. Even that did not seem like it would be enough. She was desperate to be connected to him and to show him her love. She did not want to say the words, at least not now, not after she ran away. She was not convinced that he would believe her.

"Alex," she breathed out on a sigh.

"Brie," he moaned as he fisted her hair into his hand while his other one ran over her checking her for injuries.

"I amnae hurt. Ye saved me. Again."

"Always," he breathed.

She leaned back to look at the man that she knew she would always love. She was shocked at his appearance. He looked like he had been weathered by time since she saw him that morning. He looked exhausted and harried. The day had taken a toll on him too. His eyes were bloodshot, and the laugh lines around his eyes and mouth drooped now making them resemble wrinkles more than proof of a happy life. She ran her hands over his cheeks and reveled in the rough feeling of the stubble. She drew a finger down between his eyes and over the bridge of his nose before using two fingers to smooth out the furrows in his brow. Watching him, she leaned forward and pressed a kiss to his lips. He groaned and pulled her close. The passion fired again between them until a crack of lightning followed by thunder was so loud that they knew it was too close to remain in that spot.

"I ken of a cave not too far from here. Ye made it not too far from the base of Ben Morven. We can shelter there until the rain ends, and I can get ye safely back to Dunbeath."

"Alex, I amnae going back. I canna."

"How do ye think I kenned to look for ye? I ken ye overheard Morag and Bethea talking. I can only imagine what those two auld harpies had to say. What ye dinna ken is if the clan could force them out, they would. Those two women have been the source of more marital discord than even an unfaithful husband or wife could bring upon themselves. They are notoriously harsh gossips who like to create problems where none exist. I'm sure Bethea complained that her husband, Andrew, was going to have to do too much work, and she was deeply aggrieved by it. Truth be told, he's a lazy sod and hides from her in the armory. His laziness is only overlooked because nae mon envies him having to go home to such a shew. Morag makes Bethea look kind in comparison. Morag has the sharpest tongue I have ever heard. She would flay someone alive simply for being polite if she wasna in the mood to hear it. Da canna bring himself to send them away because they're nearly old enough to be his mother, but he has made it so they live in the village. I'm surprised they were within the walls today. It could only have been to stir trouble."

"But Alex, ye didna hear what they said. Even if the threat from the Gunns wasna real, yer clan thinks I'm yer leman. They think I'm a whore."

Brighde was shaking by the time she was done. Alex could feel the tension in her body and that she was soaked through. He had to find the cave and build her a fire before he could convince her that she was wrong in her thinking.

They rode for nearly another half an hour before they came to a small cave tucked away. If they had not been looking for it, they would have ridden past. Alex helped Brighde dismount and placed her just inside the entrance before he searched thoroughly. He made quick work of unsaddling his horse and brought it inside. There was not much he could do to curry *Naomh*, so he did what he could to brush off the water with his hands.

Once he had brought *Naomh* into the entrance of the cave, he turned to look at Brighde. She had moved further inside and was looking around. She quickly found the stack of wood that sat towards the back of the cave. She looked over her shoulder as she heard Alex approach.

"It's left for travelers seeking cover like we are. I'll have to replenish it before we leave in the morn."

"In the morn? We must stay here all night?" Her bravery flagged at the thought of staying in the dim and damp cave. "What if this is something's home? A wildcat or wolf pack."

"Nae thing lives here but probably a few spiders. Harmless ones at that. If the rain stops tonight, it'll still be too dark to ride back safely. Ye are soaked through and freezing. I dinna want ye sick again."

Alex set about making the fire. He was relieved to find Brighde unharmed and to have her with him again, but he was not through being both hurt and angry that she had so little faith in him. Still.

Once the fire was going, he pulled his spare plaid from his saddle bag. He handed it to her and went to stand to look out of the entrance. Brighde stared at his back for a long moment before she began to peel her gown off herself. It was pasted to her, and it was a struggle, but Alex made it clear he was not inclined to help. She took off her chemise as well and quickly laid out all her clothes near the fire. She wrapped the plaid around her. Fortunately, Alex's height meant that he needed more material than the average man. She was able to cover herself from her neck down to her ankles.

"Alex, ye're soaked through too. What are ye going to do if I have yer spare plaid?"

Alex looked back at her, and she was surprised to see the distance and reserve in his eyes. He shook his head and turned to walk back to the fire. Brighde had not noticed that he had pulled some dried beef from his saddlebag. He handed her a couple of pieces before he pulled his leine from under his plaid. He took it off and laid it near her clothes. He sat silently before the fire, chewing on his meat and staring into the distance. Brighde did not know what to make of his silence. She knew he was not normally the brooding type, but she seemed to bring it out in him. Since there were clothes laid out on one side of the fire, there was not much choice but to sit close to him. She lowered herself to the ground, careful not to touch him. Once she was seated, she felt his arm wrap around her waist as he pulled her against him. He still stared off into space, but his warmth was a welcome reprieve from the bone-chilling numbness she felt. She remained rigid for only a heartbeat before she leaned against him and breathed in his unique scent. His presence calmed her, and she felt a sense of peace again that she only ever had when he was near.

Alex ran his hand up and down Brighde's back in hopes that it would warm her. He knew that as her blood started moving properly through her, she would be in quite a bit of pain as her limbs tingled.

Who am I kidding? I ken she needs to be warmed, but I need to touch her more. The fire would do the trick, but I canna keep ma hands from her. I just need to be near her, to ken she's truly safe and with me. I dinna ken what to do with her. If she doesnae want to be with me, then I canna and willna force her. I just wish she wanted me as much as I want her. How much I want to make a life with her.

Alex pressed her head against his shoulder and simply held her to him. Just as he thought she as dosing off, he felt her hand on his chest. It ran across his smooth skin and up towards his shoulder then back across the muscles that twitched with her touch. He almost did not notice when she unpinned the brooch that held his plaid together across his shoulder. He looked down at her, but she was looking at the wall across from them. It was almost as if she did not know she was undressing him, but Alex knew she was fully aware of what she was doing. He was just curious enough to see where it would lead that he did not stop her.

The length of plaid fell to his waist as she awkwardly pushed the brooch into his sporran. She pushed the extra fabric behind them and ran her hand all the way from his shoulder to his waist. Alex had been hard since the moment he lifted her onto his horse. He had tried all he could think of to calm himself, but her presence and her scent inflamed him. Now her hand crept dangerously close to his manhood. When she leaned forward to use both hands to unfasten his belt, he captured them both in one of his.

"Lass, what are ye doing?"

Her reply was a long, searing kiss that had him lifting her in his lap. He let go of her hands, and she made quick work of unfastening his belt. She could not pull his plaid free because she was sitting on it, but she let the plaid that had shielded her fall to the ground. She pressed her bare body to his as she ran her fingers through his hair, then up and down his back. She could not get enough of the feel of his smooth skin and the rock-hard muscles under her palms. She moaned softly as she shifted, trying to bring herself closer. Close enough to feel all of him. He flipped her onto her back, and she tugged his plaid free as their bodies pressed against one another. Alex groaned as he pulled one of her legs to his hip, and he settled between them. He could feel his sword rubbing against her moist sheath, and all he wanted to do was plunge into her.

I canna do that. She isnae mine to take. She doesnae want me, and I canna take her innocence without marrying her. I canna dishonor either of us, but dear God above, all I want is to pound into her over and over. I want to feel how tight she is. I want to hear her moaning as I make her find her release. I want to spill inside her. Dear God, I want to do that all night and then again all of tomorrow. I want to be buried inside her until she canna take it anymore. But more than aught else in this world, I want to bring her the same pleasure she brings me. I want her to ken how much I love her. That I would do aught to make her happy.

Alex fought to stay in control. The temptation was nearly all-consuming, but he would never be one of those men who claimed he could not stop. He would never take her choice away.

He is so hard. Everywhere. The feel of him bare and over me is beyond what I could imagine. I havenae ever wanted aught as much I do now. I want to ken what he feels like inside me. I ache so badly for him. It's like a slow burn taking over me. I canna stop. I dinna want this to stop. I want to feel him make love to me even if it is only this once. I want to be his and he mine for just a little while. I ken it's wrong. I ken I shouldnae, but there will never be another mon. Never. Only Alex, and if this is the only night I can have with him, then I will have him. God, forgive me because Alex may never.

Brighde grasped firmly to Alex's buttocks and shifted her hips. When she felt the tip of his cock slide into her entrance, she pulled as hard on his backside as she could and thrust her hips into him, lifting off the ground. She bit her lip almost hard enough to draw blood and swallowed her whimper of pain. Alex thrust twice before he froze. She felt him go rigid and then start to pull out. She wrapped her arms and legs around him as tightly as she possibly could.

"Please."

Alex looked down at her in disbelief. He swore this was exactly what he was not going to do. He had not taken her choice away. She had taken his. He looked into her pleasure glazed eyes and saw the same savage need as he felt. Her body quaked under him as he held himself up on his elbows. She was so incredibly tight. He never felt anything like it before. It just felt right even though his mind screamed it was wrong.

"Alex, make love to me. Please. I dinna want this night to end without kenning what it is like to join with ye. I need ye, and I think ye need me too. Let us have this. There will never be anyone else for me." She ran her fingertips lightly over his cheeks and then cupped them.

Listening to her declaration was enough to make him slowly lower back down so their chests pressed against one another. He was careful to move slowly because he knew she had to be tender even if she tried hard not to show it. As her body relaxed around him, he slid all the way to the hilt and then pulled almost all the way out. After the third glide, she thrust her hips up to him.

"Ye dinna have to coddle me. I want to feel all of ye. I want it all, Alex. Dinna hold back from me. I canna hold back from ye, so I give all of me. Please let me have the same in return."

She pressed her lips to his and ran her tongue across them. When he parted them, he thrust his tongue into her mouth, and she lightly sucked on it. That was all the permission Alex needed to begin to thrust hard into her. She could not stop the moans that escaped her. She did not want to, and the more she shared her pleasure, the harder Alex moved inside her, bringing her even more. She rubbed her sensitive bud against his hard pelvic bone and found the release she sought. It was unlike any that he brought her to before. She arched off of the ground and screamed. Alex thrust two more times before suddenly pulling out of her. He spilled across her stomach as she shook her head in displeasure. Her hips kept lifting and pressing against him. He slid a hand between them and continued to rub her engorged flesh until she went stiff again and breathed a long sigh of release.

Alex watched her throughout their coupling even though her eyes drifted closed a few times. He had never seen anything more beautiful than the glow that emanated from her cheeks as he made love to her. He had been with his fair share of women in the past, but he could not remember it ever being like this. His heart pounded as he tried to catch his breath, but he knew it was not the physical exertion that made it race. It was the depth of emotion he felt for her. He felt as though more than just his body melded with hers. He wanted to give her his heart and join their souls.

Brighde felt her eyes drift closed again. She tried to keep her eyes open throughout the entire experience because she did not want to miss a moment, but the pleasure engulfed her, and she found she could not fight it. The time that she managed to keep them open was spent looking into Alex's. Twice she looked down to watch where their bodies met. She was frustrated that she could not see more. She wanted to watch as he entered her over and over, but when she realized their position would never allow that, she went back to looking into his chocolate eyes. They took on a smoky amber tone, and she was drawn to it like a moth to the flame. He was the single most handsome man she had ever met, and he had never seemed more masculine and tender all at once than he did as they made love.

Now Brighde pressed him to lay against her. She wanted his full weight to lay on her. She needed to feel it to feel their experience was complete.

"Ye willna crush me," she whispered.

Alex gently lowered himself to her, but she knew he still held some of his weight from her. She did not want to ruin the moment, so she cradled him between her legs and brushed her hands up and down his back before settling for just holding him. His head rested in the crook of her neck and gently breathed in her scent that was now mixed with sweat and him. He felt drunk as he breathed deeper and a calm settled over him from how right it felt to hold Brighde in his arms after making love to her. His head felt both light and heavy at the same time, and he felt as though the rest of the world was slipping away from him. All he could do was focus on the woman with whom he just shared the most sensual and moving experience of his life. His fingers slowly trailed along her ribs as his other hand held her hip gently. He shivered at the feel of her fingernails gliding along his spine. His cock stirred to life again.

How can that even be? How can I possibly be ready to go again after what we just did? I havenae ever come that hard, and yet, all I want to do is sink into her and start all over again. She has bewitched me, and I canna get enough.

Alex nipped at her neck and rocked his hips forward. Brighde's reaction was immediate. She pressed her hips up to meet him as she moaned and scratched her fingernails across the muscles of his back. She turned her head towards him; her lips seeking his as she felt him reach down to guide himself into her. Their lips met as he slid back into her sheath. She sighed with pleasure as she felt him fill her to what felt like the very depth of her soul.

Alex wrapped his arms around her and rolled them over so she straddled him. He watched her sit up, and he cupped her full breasts as she slowly began to move. He let her explore at her own pace and to try rising and falling on his rod before settling for rocking back and forth. He let her find what brought her the most pleasure, and he was rewarded by watching her throw her head back as her fingers grasped onto his chest for balance. Her blonde waves hung to her waist and trailed along the tops of his thighs. They felt like feathers caressing him, and the slight contact made his skin prickle and his muscles jump. He basked in the feeling of her breasts in his hands as she stretched back. He saw the sinews in her throat work as her breathing became more labored. He felt sweat beading on his forehead as he strained to move with her without getting carried away in his own pleasure. Watching Brighde ride him was even more erotic than what they shared not five minutes earlier. His hands ran over her ribs and belly, down to her hips and then grasped her buttocks. She began to move faster as he felt her inner spasm begin.

"Alex, help me. I'm so close. I dinna ken what to do. I dinna want this to end, but I want it. But nae without ye. I dinna want to finish without ye."

Alex guided her to move faster on him. He could feel that his own release was imminent, but he would force himself to wait until she was satisfied. He thought it might very well be what finally killed him as her inner muscles squeezed and clenched around him. It took every last shred of self-control to keep from spilling inside her. The moment that he felt her relax, he thrust once more and then lifted her from him. He heard her frustrated grunt, but he was not going to risk getting her with child until they were really and truly wed before a priest in a kirk. He pulled her down to lay across his chest and lifted her hair from her neck. It stuck to her as he brushed it away.

Brighde could feel Alex's heart pounding against her own chest. She understood why he pulled out both times, and she knew it was the responsible thing to do, but a large part of her wished that he had not. She wished there was a chance, even a small one, that she might end up with his child.

Ye canna truly be that selfish, can ye? Ye would carry this mon's child, so ye might always have a part of him with ye, but ye would deny him his own first born. What kind of woman have I become? I dinna want to stay with him only because I fear for him and his clan, but I would steal from him his own bairn. I might be trying to be selfless by leaving, but instead, I could easily be the most selfish person I ken. How could I even think of doing that to him? What is wrong with me?

Brighde could not shake the feeling of self-loathing that was now putting a damper on what they shared. She had, in her own mind, managed to ruin the most incredible night of her life. She felt tears once again prick at the back of her eyes. Instead of letting them fall, she pulled Alex's arms more tightly around her. She would rejoice in these last few hours and soak in all the love she knew he felt but had not said. She would return it in even measure even though she was not ready to confess her feelings either. Alex and Brighde drifted off to sleep wrapped in each other's' arms. Sometime in the middle of the night, Alex woke long enough to pull a plaid over them before he settled back to sleep.

Chapter Seventeen

*B*righde awoke to a hard surface below her, but it was not Alex's warm body. She reached out her hand before opening her eyes, but her hand only felt cold air. She did not remember being covered with the plaid, but the cold nip in the air made her very glad for it. She slowly opened her eyes and looked around. The fire had been tended, the rain had stopped, her clothes were neatly folded next to her, and Alex was nowhere to be seen. Alex, his saddle, and his horse were missing. Brighde had a moment of panic that he had left her behind.

Did ma wantonness drive him away? Is that what finally did it? Isnae that what ye wanted after all? Mayhap nae him leaving in disgust but to leave ye alone? I didna think it would hurt so much. It was much easier when I was the one leaving. Now I ken how he must have felt. I dinna even ken where I am. He said Ben Morven, but I dinna ken where that is. I have nay idea which way I need to head. I will have to wait for the sun to rise enough for me to orient maself, but then I will lose a good chunk of the morn. But I canna walk around in circles. There isnae aught for it. I will have to wait for the sun to move into a position that I can use.

Brighde was pulling herself from her near panic and frustration when Alex walked back into the cave. She scrambled to her feet and wrapped the plaid around her shoulders. She suddenly felt shy and embarrassed. She knew it made no sense. None of it did. She knew she was the one who ran away, but now the idea of being left alone made her panic. She also knew that she was the one who left Alex behind, but the thought that he might leave her made her heart pinch within her chest. It also made absolutely no sense to suddenly find a sense of modesty after what they had done together, after what she had made them do the night before.

She was sailing unchartered waters and did not know how she was supposed to act around a man she had been so intimate with only a short time ago.

Alex entered the cave after going to the nearby stream to wash and catch a couple of fish. He looked up as his eyes adjusted to the dim light coming from the fire. He halted when he saw Brighde, more beautiful than he had ever seen standing before the fire with his plaid wrapped around her and her hair in disarray. He wanted to pull her into his arms and make love to her all over again. He suddenly felt no rush to get back home. Instead, he even thought about taking a longer route back to Castle Dunbeath so he could have more time. He could not help but smile as Brighde looked around nervously and pushed her hair back from her face. He decided to take pity on her, so he held up the fish.

"I thought ye might be a bit hungry, lass. I caught us breakfast." He smiled and moved towards the fire. "I dinna want ye getting too cold, so ye can step towards the back of the cave to dress. Ye should still have enough light to see, but I willna be able to see ye."

Alex was surprised to see a look of hurt cross Brighde's face before it was masked by a look he had come to realize was how she handled discomfort around other people. She had refined a look of serenity that might fool others, but there was a slightly tight look around her eyes. It took Alex only a moment to realize that while she was embarrassed this morning, he had awoken in fine spirits and was ready to strut like a rooster, which was not something he thought she would appreciate at this moment. He suddenly understood that his offer to escape an uncomfortable situation had seemed like rejection.

He walked over to her and wrapped one arm around her waist and pulled her to him. With his other hand, he tilted her chin up and brushed his lips against hers, gently increasing the pressure until he felt her melt against him and open for him. He plunged his tongue into the velvety warmth of her mouth as he mimicked what he longed to do with their bodies. Brighde raised her arms to snake them around his neck while the plaid sagged over his arm, and he quickly let it fall to the ground as he enclosed her in the circle of his arms. She moaned softly as she felt his hands on her bare skin, and she pressed her breasts against his chest, frustrated that his leine was a barrier between them. She reached down to push his sporran out of the way, feeling his cock brush her hand through the wool. Yet another barrier between her and what she craved. She lifted his plaid and slipped her hand underneath.

Alex was so lost in his own explorations of her body that he was unprepared for the rush of sensation that shot through him when her hand wrapped around him and began stroking. He growled as he lifted her, and she hugged him with her thighs while he took the three steps that brought her back to the wall. With another growl, he thrust into her, and her moans spurred him on as he plunged harder and faster with each thrust. She met him with equal measure. His kiss was hard and possessive, and she breathed him in as her tongue parried with his. She sucked gently on it, and when she felt Alex's control slipping, she sucked harder, grabbed his hair in one hand and his shoulder in the other.

"More."

Alex supported her with one hand as the other found her breast. He squeezed almost painfully, treading that fine line between pleasure and pain, and Bridget could not get enough.

"More."

Alex tweaked her nipple, and when he received a growl in return, he pinched harder. She pulled her lips from his and caught his earlobe between her teeth. She alternated sucking and nibbling.

Alex could feel his release coming, and he tried to stop it, but that part of him had control despite what his mind said. He pulled from her just as the first jet streamed from him. He heard her sob in frustration, and as soon as he was sure he had no more seed to spill, he thrust into her again. No longer worried, he allowed himself to completely lose control as he pounded his hips to give her the friction she craved. He had already learned what brought her the most pleasure, and he was determined to give it to her now. He pinched her nipple hard again as he tugged her hair back and feasted where her neck and shoulder met. He felt her clenching around him.

"Oh God, Alex, dinna stop. Please dinna. Alex! Alex, I need ye harder. I'm so close. God, Alex, yes!"

It was enough to cause another surge of pleasure for Alex, so he quickly pulled from her before he found his second release in as many minutes.

Bridget whimpered at the loss. Not done, she panted and writhed. Alex entered her a third time and felt the spasms deep inside her as she climaxed again. She continued to rock against him, her head sagging to his shoulders as he felt her inner spasms grip him once more. He felt his cock twitch and a mild sense of release passed over him, but he did not think he spilled any of his seed. Spent, she went limp in his arms. He twisted so his back was against the wall and sank to the ground with them still joined. He tilted his head back against the wall as he sucked in air to calm his racing heart and mind.

Bluidy hell. I just fucked her against a stone wall, and I dinna regret it at all. She's barely more than a virgin, and I took her harder than any wench I've been with. I dinna understand what is about her, but dear God, I would do just about aught she asked at this moment. It hasnae ever been like that before.

He felt Brighde quiver in his arms as he held her tightly against him, and he knew nothing could have made him let go at that moment.

Brighde felt like she was floating with her fatigued muscles still trembling. She thought their lovemaking the night before had been intense, but she never imagined that her emotions and physical need for another person could be so fervent. She vacillated between peace and belonging, and fear of being taken away by her father or de Soules. She wanted desperately to be able to accept a future with Alex, but her fear of being found had become nearly irrational. The more deeply in love she fell with Alex, the more compelled she felt to leave. She knew she had to make a choice because Alex would not allow her to leave alone, and she no longer wanted Alex to take her to Iona. She did not want to enter a convent, nor had she ever really, and she knew it would devastate Alex to make him take her. She predicted he would not be pleased with the choice she would make once they were back at the castle, but it was the best she could do.

"Mo chridhe, I havenae ever experienced aught like that before. I dinna ken what to say. I've never wanted anyone the way I do you." Alex paused to press a gentle kiss to her temple. "I didna ask last night but rather told ye that we are going back to Dunbeath. I shouldnae have done that. I shouldnae have taken away yer choice. Will ye come back to Dunbeath with me?"

Brighde leaned back to look at him. He had called her his heart. He called her his darling and his sweetheart numerous times, but this was the first time he ever made mention that his heart was truly involved. She relished it until her stomach seized.

"I'll come back. I never should have run, but I felt trapped by what I heard and what I've already worried about."

"Ye didna have to do this alone."

"I ken, but I've had to make choices to protect maself for so long, it is hard to release that control."

"Ye dinna have to protect me, but I ken you feel you have to. It's much the same for me, but we dinna have to be at cross-purposes aboot this. I want a partner nae an adversary."

Brighde knew Alex had a different plan for their future than she did, but she would not ruin this moment or the ride home with an argument or by ignoring one another.

Home. When did I start thinking of it as home? Ages ago, ye dolt and ye ken it. Ye're nae fooling Alex or yourself. Dunbeath is ma home. I need to accept it and stop trying to fight what fate decided long ago.

They rose, and Alex helped Brighde dress. He draped the spare plaid around her shoulders, and she held it closed at her throat. He had already saddled the horse. He decided the fish could wait until the noon meal and instead pulled out more dried beef. Brighde tried not to grimace, but she must have failed because Alex chuckled.

"I want to get underway before too much of the morning slides away."

Brighde leaned to look around his shoulder. The sun had just come up. She looked back at him and cocked an eyebrow.

"Fair-weather dinna wait for anyone. I ken I dinna want to travel in the rain. Do ye?"

Brighde stepped up to the horse and lifted her foot to the stirrup. Before she could hoist herself up, she felt herself being tossed into the saddle. She had just enough time to right herself before Alex was seated behind her. His strong thighs pressed against her legs, and he wrapped one arm around her waist. His thumb stroked lazy lines on the underside of her breast while the other held the rains. He spurred *Noamh* forward into a trot and then a canter. He seemed to have no trouble determining which direction to go. Brighde fully appreciated just how disoriented she would have been if she had tried to set off on her own.

They rode in silence as the sun rose higher into the sky. Eventually, Alex began to point out various landmarks that Brighde had not seen the night before. He explained that he and his siblings, including Mairghread, would come to this area to camp underneath the stars as children. For the boys, it had been survival training, but for Mairghread, it had been a refusal to be left behind or outdone. Brighde found herself longing to reconnect properly with Mairghread. There was so much from each other's lives that they missed during the years they had not seen each other. Between Mairghread and Siùsan, she finally felt like she had friends and a place where she was wanted and fit in. It was so unlike her father's home that at times she found herself waiting for the rug to be pulled out from beneath her.

I keep waiting for something to go wrong, but the only thing that has gone wrong is ma own foolishness. I have been so worried about everything from the way the wind blows to what people think that I am missing what is clearly just beyond ma nose. I am taking for granted friendship that is being offered up freely and a mon who would devote himself to me. I canna keep on this way. I maynae be in a position to truly be Alex's wife, but I dinna have to run from him either.

Brighde felt the peace of mind settle over her as she reconfirmed the choice she made when she agreed to return to the keep with Alex. More relaxed, she was able to enjoy the long ride held securely in place by Alex.

They stopped for a noon meal, and Brighde surprised Alex with her ability to prepare and cook the fish over an open fire. He knew she spent a fair amount of time in the kitchens, and her skills were praised, but cooking over a campfire was not the same.

"I clearly didna starve entirely while I journeyed north. I did keep the wolf from the door, and it wasna just by foraging or nabbing things from local farmers. I would build a fire when there was enough light that the smoke would not show. Then I cooked and ate as quickly as I could. I also picked places where there was enough dirt that I could cover the hot embers and wipe away the fire ring."

"Ye were wise to do this. How did ye learn how to travel without leaving tracks? Was it just obvious to ye, or did someone teach ye?"

"As a young lass, I showed interest when I traveled with ma grandparents. Ma grandfather was always careful to leave as little a trace that we stayed overnight anywhere as he could, and he made sure his men cleared their tracks before we moved on. The Campbells are not always a well-liked clan, so Grandda was extra cautious when he traveled with his family. He wanted naught to happen to me or Grandmama. As I grew older, I paid more attention, and his men showed me different tricks. When Grandda discovered ma interest, instead of scolding me, he made a point of taking me out to the woods near the keep teaching me all that he could. When I ran from ma father the first time, I was too panicked to remember what I had been taught. I didna be careful enough and made it too easy to be tracked. When I ran from him and de Soules, I kenned ma life was truly in danger. I didna have the luxury of being careless. I was ever vigilant. It was exhausting beyond just the physical strain of the travel, but it is what kept me alive. Neither ma father and de Soules nor any lawless men found me."

At the thought of Brighde running into any criminals who had no clan or alliance, usually ones banned from their clans, his arm tightened around her. She ran a soothing hand along his forearm and covered his hand with her own. Alex relaxed only slightly. He would not say anything because he knew she understood his feelings. He just held on a little tighter for a little longer.

By midafternoon, they rode into the bailey. Brighde was nervous about how she would be received after she caused such a disturbance. She knew that Mairghread and Siùsan probably were looking for her, and one of Alex's brothers probably alerted him. Laird Sinclair must have worried about his son tearing off into the night alone and with few supplies.

When Alex lifted her from the saddle, she angled herself slightly behind him. He reached an arm backward and wrapped it around her waist.

"Dinna fash," he whispered.

She had no time to respond before Siùsan and Mairghread ran down the steps from the keep and across the bailey. Each of them holding their skirts at a nearly indiscreet height to make it easier for them. They pulled Brighde from behind Alex and engulfed her in a hug. They both ran their hands over her as they gabbled next her ears. She could not make out what they said, but she felt their concern in their ministrations.

Before Alex could say anything, his sister and sister-by-marriage whisked Brighde into the keep. She looked over her shoulder for a long moment before she had to focus on the steps in front of her.

"What is it about our wayward women, brother?" Callum clapped him on the back and pulled him into a hug. The brothers had tussled for years and probably always would, but their love for one another ran deep, and they were never embarrassed to demonstrate it. "I ken it isnae about the chase either because I have Siùsan now, and I still canna get enough of her."

"Aye, and that's why she already has her head over a chamber pot every morn." Alex laughed.

Callum simply shrugged with an unrepentant look on his face.

"So ye found her. How far had she gotten? It's midafternoon already, and ye are just getting back."

"She almost reached Ben Morven. It was dumping buckets by the time I found her. We sheltered in the cave."

"That isnae nearly a day's ride from here. Ye should have been back closer to the nooning. Ye didna get lost, so why did it take so long? Get a late start?" Tavish nudged him as he came up to his two older brothers. He inserted himself into any and every conversation that struck his fancy.

"Nay. We didna get a late start," Alex could not help but blush slightly, "I just didna feel the need to rush back once I kenned she was safe. I showed her around our land a bit."

"Does she ken ye took the scenic way home just to keep her to yerself a while longer?"

"And why are ye blushing, brother?" Magnus now joined in.

"I dinna blush. The sun has been out all day, and I am just a little warm."

"Dinna give us that shite. Ye ken nae one of us is going to believe that." Callum stepped in front of his brother and turned to look him in the eye.

"I think ye did more once ye found her than ye ken to admit. What say ye?"

"Little brother, I say ye keep yer neb out of ma business. It isnae any of yer concern." He purposely tried to distract Tavish by hitting on a sore spot for him. He truly was only a hairsbreadth shorter than his brothers, but Alex and Callum had always taken advantage of it, especially as he grew to be barrel-chested like their father and easily able to challenge either or both of them.

"Dinna skirt the issue, Alex. Ye arenae telling us all, and ye would be better off telling us the truth than leaving our imaginations to make up the rest," Magnus grinned wolfishly. The largest of all the brothers in height and width, Alex knew that Magnus was fierce in battle, but he was also a gentle giant who was giving his brother a fair warning hidden in jest.

Alex sighed and ran his hand through his hair. He looked out towards where he knew the beach was and his favorite escape. He longed to be there now. While he was with Brighde, he basked in the afterglow of their couplings, but now, standing in the bailey with his brothers, he was ashamed of his actions. He took what was not his to have, at least not yet. He dishonored them both and did not want Brighde to think when he offered for her, it was done out of obligation.

Alex looked over at his brothers and hung his head shaking it.

"Dinna make me say it aloud," he said quietly. "I dishonored us both."

His brothers wisely stayed quiet until he entered the keep. Then they looked at one another.

"Looks like Siùsan is going to win that wager. It'll be at least a moon before he gets her to the kirk."

"That may be true, but I just hope she doesnae break him in the process."

The brothers sobered as they looked at the door that had just closed behind him.

~ ~ ~

Brighde let the two women lead her up to Alex's chamber where a steaming bath was already awaiting her. She marveled at how it could already be full.

"The watch announced ye approach when ye were spotted coming over the last rise," Mairghread explained as she helped unlace Brighde's gown while Siùsan gathered oils and soaps for her. Brighde's eyes traveled to Alex's bed, and her stomach knotted. While she slept there ever since she arrived, she knew Alex would never join her there. Eventually, she would have to relinquish it because she knew Alex reserved it for his wife. He would never share that bed with anyone who he was not wed to. She turned back to the bath and found the two other women watching her. She shook her head slightly and stepped into the tub. She sank into the hot water and bubbles allowing herself to drift away. Mairghread and Siùsan both slipped out of the chamber and left her to her thoughts.

Brighde soaked until the water cooled enough for her to start to feel chilled. She finally dragged herself from the tub when her fingers and toes had completely shriveled, and she began to shiver. She dried herself off, and an overpowering sense of fatigue settled upon her. She toweled her hair dry and ran a comb through the tangles. She slipped a chemise on and slid into bed. She resolved this was the last time she would sleep in this bed. Before the end of the evening meal, she would be moved into a guest chamber. Her last thoughts before drifting off were that she would miss his scent that lingered permanently in the room despite how long she occupied it.

.

Chapter Eighteen

*B*righde awoke to a soft knocking at her door. She stretched as she tried to understand what disturbed her sleep. She heard the knock again and flung back the covers to pad over to the door. Before she could ask, she heard Alex call out to her quietly. She opened the door just enough for her to be able to stand behind it and still look out.

"Lass, the evening meal approaches, and I thought ye might be ready for something a bit more substantial than dried beef and thin fish," Alex said with a smile. Brighde took in the crinkles around his eyes when he laughed and how he had bathed and shaved. She was never sure which she liked better, Alex with stubble or smoothly shaven. She decided that she would happily take either or both.

"I will be down shortly. Thank ye for waking me."

Alex looked like he was about to say something but thought better of it. He just nodded and turned away. Brighde watched as he walked down the passageway before she closed the door. She hurried to get dressed and arrived in the Great Hall just as the rest of the Sinclair family stepped onto the dais. She slid into her spot next to Alex. Once the blessing was said, Alex began to fill their trencher placing far more food on her side than she could ever eat.

"Alex, I wasna gone that long. I canna eat that much. Ye must have some too. I dinna want it to go to waste, but I'll be ill if I try to eat all that."

Brighde discreetly pushed some of the food into the center of the trencher and onto Alex's side. He then picked the choicest pieces and moved those to her side while moving the rest to his. She tilted her head up to look sideways at him, but he looked unrepentant and simply shrugged.

"Eat what ye can, and what ye dinna, I will." With that, Alex began to eat his meal. Brighde looked back at the trencher and found a few pieces of food that she could manage. Sitting next to Alex again was fraying her nerves. Between her attraction to him and her knowledge of what they had done the night before and that very morning, she was sure that everyone around them could sense that she was no longer a virgin. She had just taken a rather large gulp of wine when Laird Sinclair's words nearly made her choke.

"So, lass, ye have finally agreed to make Dunbeath yer home. Ye plan to make this permanent, dinna ye? I canna think of aught better for this family."

Short of announcing a betrothal right there and then, there was no doubt Laird Sinclair meant she would be marrying into the family, that she would be marrying Alex. She tried to swallow without any of the wine dribbling from her mouth. She felt Alex's hand rest on her thigh before giving it a gentle squeeze. She knew he meant to reassure her, but it did everything but. She finally managed to swallow several times before she responded.

"Aye. I hope to make ma home here at Dunbeath for as long as I can." Her noncommittal answer did not slip past Alex. He pulled his hand from her leg, and she could feel his eyes boring into her. She refused to look at him, and instead, she looked back at Laird Sinclair. "Thank ye, ma laird, for the ongoing gracious hospitality. Ye have made me feel welcome and at home."

She purposely avoided saying anything about being part of the family. Her eyes skidded to each member at the table and could see the varying levels of confusion, disbelief, and sympathy. Sympathy that was clearly directed towards Alex and not her. She dared to look at Alex and caught the stricken look on his face before a mask of stone dropped into place. It was only the slightest of motions, mostly likely undetectable by anyone else, but Brighde felt him shift away from her.

For the rest of the meal, Alex ate in silence only speaking when spoken to. His tone was polite and even friendly, but his answers were short and to the point. He minced no words and initiated no conversations. Brighde felt wretched and had hoped she could speak with Alex and offer her solution first, but that opportunity had come and gone. She was not going to lie to Laird Sinclair or his family. At least not anymore.

The meal was just coming to an end when a party of four haggard men wearing Mackay plaids stormed into the Great Hall. Tristan rose and came around the table to receive his men. Mairghread stood by her chair with Wee Liam in her arms. She looked to her husband, and then her father, and back to Tristan. Tristan was speaking softly with the men, but the entire scene spoke of bad news. Tristan sent the men to the kitchens for a meal, and he turned back to the table where eight sets of eyes watched him with concern and foreboding. He returned to the table and helped Mairghread back into her seat. He lifted their son into his lap before speaking.

"The Gunns and de Soules attacked one of ma villages and fired the fields. The entire crop was lost. They head this way and have been terrorizing everyone who crosses their paths. Fortunately, most of the villages in the surrounding area were vacated, and the people safely locked behind our castle walls. They lost their homes, but they didna lose their lives or their livestock. Neither of them is daft enough to try to lay siege to Varrich. They ken we will outlast them, and they would most likely lose more men than they can spare. They are only a day out."

Brighde gasped and looked to Alex. He may have been distant the entire meal, and he might be displeased with her, but her instinct was to turn to him. He took her hand and pulled her from the table. He led her down a passageway to a set of stairs she knew would take them eventually to the battlements. Alex did not say a word until they were outside. Once on the wall walk, he checked to be sure no one was within earshot before turning to her.

"Ye heard the same as I did. Are ye really going to continue to avoid what must be said? I didna want it like this at all. I never wanted ye to think that I would marry ye out of obligation or because ye have nay other choice. I wanted ye to ken that I marry ye because I want ye and nay other. Nay other ever again. It is ye and only ye nay matter what." Alex held both her hands in his. She knew they were cold even though they felt clammy to her. She licked her lips before answering. This was not how she had wanted to offer her solution either, but she had little choice left.

"I will stay on here and accept yer offer of protection. As ye leman nae as yer wife."

To the day she died, Brighde would never forget the look of excruciating pain that crossed Alex's face. She knew at that moment what it was to watch someone's heart break. Hers felt the same way as he dropped her hands and stepped back.

"How could ye even suggest something like that? What kind of mon do ye think I am? Have I so dishonored us both by taking yer innocence before we wed that ye think that is all ye can offer? Ye think I would continue to dishonor ye? I have never had a leman, and I have nay intention of having one now. I intend to have a wife."

"Alex, I canna marry ye. I dinna ken if I'm precontracted," Brighde's voice came out hoarse and strained. "This is the best that I can offer ye. Do ye want to marry me only to find out that ye must set me aside because another mon claims me as his bride? I canna be aught more than a leman. Perhaps kenning that I have been with another mon will be enough for de Soules to give up, but I doubt it. Nae where money is concerned."

"So ye would marry me once we ken where de Soules stands when he kens ye have laid with me?"

Brighde's pause was all that Alex needed. He shook his head as he looked at her in disgust.

"Do ye really believe that ye can stay on as ma mistress forever? If I dinna wed ye, then one day I will have to wed someone else. I willna have a choice. Do ye think ma bride deserves to enter a home where I keep a mistress or where I slip off to bed another woman in a croft she and I share? Do ye really think that I would ever stray from ma marriage vows once made? To anyone? And what if I was to sire a child on ye? What then? Ye would have our child named a bastard and ruin their life before it ever began. Can ye stand the idea of watching me wed someone else and watch as ma bairn grows in her belly? I ken I could never set ye aside to watch ye take up with another mon, to watch his seed grow into the family I will always ken I should have had with ye. I'd kill him before sharing with any other mon what has only been mine. What should only ever be mine. I canna keep doing this with ye, Brighde. This isnae aboot any precontract. This is only aboot ye and yer unwillingness to believe I can make ye a good husband. Yer refusal to trust me to be faithful. Instead, ye would have me become exactly what ye hate. It's be ma wife or naught at all." Alex choked out the last of his speech before spinning on his heels, so she could not see the tears stream from his eyes. He stormed away leaving Brighde alone. She fell back against the wall and watched him walk away.

What have I done? I have ruined nae only ma life but his too. He doesnae deserve me playing him for a fool. He is right, and I ken it. I kenned it before I even suggested it. How could I have ever thought he might consider keeping me as a mistress? I didna even think one day he might marry someone else. I thought we could live much like a married couple without risking our vows being set aside. I've never had any intention of leaving with de Soules nae matter what. I canna keep using that as an excuse.

It's about bluidy time ye were honest with yerself. Ye've kenned all along that ye were lying every time ye blamed possibly being precontracted as yer reason. Ye have feared he would turn out to be like yer father, and he would betray ye just as yer father betrayed yer mother.

Except I have kenned since the moment that I awoke in his chamber with him holding ma hand as he slept there to guard me that he is naught like ma father. He has proven at every turn he couldnae be more opposite than ma father. Ma grandmama warned me that men stray, but instead she should have taught me to look for a mon like Grandda because that is exactly what I have found. And now what I have lost.

Ye're a coward, Brighde Kerr. Ye made this mess through willful blindness and selfishness.

I have to fix this.

"Alex! Alex, wait!" She ran for him, but he refused to do more than turn his ear towards her. He kept walking away from her. It started to drizzle while they talked, and now the stones were slick. She tried to carefully pick her way around the slippery stones as she kept running. Her footsteps must have been enough for him to turn around.

"Dinna run--" Alex did not have time to finish his warning as he watched Brighde slip and lurch towards the ledge of the wall. He pushed himself into a sprint and lunged forward to catch her before she could go over the wall or hit her head against it as she continued to slide. He caught her and pulled her to him.

"Alex," she sobbed almost uncontrollably. "I'm sorry. I'm so vera sorry. Please dinna leave me, too. Please dinna let go, too." Alex could barely understand her, but he caught the word "too." He tried to think who else had left her, and he realized everyone left her at one time or another. It began when her mother died, and her father rejected her. Then her grandparents died, and she returned to a mon who deserted his role as her father.

"I love ye, Alex. I love ye, and I dinna want to ever be with anyone else. And the idea that ye could marry someone else makes me feel wretched. I dinna want to live if I must ken ye are with someone else when it could be me. Alex, I'm sorry. So, so sorry." She kept repeating the last part over and over as though it was a mantra. He cradled her in his arms as she shook from head to toe.

"I love ye, too, lass. I have from the vera start. I only wanted ye to realize ye could feel the same way. If I couldnae have ye, there would never be anyone else. I couldnae do it. It's ye or naught. Ye've had ma heart since ye collapsed in ma arms in a storm." He smiled down at her as he wiped her tears away. "Ye seem to be making this a bit of a habit."

She offered him a wobbly smile as she sniffed. Through trembling lips, she retorted, "It isnae ma fault it rains every day in Scotland."

"Mayhap, but ye arenae denying that ye keep falling into ma arms."

"Aye, and I will for the rest of our lives if ye will let me."

"*Tha mi a 'guidhe gach rud a tha mi agus a h-uile rud a th' agam.*" I love you with all that I am and all that I have. "From this day forth, there is naught that will pull us apart again."

"Alex, I am so sorry. I have caused ye so much pain when all ye have ever done is stand by me, catch me every time I fall, and love me. I've lied to ye and to maself. It hasnae aught to do with the precontract or even de Soules really. It has been the nagging and constant fear that ye might leave me just as everyone else I've loved has. I thought if I could keep ye at arm's length, then it wouldnae hurt so badly when ye finally left too. Except, I have never felt such a supreme pain as I did now as ye walked away. I kenned ye wouldnae come back. I kenned I could only push ye so far or so many times before ye wouldnae keep subjecting yerself to ma rejection. I dinna think I could ever survive the feeling of watching ye walk away. Dear God and all the angels, I dinna ever want to see that look of pain on yer face again, and to ken, I was the cause of it. I will never be able to properly show ye just how much I regret ma words, ma actions, ma choices."

"Aye, ye can. Marry me. Pledge yerself just as I would pledge maself to ye. I would never let ye go. I will always come back."

"Alex, I couldnae want aught more than to marry ye. I would marry ye right this moment. Aye, I will marry ye." Brighde looked into Alex's smoky eyes. She wanted to be sure he understood the significance of what she just said. The look of happiness assured her that he did.

Alex felt his chest expand painfully as his heart swelled. Only moments ago, he thought his head might explode as his heart shriveled into a pebble. He had never felt the kind of pain that Brighde had inflicted upon him, not even in battle. His mind whirled as he tried to make sense of everything that happened since they stepped onto the battlements. He looked into her luminescent silver eyes as he stroked her hair. The hair he could not wait to have strewn across his pillow that very night as he made love to her over and over. He understood the significance of what she said. She declared three times her desire to marry him. They were now married by consent. In Scotland, marriage by consent was even more binding than a handfast and nearly as much as being wed by a priest.

Alex pulled them to their feet and lifted her into his arms before carrying her to the door. He pushed through and began making his way down to the floor with the family chambers. He was looking forward to reclaiming his bed and making it theirs. Finally. He just stepped off the last stair when Magnus and Tristan came barreling towards them.

"They've been spotted just on the other side of the last hill. They made better time than we could have anticipated." Tristan announced.

"The others are in the armory already," Magnus noted.

"Alex, do ye really think they would attack in the dark?" Brighde gripped his sleeve.

"Nay. Nae outright, but they'll put their archers up in the trees to lob a few arrows to test our defenses. They will wait until they can see as our wall design is too thick and complicated with its angles and twists to try to scale in the dark."

"Alex, we have to go. Da is waiting for us."

Alex pulled Brighde in for a hard kiss before letting go slowly.

"Wait with Mairghread and Siùsan. Mairghread kens what to do." With that, he was gone and Brighde was left standing alone watching his retreating form as he rushed down the stairs. She looked down the passageway and heard voices from one of the chambers. She recognized them as Mairghread's and Siùsan's.

She approached, but when she heard more of their conversation, she paused. The door was ajar, and she could hear everything clearly.

"It's about bluidy time she pulled her head from her arse. Alex is an excellent mon and would make a better husband than just about any mon I ken, including ma own. I love Tristan more than I can explain, but he was as utterly clueless as yer husband when he courted me, and that's all thanks to the woman he was diddling before he met me. Alex isnae like that at all. There willnae ever be a woman coming out of the woodwork to ruin things."

146

"Ye have the right of that. Yer other brother was a right arse as well when he was wooing me. I dinna ken how men who are so brilliant in war can be so completely and totally stupid in peace. Callum couldnae see the trouble he had until it was nearly too late to stop it. She should be praying a rosary daily that Alex doesnae believe in mistresses and doesnae have a long line of women trying to snag him into marriage."

"It's a good thing I like her so much. I dinna ken if I could have put up with her dithering about if I didna ken how sweet and kind she normally is. She's perfect for Alex."

"Ye ken that, I ken that, Alex kens that, and the whole damned clan kens that, but it certainly took her a far sight longer than anyone else to see it."

"I wasna quite sure what to make of her little announcement at supper, and I thought Alex was going to have apoplexy. Then he dragged her off. If ye hadnae sent Callum up to check on them, I dinna think any of us would be so calm aboot the men going out to stand watch. I dinna worry aboot them now I ken they arenae having to talk Alex down from any ledges."

Brighde had stepped into the doorway by this point and cleared her throat softly. The two women looked up from their sewing completely oblivious to anyone who might have been listening. Neither of them blushed or seemed embarrassed to be talking so openly about the woman who caught them.

"Come in and grab a leine. I dinna ken how they manage to rip so many shirts in so short a time. Tristan has already ripped three while in the lists. He claims his muscles just dinna fit." Mairghread snorted at that. "More likely, he needs to pay more attention and show off less. Then they wouldnae get nicked."

Brighde approached the women, wary after what she just heard, but willing to join them because she did not want to be alone.

"I ken ye heard us, Brighde. There isnae any reason to tiptoe around it. We are glad ye are finally going to be joining the family. We've been mighty impatient for ye and Alex to get on with things. We thought once ye rode back in after spending the night together that ye resolved things. A little time for intimacy usually works things out, but that didna seem to be the case for the two of ye."

Brighde was taken aback yet again by Siùsan straightforward approach to her relationship with Alex. She hoped to keep some things private.

"Dinna be embarrassed. Truly. Both Siùsan and I shared intimacies with our husbands before we wed, and Siùsan handfasted before she said her vows before a priest." Mairghread shrugged. "So what if ye did things a bit out of order. If it works for ye both, then I amnae going to question it. Alex clearly loves ye and adores ye. We could all see ye felt the same way. We were just growing a bit impatient with ye after we each promised nae to meddle."

147

Brighde picked up a leine that she recognized as Alex's and sat beside Mairghread on the window seat.

"When ye put it that way, I do sound nae only pigheaded but rather nitwitted. I feel horrible for how I've treated Alex. I dinna ken why he still loves me."

"He loves ye because he sees past this to who he kens ye really are in yer heart. Callum saw how vulnerable I was to rejection and that I feared it at every corner, but he also saw more in me than I saw in maself. In turn, I had to look beyond his thoughtless words and careless choices to see who he was trying to become for me and for this clan. That's who I fell in love with even though it certainly wasna easy."

"But Alex is already the mon he needs to be, so why would he be so intent upon having me. I come with nay dowry, I have nay clan alliances for the Sinclairs to gain, and I'm bringing a war to yer doorstep. How can any of ye want me to stay?"

"I didna have a dowry either. Callum kenned it and still agreed to the betrothal. I ran from him and caused him to break his arm and dislocate his shoulder, and he still kept coming for me when I needed him most. Ye canna always pinpoint just what it is that makes someone love ye. Sometimes it's the smallest pieces combined that make ye loveable. Dinna question it and dinna take it for granted."

Brighde thought about Siùsan's final words and the wisdom in them. She appreciated the frankness the other two women used when at first it stung. Now she realized she was a part of a family who wanted her and valued her enough, to be honest.

The minutes slipped into hours as the women waited for word from the Sinclair men and Laird Mackay. They each took turns pacing. When they finished all the darning, they each read from a book Mairghread started during her confinement but never had time to finish. When none of them could keep their eyes open any longer, they climbed into Callum and Siùsan's oversized bed. Brighde thought about how many nights she spent in Alex's bed. This was the first time she would sleep somewhere other than his chamber. She was glad for the company and did not want to be alone in a bed that reminded her of him when she did not know what was happening. But all the same, she wished that she was sharing the enormous bed with Alex and making love to him instead of dozing fitfully, waiting to hear whether she brought half the Highlands and Lowlands to the Sinclairs' door.

~ ~ ~

The sun was just above the horizon when Callum, Tristan, and Alex quietly peeked in on the women. All three were still asleep. Callum removed his boots and sword while Tristan and Alex each lifted his lady into his arms. They nodded to one another before moving to their own chambers. Alex opened the door to their chamber, that is how he thought of it now when Brighde's eyes fluttered open.

"Alex," she said in a groggy whisper.

"Aye, lass."

"Is all well?"

"It will be, come morn. Sleep, mo leannan."

Brighde craned to turn her head towards the window where she could see hues of pink and blue telling her that it was already morning.

"What has happened, Alex?" She struggled to sit more upright in his arms. Instead, Alex sat down on the bed and shuffled his way to leaning his back against the headboard. He played with a lock of her hair before answering.

"It was as I suspected. They lobbed some arrows at us to see where our defenses might be weak."

"Was anyone hurt?"

"Nay, the drizzle doused most of the flames before any landed, and the fire made it easier to see the arrows approach."

"Flaming arrows!" Now Brighde truly struggled to free herself from Alex's hold. She pushed herself onto the mattress in front of him but continued to look at him. She could not think clearly while snuggled in his arms.

"Haud yer wheesht. It's a common enough tactic and one we were prepared for. It didna come as a surprise to anyone, and so nay one was hurt. At least nae on our side. They sent a few men with ladders to try to scale the walls, but they were either shot, broken when the ladders were pushed back from the wall or stabbed as they tried to come over the wall."

Brighde attempted to take in everything Alex told her. Once again, her gut insisted she flee. To take all the danger and strife with her, but she knew it was completely illogical. Not only would she put herself at risk, but Alex too since he would undoubtedly chase her. Beyond that, the Sinclairs had harbored her for nearly two moons. Even if she was no longer there, de Soules would not easily forgive what he would see as a slight against him. He would still seek to punish the clan that hid his prize from him.

"Was ma father with him? Did either of them say aught?"

"It was too dark to tell, and neither sent a message other than their intention to attack."

Brighde shrank into herself, pulling her knees into her chest and wrapping her arms around them. She rested her cheek against the top of her knees. Alex adjusted his position, so he had a leg on either side of her. She had not even noticed when he shed his boots or his sword. He took her hands in his and gave them a gentle squeeze.

"Brie, I have told ye already that we are well equipped to withstand an attack or even a siege. We are one of the largest clans in the northern Highlands, and we have several of the Mackays here with us. I amnae worried, so neither should ye."

What Alex would never admit was that he feared the same thing she did. He worried de Soules would bring a falsely signed betrothal document, or one signed well after Brighde escaped, and his own clan's priest, Father Peter, would have to declare Brighde legally de Soules's bride. He did not fear for a moment that she would ever leave his side. He feared instead what would happen if he had to kill her father or one of her half-brothers in battle. She might not look at them as her family now, but if he was responsible for their deaths, she might not feel so distant from them after all. He also worried about the position Father Peter would be in if he declared Brighde legally de Soules's, and Alex refused to hand her over. He worried about a great many things, but the concern that Brighde would never be his wife never entered his mind. To him, it was a fait accompli. There was nothing left to argue because she was already his wife.

Alex ran his thumbs over the tops of her hands and leaned forward to press his forehead to hers. He kissed it gently before rubbing the tip of his nose against hers.

"Brie, ye arenae going anywhere. Ye are home, in our chamber, where we both belong." With that, he pulled her to lie down with him as he spooned her from behind. She drifted back to sleep thinking that it had been far too long since Alex last called her Brie, and how she missed hearing it.

I need a name for him that is mine alone. Nay one calls me Brie but him. I want something that is mine alone too. I shall have to think aboot that.

Alex felt the rhythmic breathing slow and become evener. He waited until he was sure Brighde was completely asleep before whispering his prayers.

Heavenly Father, watch over all of those whom I love and care aboot. Watch over ma brothers by blood and by marriage. Watch over Da. Nay one is ready for Callum to be laird. It just isnae time yet. And Lord, watch over this woman, ma wife, who lays beside me. Help her to find peace with this, and Lord keep her far from harm. I dinna want to live another day without her. Thank ye for the blessing of bringing her into ma life, and the many other blessings ye have given me and this clan. Watch over us and guide us. All of this I pray in yer name. Amen.

Alex finally closed his eyes and allowed himself to catch a couple hours of sleep before it was time for him to return to the watch.

Chapter Nineteen

lex's internal alarm clock would not allow him to sleep much more than two hours. He was aware it was approaching the time when the sun would fully rise, and both sides would be preparing for battle. He knew it was his turn to stand guard, and he would lead the Sinclairs and Mackays. His father agreed the night before that he and Callum would let Alex determine and execute their battle plan as it was Alex's wife who they fought to defend and keep. Tristan was also willing to have Alex lead their side, but he maintained control over his own men. Alex understood it was more a matter of logistics than whether Tristan trusted him. Before his sister married him, Alex crossed swords more than once with Tristan while they each defended their villages or raided the other. The Sinclairs and Mackays had been formidable foes and were now unstoppable allies. Everyone knew de Soules and whichever Kerrs traveled this far north seriously underestimated the battle-honed skills and tenacity Highlanders possessed especially in the harsh climates near the Orkneys. Living here was not for the meek. The weather and terrain shaped these warriors, and Lowlanders were no match in size, strength, or skills because the Highlanders fought with more than just their swords. They fought with poleaxes, battle axes, double-handed broadswords, dirks, and anything else they could find. There was not a man in the Sinclair army who could not toss a caber, but it was not only about brute strength. To win this battle, Alex would have to employ every strategy he could think of to keep them one step ahead of their opponents.

Alex slipped from the bed and looked down at Brighde. They had both been too exhausted to do anything but sleep. He regretted their first night together was only a couple of hours snatched from the early dawn. He would make it up to her that night and every night to come. He pulled an extra plaid over her and watched as she drew it to her face in her sleep. He watched her relax further once she smelled his scent on the half that covered him during his nap.

When he reached the door, he considered waking her to make her bar it from the inside, but he could not bring himself to disturb her, and he did not think the situation was dire enough for that. At least not yet.

When Alex reached the Great Hall, Hagatha met him with a plate of warm bannocks. He snagged four, gave her a peck on the cheek, and headed to the armory. The bailey was overflowing with livestock just as the Great Hall had been overflowing with bodies. The elders were warned in time, and the villagers were able to seek shelter within the walls before the enemy made it over the last rise. So far, the fields had not been touched. A few of the farmers had stayed behind to lift the dams that had been built in case of this emergency. The fields flooded slowly, but it would make them less likely to catch fire. The men entered through the postern gate just as the first arrows began to land just short of the wall. There was no doubt they were spotted and were the archers' targets, but with the light rain falling, it was extremely difficult for any of the archers to line up a clear shot. The only injury was a twisted ankle when one of the men tripped coming through the postern gate.

Alex made his way to the top of the wall closest to the portcullis. He joined Magnus and his father who he expected to see looking tired from the long night, but Laird Sinclair was not yet past his prime. He looked ready to head into battle, and for a moment, Alex felt a wave of pity for anyone who squared off against his father. There was little chance that the other man would survive.

"Have they sent any messages or made any moves yet?"

"Nay more than they had last night. We can see them starting to move aboot their camp. They are late risers. Apparently, Lowlanders dinna see a need to rise with the sun even for battle. We have scouts out to make sure that they have nae broken into smaller raiding parties or tried to approach from other sides. So far, the signals have been all clear. We ken where each scout is, and there hasnae been aught happening yet." Magnus reported.

"Da, do ye think they will try to parlay first or just attack?"

"I think they will try to haggle and barter before launching a full attack. They ken they are outnumbered now that de Soules and Kerr have seen our keep and have a better idea of our numbers. Gunn was a fool to lead them here or too incompetent to convince them this was a fool's errand. Either way, they shall all regret making the trip out here. It willnae go the way they planned."

The men stood silently until the others joined them. Even when Callum, Tavish, and Tristan came to survey the impending forces, they remained quiet. They discussed their plans and rehearsed them several times the night before, so there was no point in rehashing them again. There was little more they could do than wait. They each kept unwavering sight on the enemy camp and scanned the periphery for any movement that could signal a sneak attack.

Hours passed before any significant movement was noticed coming from the camp. Men had been up for hours and cook fires could be spotted, but no one was preparing for battle in any type of hurry.

"The bells will be ringing for tierce soon. The morning is wasting away. Do ye think they are doing this on purpose to wear us down or make us impatient enough to initiate the fight?" It was nearly nine o'clock, and Alex was beginning to feel on edge which he knew was exactly what the enemy was hoping for. He drew in a few deep breaths.

"Mayhap. I dinna totally underestimate de Soules's battle skills nor Kerr's. Neither of them is untried. De Soules has been fighting for both sides of the border for years now, and Kerr is a known border reiver as his kinsmen have been for generations. Their strategy may vera well be to wait us out and wear us down until we are so impatient we are careless." Laird Sinclair moved to stand beside Alex. He placed his hand on his shoulder and squeezed. He wished during moments like these that his children were not yet adults and were instead still weans that he could shield from these types of duties and worries. However, he knew it was inevitable they would grow up. He wished he could save them the heartache and keep them from danger.

"Do ye want to check on the lass again?" Laird Sinclair whispered to Alex.

Alex looked at his father, a man he tried to emulate his entire life. He saw kindness and understanding there. There was no mocking or patronizing, but instead, a father who knew how his son felt.

"Nay, Da, but I thank ye all the same. Brighde is better off inside. If I go back in and must leave her again, neither of us will fare well. I dinna want to leave her in there, but it is better for both of us."

Alex, along with the other men, were becoming restless to the point where more than one of them wanted to pace, but it would be visible from the height of the battlements. It was nearly another hour before they saw three men mount up and lead a small contingent of riders and foot soldiers towards the castle.

Alex, the Sinclair, and the Mackay mounted their own horses with Magnus, Tavish, and Callum following slightly behind with ten other guardsmen. While they agreed outnumbering their foe too early on might play their hand too soon, they also wanted to form an early impression that regardless of how many men hid among the trees, there were far more waiting behind the gate.

The Sinclairs rode within a safe distance of the gate. They did not want to go beyond the reach of their archers, but neither did they want to be so close to the portcullis that the enemy might try to storm the entrance.

"I believe you have something of mine, and I should like to have it back." A tall man wearing mail like an English knight called out when both parties stopped with a spacious buffer of land between them.

"I havenae aught that was ever yers. I take better care of what I'm entrusted to protect." Alex shot back.

"I wasn't talking to you, welp. Unless of course, your father prefers letting others do the talking for him." He sounded as English as he looked.

"Ye seem to be doing enough talking for the lot of us. Ye heard ma son. We have naught of yers. "

De Soules looked over his shoulder at a large man with graying hair. There was little that would make anyone guess he was Brighde's father except for the piercing gray eyes. Alex assumed when Brighde said she inherited her looks from her mother, she meant all of them. Laird Kerr felt around inside his doublet. He produced a scroll he flourished before them. He began to read the betrothal decree that made Alex's vision begin to blur with red dots dancing before his eyes. He listened to the very end when Laird Kerr read the date. It was conveniently dated before the ambush on their party.

"I heard the date that ye read as to when the agreement was drafted and signed by ye, but what was the date when Lord de Soules signed the agreement?"

"Why the same day as I signed it, of course."

"How can that be when ye were traveling with yer daughter to deliver both her and the betrothal agreement to de Soules? He hadnae signed it yet, and yer daughter went missing during an ambush. De Soules, ye signed a marriage agreement when nay one kenned where yer bride might be? How vera optimistic of ye. More likely it didna matter whether she was alive or nae so long as the money exchanged hands. When word got back to ye that she might be alive and well, ye only wanted her back for the sake of saving face and to punish her."

"I don't know what you are talking about. I love my daughter and only want what's best for her." He was worse than de Soulis and sounded far more English than Scots.

At that, all the Sinclair men and Laird Mackay could not help but laugh. There was nothing remotely plausible about what Laird Kerr had just uttered.

"Even if I didna already ken that to be a lie, ye can barely say the words without grimacing, and ye are looking over our shoulders rather than trying to lie to our faces. Ye ken even ye canna pull off such a falsehood." Tristan spoke up.

"Are you questioning my honor?" Laird Kerr sat up taller in the saddle. He was already a large man, but he was nothing in comparison to the wall of Highlanders who stared back at him.

"I dinna need to question it. I already ken ye havenae aught." Tristan fired back.

"Your honor, his honor. None of that is what matters at the moment. What does matter is that you are holding my bride hostage, and I expect her to be returned to me just as you found her."

Alex could no longer hold back.

"Just as I found her? Battered and bruised with fingerprints pressed into her throat, ribs cracked, and feet torn to shreds as she fled a father who beat her and a *potential* husband who arranged for her murder. Nae, I dinna think so. I will never allow her to return to the condition in which I found her."

"You admit now that you lied, and you do have what's mine."

"I dinna lie. She isnae yers never was and never will be, therefore, I havenae aught to give back. Ye forfeited any claim on her when ye attempted to kill her. And if nae then, when ye left her for dead at the bottom of a ravine rather than going to her aid, ye forfeited any claim to her."

"You cannot deny a betrothal that was witnessed by a priest and sanctioned by the king!" de Soules bellowed.

"And just which priest signed those papers? Is he willing to swear to its legitimacy before a bishop or in a letter to the pope kenning he faces excommunication for falsifying such a document?" Laird Sinclair was looking past de Soules and Kerr to a nervous man riding on a donkey next to Laird Gunn. The man looked ready to wet himself or collapse, perhaps both.

"What say ye, holy mon? Were these papers signed just as Laird Kerr and Lord de Soules claim? The bishop of the Orkneys isnae that far from here. He could be reached in less than a day's ride. Mayhap ye would care to make yer confession before him?" Laird Sinclair cocked his head to the side and raised an eyebrow. Even with the reins in his hand, he was easily able to cross his arms without his horse moving an inch. As though a silent message floated through the air, all the Sinclair men crossed their arms simultaneously. Laird Mackay had been part of the extended family long enough to pick up the habit as well. An impressive sight when they all stood on the ground, but on horseback, it was like looking at Druid monoliths that had not moved in centuries. They seemed rooted to the spot and impenetrable.

"Nay. I dinna want to make ma confession before the bishop." The priest looked at the men who surrounded him and then down at the donkey on which he rode before looking back at Laird Sinclair.

"I ken when the documents were signed. Laird Kerr signed just as he said." He pulled back on the donkey's reins, and it sidled behind the Gunn's horse. The stallion did not like having another animal so close behind it and tried to kick out its hindquarters. The donkey brayed as it tried to avoid the much larger, angry horse.

"Get yer arse under control, ye lackwit," Laird Gunn snarled.

The priest continued to draw his donkey further back and away from the now three irate lords. He brought the animal alongside Laird Gunn, but when the stallion whinnied again and pranced in place, the priest spurred the donkey forward. He attempted to flee to the Sinclairs' side, but an arrow sailed through the air from the hillside and lodged itself cleanly in the center of the man's back. The priest fell to the ground, dead before he reached it.

"Ye would have a holy mon killed to hide yer secrets. There will be a place in hell marked just for the two of ye. Ye will be able to spend eternity bound together through yer evil deeds rather than by marriage." Laird Sinclair did not bother to hide his disdain and disgust. "Enough clishmaclaver. We arenae giving ye the lass, and ye dinna have any proof now that the document isnae a forgery or fake. The only person who might have validated yer claims is now dead. Leave ma land now, peacefully, or ye willnae leave alive."

The Sinclair signaled his men to fall back. None turned their backs to their enemy but still made their way back towards the gate and the safety of the wall.

"Alex, I ken we agreed ye would lead this parlay, but that just isnae how the conversation went. Ye ken it wasnae because I thought ye couldnae do it?"

"Da, dinna fash. It played out for the best. A battle was inevitable from the moment they showed up on our land. They werenae looking for any other solution. They ken we wouldnae ever give Brighde over to them. They dinna really want her, so much as they want vengeance. If they have a forged document, then they have all they need for the money to remain theirs. The only reason for Brighde is to keep her from telling anyone of their bargain. They want her, so they can silence her. De Soules probably intends to bed her until he is bored before doing away with her just as he did his previous wives."

They were near the gate when a flash of silver darted out and ran towards them. Alex pushed his horse forward trying to align himself with her path in the hopes it would block the enemy's sight of her. It was too late. He heard the hooves pounding behind him. He leaned low and swept her up in his arms. The other Sinclairs formed a circle around him facing outwards to guard her. More Mackays joined them from just outside the wall and formed a second, outer circle.

"Brie, what the bluidy hell are ye doing out here?" Alex growled. "I left ye inside where ye were safe. I didna think I had to tell ye nae to come out here. Where is yer common sense, lass?"

Brighde looked up at Alex and then twisted around to see her father, de Soules, and another large man she had never seen before approach.

"I knew you had what belongs to me. Hand her over now, and there will be no siege on your castle. This can all be done with, and we will return home. My bride by my side."

"She canna be yer bride when she is already ma wife," Alex said evenly. He saw even a few of his men and his brothers freeze at this pronouncement.

"She cannot be your wife as she is already contracted to be mine. You heard the betrothal agreement. Enough of this ridiculousness. You cannot claim what is not yours."

"What is mine is the babe that is surely growing within her womb already. What is mine is ma wife who wed me by consent. In this part of Scotland, that is as binding as a kirking. Ye didna contest the marriage before it took place, and now it has been consummated. There is naught ye can do." Alex looked down at Brighde's face. She no longer looked at her father or de Soules. She was not even looking at him. Alex knew she was mortified he would admit what they had done before all these people, and she knew there was almost no chance at all that she was carrying his child, but she also knew she would say anything to keep him alive.

"Alex, dinna do this," she whispered. "I dinna want ye to go into battle. It isnae too late to let me go."

"Brie, I ken ye fear I willnae come back and I will leave ye too. I canna make ye such a promise as I canna control all that happens on a battlefield, but I can promise ye that I will do all that is within ma powers to always come back to ye. But if I should perish here today, this is yer home. This is yer kin and yer clan. Nae just as ma widow, but in yer own right. Mo ghoal, go back to the keep and dinna come out until I come for ye."

"Alex, nay. Dinna do this. I havenae a good feeling aboot this. Love makes ye rash in battle. I dinna want ye doing aught impulsive only to get yerself killed."

Brighde looked around in confusion and irritation as she heard more than one strangled laugh that came out more like a cough. When she felt Alex's chest rumble with laughter as well, she scowled at him.

"Mo ghoal, I have been called many things in ma life but never have I been called rash or impulsive. The men laugh because they ken that is the last way anyone would describe me. Love doesnae make ye rash in battle, nay, love makes ye keep sight of the goal. I will come back to ye," Alex leaned in to whisper in her ear, "I will make love to ye the entire night. Rest now for I willnae leave ye alone until I have shown ye every way a mon and woman can come together. Until ye are screaming ma name again in ecstasy. I will teach ye all I ken aboot love play and we can make up more as we go along, but I canna do that until this is done." Alex sat back up and turned to Tavish and the guardsman next to him, Lewis.

"Tavish, ye and Lewis take Brighde back to the keep and make sure she returns safely to our chamber." He spoke quietly to his brother then looked down at Brighde and tucked hair behind her ear. The intimate gesture was heartfelt but also done to show his claim to her.

"Bar the door and dinna open it for anyone but me. Have a bath waiting since I'll need ye to wash ma back." He kissed her soundly on the lips. "I'm sorry, mo leannan, but I willnae have anyone doubt that ye are mine. I dinna want to embarrass ye, but I must make ma claim obvious before the battle begins." The words came out so softly that she felt them more than heard them. She nodded her head just enough for him to know she understood. He moved his horse towards Tavish's and passed her to him.

"To *our* chamber, lass! Dinna forget." Alex called as the circle opened and Tavish, along with Lewis, raced back to the keep. The two circles broke apart as more men rode out from the bailey. Nearly threescore men now formed three lines of defense with Alex, the Sinclair, and the Mackay back in the lead. Callum and Magnus were in the second line, one on each side of their family members. The Mackays formed the third line with the laird's personal bodyguards beside him in the front. Each man had a targe they now lifted before them. A soft whistle from Alex had the men beating the hilt of their swords against their targes in a rhythm that echoed across the field to the men who awaited orders from their own leaders. The three lines of Highlanders slowly advanced, the drumming never ceasing. As they neared de Soules and Kerr again, Alex raised his fist. The men halted and beat their targes more lightly. Alex starred at de Soules, challenging him to refute what they all clearly heard.

Rather than take the bait, de Soules threw down his own gauntlet.

"I take it she's your whore now. I don't believe for a moment that she is your wife. How long did it take before she was spreading her thighs for you? A few days, a week at most. You ravaged my bride and took what was mine. You owe me recompense for your theft. I will have it in blood."

His words fell on deaf ears as Alex tuned out the sound of any voices around him. He homed in on how de Soules held the reins to his horse, how his feet hung in the stirrups. He watched de Soules's hand hover over the hilt of his own sword. He took in the kind of sword the man carried. Then his eyes slid over Laird Kerr and Laird Gunn. All three men could be formidable opponents, but it was only Laird Gunn who caused him a moment of pause. The Gunn was the only Highlander among the three of them, and the only one who would fight much as he would. He knew Kerr was an experienced warrior as a border reiver, but he was most likely used to the way the British fought. De Soules might claim himself loyal to the Scottish crown now, but he was more English than most Sassenach. His eyes next slid to the movement that was occurring behind the three men and their small entourage. He took in how the men arranged themselves as they began to descend the hill and cross the open field that separated them from their leaders and their opponents. He looked into the trees and counted the darker spots that sat motionless, knowing they were archers. All this information was taken in within the mere moments de Soules taunted him.

Before de Soules could say more than he wanted blood, Alex roared the Sinclair battle cry, "Girnigoe! Girnigoe!" a word that harkened back to their Norse ancestors who settled the Orkneys.

The Sinclairs and Mackays surged forwards with the Mackays shouting their own battle cry, "Bratach Bhan Chlann Aoidh," or the "White Banner of Mackay."

They charged forward as archers began to fire on the approaching enemy. Being on horseback came nearly as naturally as holding a sword for these warriors of the north. They maneuvered their horses forward while continuing to bang the hilt of their swords onto their targes, once again creating a cacophony of sound that was meant to intimidate and warn their opponents. It was clear that it was duly noted by many of the inbound warriors who slowed their own horses before entering the forming melee.

As Alex plunged into battle, Tavish and Lewis raced through the nearby gates and brought their horses to a halt in front of the stables. Tavish turned his back for only a moment to pass the reins off to a stable boy. Before he could turn back, Brighde dismounted and was running to the stairs by the gatehouse that led up to the battlements. She lifted her skirts all the way to her knees as she ran as fast as her legs could manage. Never had the top of the wall seemed so far away. When she finally reached the top, she dropped her skirts and looked around. She spotted a bow that an archer laid aside when he went to fetch more arrows. There was a quiver standing next to the bow with not many arrows left in it, and Brighde scanned to see how far the bowman was and how soon he would return with more.

Brighde snatched the bow and ran to an opening in the wall directly facing the ensuing battle. She scanned the utter chaos looking for one dark head in particular. She spotted Callum and Tristan who fought back to back. Then she saw Magnus who alone was plowing through men as his sword continuously swung from side to side leaving a wake of dead or broken men. Next, she spotted Laird Sinclair and to his back was Alex. She breathed a silent prayer of thanksgiving as she lifted the bow. It was much heavier than the one she used as a young girl and sporadically since her return to Clan Kerr. She nocked an arrow and pulled back the string as far as she could. She was surprised she was able to pull it almost to its full tautness. She took a deep breath in, and as she slowly exhaled, let the arrow fly. It traveled true to her target and landed in the throat of a man who was charging towards the Sinclair and Alex. She pulled another arrow and shifted her sights to a man on horseback who was barreling towards Magnus. She loosed her arrow and was already nocking another as the arrow she just shot landed between the eyes of the horseman. She aimed for one of the two men who Magnus fought off. That man received an arrow through his chest.

She did not notice as Tavish ran up behind her and tried to pull her away from the wall. She thrust her elbow back into his stomach and faintly heard the whoosh of air leave him. She rapidly fired off the last two arrows that were in the quiver. Once again Tavish reached for her, but she snarled, "More. I need more."

A brief memory of yelling out something similar under very different circumstances flashed through her mind before she pulled an arrow from the quiver that appeared next to her leg.

Tavish could only stand behind her and watch. At first, he was anxious to move her into the keep as Alex instructed, but as he watched her fire one arrow after another, he was incredulous at her strength and aim. He knew he would incur Alex's wrath and would deserve it, but Brighde was taking down as many men, if not more, than any of the other archers. Before Tavish knew it, he oversaw that Brighde constantly had a quiver of arrows at the ready. When a few stray arrows made their way over the wall, Tavish yanked her down and covered her with his body, his targe left in the bailey attached to his saddle. As soon as the threat ceased, he allowed her to resume her place. For Brighde, the battle seemed to last an eternity. She could feel her strength flagging, but as long as Alex fought below her, she refused to put down the bow and rest.

Chapter Twenty

*A*lex was aware of arrows flying down with remarkable speed and accuracy, but he could not afford to take the time to see who the superior archer was. He continued to fight at his father's back as they made steady progress through the men who came at them and the men they attacked. They called out warnings and instructions to one another, working in tandem to win and most importantly protect one another. Sometime during the middle of the battle, Magnus made his way over to Alex and Laird Sinclair. He quickly dismounted and slapped his horse on its hindquarter. It reared and took off for the safety of the keep and its stall in the stables. Now the three of them fought back to back.

Sweat dripped from Alex's forehead stinging his eyes as it made its way to the tip of his nose. There was no time to wipe it off or to brush his hair back from his forehead. He settled into his cadence of swinging and thrusting his sword. He was both hyper-focused on the man he fought, unaware of what happened around him, and situationally aware, always sensing when another enemy approached. It was as though he had tunnel vision making his other senses heightened to his surroundings.

At one moment, the sweat blurred his vision, and he stumbled a few steps. He became separated from his father and brother. He and his father dismounted early in the battle, and now he no longer had the protection the height of a horse gave him or the powerful hooves a warhorse was trained to use. He prayed fervently that *Noamh* made it safely back to the stables. As he swiped his sleeve across his eyes and forehead, his vision cleared to show he was now surrounded by four men, two Kerrs and two Gunns. He was confident in his ability to fight off four men, even when two of them were Highlanders. His battle lust still coursed through him, and he was unaware of a slash he took moments ago from a now slain foe. He did not notice it until he tried to lift his arm higher than his waist. The pain flashed through him like a red-hot poker. He moved to switch sword hands. His father insisted they all learn how to be ambidextrous for this exact reason. As the sword settled into his left hand

and he pulled a dirk from his waist, arrows sailed over his head marking each of the four men dead on the spot. Arrows lodged in throats, foreheads, eyes, and chest. Each received two arrows just for good measure. He glanced back over his shoulder but could not make out any of the archers with the sun shining from behind them.

Alex pushed forward until he was able to rejoin his father and brother. By this time, the battle was waning with the Sinclairs and Mackays as the clear winners.

Alex scanned the battlefield and spotted Tristan taking on Laird Gunn. It was clear the Gunn was flagging, and it would not be long before he fell. Tristan toyed with him to wear him out before seizing the opportunity to cut him down. Alex spotted Laird Kerr laying on the ground with his throat slit. He thought for an instant that he should feel a moment of regret for the death of Brighde's father, but he could dredge up none. He was about to make his way back to his family when he spotted de Soules charging towards him. He forced himself to raise both arms and noticed that the pain in his side was no longer as noticeable. He did not question it and met the man as their swords clashed together. De Soules had the advantage of chain mail which made it harder for Alex to find places to strike and his weapons did not penetrate the armor, but at the same time, the extra weight already began to tire the man. They went back and forth until Alex managed to knock the shield from de Soules's hand. De Soules turned his head for only an instant, but it was the opening that Alex needed. He raised his dirk and plunged it into de Soules's neck at the very same moment an arrow whizzed past his ear and lodged itself through the eye opening of de Soules's helm.

Alex spun around to see who fired an arrow so close to his head and with such precision. He wanted to know who had such self-confidence that they would risk hitting the Laird's own son to kill the clan's main adversary. As he squinted and tried to shade his eyes, his father, brothers, and brother-by-marriage stopped beside him.

Tristan nudged him before pointing up to the battlements.

"Looks like yer wee bonnie bride is the one who kept yer arse in one piece. She had a keen eye and some bullocks on that last shot."

Alex followed Tristan's finger and spotted Brighde on the battlements. He ran towards a horse that had stopped nearby and swung into the saddle, spurring the animal on before he had both feet in the stirrups. As he approached the gate that was open only halfway as a defense, he laid low and passed underneath, barely clearing the sharp teeth that pointed to the earth. He pulled the horse to a stop just before the stairs leading up and dismounted on the wrong side. He took the steps three at a time. When he reached her, he yanked the bow from her hands and scooped her over his shoulder, marching back to the steps.

"Put me down, Alex." Brighde's protest fell on deaf ears. She tried again, but he still did not seem to listen. "Put me down, or I'll kick ye in yer cods. Ye ken I will."

Unceremoniously, he dumped her on her feet just before they reached the stone steps.

"How dare ye humiliate me like that," she ground out between her teeth as her eyes darted about to see who watched. Before she could say anything else, Alex tugged her to him and covered her mouth for a savage kiss. It was demanding and almost too much as Alex filled her senses with his touch, his taste, and his smell. She fisted his leine as she tugged him closer. She bit his lower lip while he licked her lips. She released his lip and opened to his thrusting tongue. When they could no longer go without taking a breath, they finally pulled apart.

Alex recovered from their kiss faster than Brighde did. He grasped her waist and pinned her to the spot.

"God damn it, Brighde. Why the bluidy hell couldnae ye go to our chambers as I said?"

At first, she thought his trembling was leftover battle lust or even anger, but she looked into his eyes and saw fear. Pure, unadulterated fear. Fear for her. The battle on the field died down, but they both knew archers still hid in the trees, every so often trying to pluck off another archer or warrior. She ran her hands over his chest. She tried to soothe him, and she felt the rise and fall of his chest slow.

"I warned ye that love makes ye rash in battle. I couldnae leave. I had to be sure ye were alright. That ye would be coming back to *our* chamber." She grinned, "Och, aye, I heard ye and remembered what ye said. Our chamber, indeed. I'd rather be there right now than here. I dinna want to argue when I'd rather be making up."

She stood on her tiptoes to kiss him, swiping her tongue across his lips.

Alex growled before picking her up. This time, he scooped her into his arms and carefully made his way down the steps. They entered the keep as Mairghread and Siùsan rushed towards the large double doors. They both carried baskets filled with linen strips and medicinals. They would have stopped to ask Brighde to help, but they could tell she had very different plans. Mairghread whispered to Siùsan and jutted her chin towards the blood that was quickly seeping through Alex's leine. "She'll notice soon enough and most likely will have to stitch him up." As the women passed them, Alex paused.

"They're both safe. Naught more serious than a few nicks and scratches."

Alex and Brighde saw the tension immediately ease from both women as they rushed forward to find their husbands and help the wounded. As they approached the stairs leading them to their chamber, Alex felt his strength waning. He could not take the steps two at a time like he normally would.

It must have been that dash up the stairs to the battlements. The battle lust has worn off and those steps must have sapped ma last reserve of strength.

However, Alex felt light headed and saw flickering dots dance before his eyes. He barely made it to their chamber door before he had to put Brighde down. Brighde looked up at him in concern and pushed the door open. When they entered the chamber, the room was flooded with early afternoon light. She looked back at him and screamed when she saw his leine was completely saturated with blood. She glanced down and saw it covered one side of her gown. She unfastened the brooch on his shoulder and dropped it to the ground. She tugged at his belt and pulled down the plaid. She tried to yank the leine up and over his head, but she was not tall enough, and he had no energy left to help. She pulled the dirk from the hidden pocket in her skirts. Alex was barely aware enough to look questioningly at her.

"I put a few on me when I discovered ye already left for the bailey." She explained quickly. She sliced open his leine on his good side and pulled it down over the wound.

She thought she was going to be ill when she saw the gash that ran from just below his chest across to his ribs, and down the length of them to where his belt must have stopped the blade.

"It isnae all that bad, bhean." At any other time, Brighde would have delighted in hearing him refer to her as his wife, but the moment the words were done crossing his lips, he collapsed into a heap at her feet.

Chapter Twenty-One

*B*righde's heart nearly stopped as she watched Alex crumple before her. She rolled him onto his back and checked to be sure he was still breathing, then she ran to the door, flinging it open so hard that it slammed into the wall and bounced back.

"Help! *Help! Callum! Tavish! Magnus!* Someone come help! Get the healer!"

Brighde did not wait to see who might answer her call. She ran back to the small table that held a bowl, ewer of fresh water, soap, and linens. She fell to the ground beside him and began to gently and methodically wash away all the dirt and grime that surrounded the wound. She switched to a clean cloth to wash the actual wound. She could see it was far deeper than Alex probably thought and explained why he lost so much blood so quickly. She could see all the way to the bone in some spots, so she did her best to get as much of the remnants of his blood, sweat, fabric, and dirt from inside the wound. She was terrified by the fact Alex never moved, not even flinched, during the entire time that she was manhandling him. She looked around and remembered there was a bottle of whisky in one of Alex's chests. She ran to the one that she thought held it and said a prayer of thanksgiving when she found it under a layer of fresh leines. She brought it back to Alex, and after a healthy swig, she poured it over his wound. Only then did he groan and try to twist away. Brighde felt miserable that she was causing him any additional pain, but the fear of him dying from infection was far stronger than any remorse for being responsible for his discomfort.

What is taking everyone so bluidy long to get here? Did they nae hear me? I canna lift him onto the bed by maself. I need his brothers to help me, and I canna leave him here on the floor alone. St. Columba's bones, where are they?

Brighde was ready to yell for help again when Magnus and Tavish ran into the room.

"We heard ye yell--" That was a far as Tavish got before he spotted his brother on the floor. He reached out for Magnus and gripped his sleeve. They both looked down at Alex who was not only unconscious but now deathly white.

"He isnae dead. Please, I need yer help. I canna get him to the bed alone. Hurry."

Magnus and Tavish surged forward each lifting from below his shoulders and thighs. They carried him to the bed and gently placed him in the center.

"Take his boots and stockings off and remove his belt and plaid while I find ma sewing kit." Brighde did not bother looking at the brothers as she barked orders. She knew they would do whatever she asked.

She had just found her needles and thread when Laird Sinclair and Callum entered the room.

"The healer?" Brighde asked as she moved towards the fire. She threaded the needle and used the string to dangle the needle over the flames. She did not know why heating the needle almost always seemed to help fight infection, but she did it anyway. Once the needle was almost glowing red, she let the string swing until the metal was cool enough to touch.

"Where is Aileen?"

"She is in the Great Hall seeing to some of the other men. She will be up as soon as she is done stitching up one of them."

Brighde could only nod. Alex may have been the laird's son, but she could not very well insist that the healer leave one man to tend to another simply because of birth. Her grandmother had taught her how to treat wounds and stitch them closed just before her own death. Brighde had still been very young at the time, but she had paid close attention. She was an adept seamstress and excelled at embroidery even though she rarely liked to sit still long enough to finish a tapestry or banner. Her sewing skills had been called upon more than once for her half-brothers who seemed to constantly be getting injured. She sewed plenty of cuts together, but this was the worst wound she had ever seen.

She poured whisky over the needle and the length of string she would need to begin stitching the wound closed. She examined Alex's side to try to determine the best angle in which to reach him.

"Can ye roll him onto his good side? And hold his arm and legs still? I dinna ken how much of this he will be able to feel, and I dinna want to pour any whisky down his throat for fear he may choke."

Callum and Tavish stepped forward to hold Alex down while Magnus moved to the window embrasure and pulled the cover all the way back. Bright sunlight streamed in, and Brighde nodded her head in thanks as she focused on the man she loved beyond reason and the wound that could very well take him from her.

The next hour was spent making tiny, neat stitches that ran from the center of his right chest muscles to just under his armpit and down his ribs to his waist. Alex had been unbelievably lucky that while the cut was deep, it had not severed any major veins or arteries. Brighde had to keep blowing the hair from her face as she sweat from the tension and strain of her task. She had not heard Mairghread or Siùsan enter until Mairghread gently pulled her hair back and tied it with a ribbon while Siùsan mopped her forehead. She was nearly finished when Aileen entered. The healer looked over her shoulder and murmured her agreement with Brighde's suturing.

"Ye have done well to sew the wound shut from as close to the bone as ye could. We will pack the wound with yarrow to help fight infection, but we shouldnae stitch it closed at the top. The skin must grow back together from bottom to top. Stitching it shut on the surface will not allow the skin to knit back together properly and will either kill him or maim that side of him." Aileen set about placing her various tools and medicinals on the small table where the pitcher and bowl had been. She made a poultice to pack his wound with and a tincture that would ease the pain to keep him asleep.

When Brighde finally finished stitching Alex closed, she sat upright and stretched her back. She rolled her shoulders and looked to Aileen who traded spots with her. As Aileen tended to Alex and applied the poultice, Brighde looked around the room for the first time since she had begun sewing the wound together. The Sinclair men wore expressions of varying degrees of worry and fear for Alex. Brighde had never seen a group of men who were more candid about their feelings for one another. She did not completely understand the depth of their bond because she was not close to any of her half-brothers and could not imagine what it would feel like to love a brother as these men clearly loved one another, but she could appreciate the sincerity of their emotions. She watched as Siùsan held Callum and ran a calming hand up and down his chest. She saw Tristin's arms wrapped tightly around Mairghread who leaned heavily against him, and it was clear to see that the love the brothers shared was felt deeply by their sister too. Finally, she looked over at Laird Sinclair who she was surprised to see was watching her instead of Alex. He opened his arms to her, and before she knew what she was doing, she flew into them. He enclosed her in a cocoon of warmth and security that she had only ever found with Alex. He was the same height as Alex, and it was clear where he had inherited his breadth of shoulders. Laird Sinclair was still all hard and defined muscle, but there was a softness to his embrace that felt like home to her. She burrowed her head into his chest and finally allowed the tears to fall. Her greatest fear had come to pass: Alex was grievously injured, and it was her fault.

Laird Sinclair stroked her hair and rocked her slowly as if she were a wean instead of a fully-grown woman.

"Wheest. Dinna fash, nighean. It wasna yer fault."

Brighde sniffled as she tried to stop crying, but the tears refused to abate.

"How can ye think of me as yer daughter when I may have gotten yer son killed?"

"Brighde, ye didna cause Alex's injuries. Nae directly or indirectly. Havenae yet noticed other scars on his body?" When Brighde nodded slightly, he continued, "Lass, he is a warrior, and unfortunately this is neither the first nor the last time he's been injured. He has recovered from other wounds such as this. Have ye nae seen the scar that runs down his left thigh? That sword slice was so deep we thought he might lose his leg."

Brighde tried to recall whether she had noticed that particular scar, but she had to admit to herself she had seen and felt numerous other scars that crisscrossed his chest and back. He had fine white lines all over his arms from nicks and slashes. She swallowed as she tried to accept Laird Sinclair's reassurance, but she still felt enormous guilt.

"That may be so, but this wound wouldnae happened if I never came here."

"Mayhap, but neither would ma son be in love with a woman who couldnae be a better match had I planned it maself."

Brighde rested her cheek upon his chest and watched as Aileen finished administering the tincture to Alex's lifeless form. He had not stirred once or made a sound during the entire time she pushed and pulled a needle through him. It was only the rise and fall of his chest she had to work around that reassured her that he still lived.

Chapter Twenty-Two

The next fortnight was a personal hell for Brighde that she felt she would never escape. Those two sennights were harder for her than the entire northern trek she made while evading pursuers and avoiding being assaulted as she traveled alone.

Alex's fever began within hours of when she finished sewing him closed. It raged daily and spiked at night. He mumbled incoherently throughout the day but suffered horrible night terrors where he screamed her name over an over as he dreamed that he had to rescue her. The first time she tried to soothe him, he lashed out and sent her flying halfway across the room. Fortunately, Magnus was in the passageway and heard the clatter as Brighde knocked over the wash basin when she fell. Magnus was able to pin Alex down and kept him from ripping his stitches. From that night on, at least one of the Sinclair men or Tristan kept watch with her. Brighde refused to leave his bedside. She took all her meals there and could not be convinced to leave the room for fresh air. She argued that she could breathe just as deeply standing by the window as she could in the bailey. When her refusal almost came to blows with Callum, they finally all relented. Her new family by marriage did all they could to comfort her and provide anything she might need or want, but the days passed by in a blur to her. She was not truly aware of what anyone else did around her. Her only respite was each evening when Hagatha arranged for a steaming hot bath to be brought to the chamber. She moved around silently as she ensured Brighde had everything she needed. It was the second evening after Alex's injuries when Hagatha assisted Brighde into the bath. Brighde was so exhausted that when Hagatha saw her struggle to undress, she offered to help her. Once settled into the warm water, Hagatha again took charge and washed her hair. During that brief reprieve before the night terrors began, the older woman shared stories of Alex and his family from when the children were young. She recounted tales of the great love that developed between Laird and Lady Sinclair. It became their routine over the course of the following two sennights. While Hagatha helped Brighde learn more about the Sinclair family and the clan's history, it was more the quiet company that helped Brighde prepare for the onslaught of rants and thrashing that was sure to come as Alex's fever peaked each night.

Brighde finally understood the hell Alex must have experienced when he cared for her for nearly a full moon. The difference was, while Brighde's illness lasted longer, Alex had not yet fallen in love with her. Brighde loved Alex with a fierceness and unwavering devotion that scared her at times. She could no longer picture a life without him.

By the eighth day, Alex's fever broke, but he still did not awaken. This scared her more than the raging fever and night terrors. He barely ate or drank anything in over a week. She spooned barley and beef broth into him throughout the day, and he managed to swallow Aileen's tincture despite their wretched smell and what Brighde was sure was a horrendous taste. He clearly lost a good deal of weight during his illness. He seemed to deflate right before her eyes. When his cheeks were not flushed from fever, he had a greyish pallor that looked nearly ghostly. She tried not to bombard Aileen with questions when she came to check on Alex twice a day, but she could not help it. She wanted to know why he had not yet awoken when his fever ended two days prior. She wanted to know what damage might happen to his mind if he remained unconscious any longer. Aileen was patient with her as this was not the first anxious family member she had dealt with, so she kept reminding Brighde that she, herself, had been sick for much longer and had survived without any lasting effects.

Brighde tried to keep that in perspective, but it was difficult when she feared she was watching Alex's life slip away. The end of the fever and night terrors meant she felt safe climbing into bed next to Alex each night. She was careful to never jostle him, but she did sleep with one hand on his good side as a reassurance that he was still there.

"Bhean, are ye nae going to wake, so I might see yer beautiful face?" It was the morning of the fifteenth day after Alex was injured, and Brighde could not understand why there was such a heavy weight pinning her to the mattress as she woke. She could hear a soft voice near her ear but could not quite understand what she heard. Her eyes struggled to open, but when they did, she found herself staring into a pair of mahogany eyes that twinkled with mirth.

"Bhean, I thought ye were never going to wake. Ye sleep like the dead." Alex teased as he pulled her closer. Somehow his good arm had snaked beneath her neck and now wrapped around her waist. He kissed her forehead as his hand wandered lower. He grunted in frustration when his arm was not quite long enough to reach her bottom. He pulled her onto his chest and grinned when he could finally reach what he wanted. He snagged the hem of her chemise and lifted it, so his bare hand could touch the silky skin of her bare bottom.

When all she could do was stare, open-mouthed at him, he gave her a pinch and a tap on the backside. He tried raising his other arm to cup her face, but the skin felt too taut to move his arm that high.

"Kiss, Brie," he murmured.

Unblinking, she lifted her mouth to his. She watched him as she felt his tongue slide along the seam of her mouth. She opened to him immediately and nearly sobbed when she felt his tongue glide along hers and then explore the recesses of her mouth. She cupped his face and held it to her as she nearly devoured him.

"Easy, lass, unless ye plan to finish what ye've started." Alex chuckled as he squeezed her buttocks again.

"Heavenly Father and all the angels, thank ye, Lord, for bringing him back to me." Brighde again latched onto his mouth as she tasted him for the first time in a fortnight.

"Brie, I dinna think I am ready to bed ye properly, but if ye keep this up, I will certainly try."

When Alex's words finally permeated her scattered mind, she pulled back and settled for stroking the beard that had fully grown in during his illness. She had attempted to shave him the first few days but decided that it was pointless.

"Alex--" That was as far as she got before the lump in her throat kept her from saying anything else. Her fingers flexed along his jaw, and one hand ran down lightly over his throat to his shoulder, and then back up and into his hair. She feathered kisses along his forehead, his nose, his cheeks, and jaw, and finally, she nibbled at his chin.

Alex growled as he attempted to flip her onto her back. Pain like a smelting iron being pressed against his side made him pull back. He lifted his arm to get his first good look at his wound, but it was covered with bandages. He saw a few specks of blood beginning to brighten the white linen. Brighde saw this too and pushed at his shoulder until he lay on his back again.

"If ye've ripped any of ma stitches, I willna be pleased with ye." She bounced off her side of the bed before Alex could stop her. She came around to his side and slowly peeled the bandages away. Alex pulled his arm over his head to give her space to look. The pain was nearly mind-numbing until he caught sight of his wife's full breasts as her chemise gaped when she leaned over him.

He had only been conscious again for a matter of minutes, but his cock was fully alert. He dreamed of her over and over as he tried to fight through the blackness that enveloped him for what felt like years. He saw her so clearly and reached for her so many times, but she always managed to slip beyond his grasp. He saw her in his mind running away over and over, but she was not running from him. Instead, she seemed to be trying to find him. Each time he searched for her and nearly rescued her, only to watch a faceless man in chain mail ride off with her. She always reached for him and mouthed the words, "I love ye," as she was carried away. Now that she was within reach, he intended to savor every moment he could spend touching her.

"Brie, I am fine. It isnae bleeding, just a few spots. Come back to bed." He lightly grasped her wrist and tugged her towards the bed.

"But Alex, I need to look more closely."

"And I need to feel ye in ma arms again. Brie, please."

Brighde looked up when she heard the note of pleading in his voice. She glanced down once more and nodded. She walked back around to her side of the bed and climbed back on more gingerly than she had gotten off.

"I amnae going to break." He scowled as she slowly inched closer. Impatient, he scooped his arm under her again and pulled her over him. She landed with an "oomph" as she tried to brace herself from putting her full weight on him.

"Alex, ye have been seriously ill and badly injured. Do ye ken how long it has been since the battle? Ye have been unconscious for a fortnight."

"Aye, and it has felt more like a century. Brie, I need to hold ye. I dreamed over and over that ye were taken from me. I chased after ye, but I was on foot and the mon was on a horse. I ken it was de Soules who I could see so clearly. He had ye even though ye fought against him, fought to get to me. Brighde, I need to feel ye now to ken the nightmare is over." He held the back of her head in the palm of his hand and pressed gently to bring her closer. Their lips met, and this time it was tenderness that passed between them. It started out softly as they stroked one another's tongue and explored each other's mouths. Again, Alex pulled Brighde's chemise up, so he could reach her satiny skin. His other hand found the neck opening and plunged below the collar to reach for her breast. His groan of pleasure encouraged Brighde to straddle one of his legs. The pressure of his firm thigh against the sensitive skin between her own thighs made her writhe. Alex's hand pressed against her backside and guided her into a rhythm that had her riding his leg.

"Alex, ye arenae ready for this. It's too soon." She panted as she felt his fingers slide down between the cheeks of her buttocks. They found the damp entrance and plunged inside. She could not stop the throaty moan that escaped her. "Alex, too soon," was all she could manage before he plunged his tongue into her mouth and matched the pace of his fingers. From then on, she was lost. All she could do was rock back and forth. Alex pushed the bed sheets all the way down and then kicked free of them. Her hand slid down his front and encircled his erect shaft. He felt like hot steel covered in silk. She held firmly as she stroked him. The harder he pressed into her sheath, the faster she stroked him.

"Climb on."

"Nay, ye canna do this yet. It is too soon, Alex. I will hurt ye."

"The only thing ye will hurt if ye dinna is ma cock. It's ready to explode, and this time, I will be spilling ma seed into ma wife and nae onto a blanket."

"Alex, I'm scared of hurting ye."

"Then be gentle."

"There isnae aught that is gentle aboot what I want to do and feel."

"Then just be careful."

He lifted her up so that she straddled both of his hips. He watched as she pulled her chemise over her head and leaned forward. He feasted on her breasts as though they might be his final meal.

I could die now, and I would be satisfied that they were ma last supper. They are indeed divine.

He kneaded and massaged the flesh as his thumbs ran over the peaks of her nipples making them into darts that he laved and swirled with his tongue. He felt her take hold of his rod again and nearly climaxed the moment he felt his tip brush against her now soaked slit. He pressed upwards as she pressed downwards until she was fully seated, and he was sheathed to the hilt.

Brighde was still frightened that she was going to hurt Alex, but he demanded no quarter. His hands gripped her hips as he pushed and pulled her into a slow slide back and forth. The barest movement was all it took for them. Their inflamed and sensitive skin had gone too long without finding release with each other. Alex could feel the tingle begin at the base of his spine as Brighde felt the tightening of her core and the wave of pleasure beginning to surge. Alex thrust into her once more and they both peaked.

"Brighde!"

"Alex!"

Brighde collapsed to the uninjured side of his chest as he held her snuggly to him, both basking in the remaining tremors of their release. Brighde tilted her head back, and they pressed their lips together softly. They were still joined together as their breathing began to slow. While she was still lost to the euphoria, he heard boots in the passageway and then the rattle of the door handle. He snatched up a blanket and tossed it across Brighde just in time to shield her from Tavish and Magnus who jostled one another to get through the doorway. Once inside, both brothers froze as they realized the newly married couple had just finished making love. Alex lifted his head and tucked Brighde's more firmly against his chest. He cocked one eyebrow and challenged his brothers to dare say a word that might embarrass his wife.

"We, uh, heard screams and worried something might have happened." Magnus choked out.

"Aye, something happened alright," Tavish said under his breath. To Alex, he said, "it is good to see ye awake and up." He could not keep from smirking. The double entendre was not lost on any of the brothers, and from how Alex felt Brighde freeze, she understood the innuendo too.

"I am hail and well taken care of, by *ma wife*," Alex stressed, reminding his brothers that this was not some barmaid they walked in on. Both men nodded their heads and backed out of the room, shutting the door as they left.

"Wonderful. Now yer brothers are going to think me wanton for bedding ye within minutes of coming around."

"Or they will congratulate me on ma prowess for being able to satisfy ye so soon after being out cold for a fortnight." Alex grinned. He looked so boyish in his good humor that Brighde forgot to be embarrassed or upset. She settled next to him and ran her hand lightly over his chest as her eyes suddenly felt heavy again.

"An duine agam," *my husband* she breathed out on a sigh as she drifted back to sleep.

The dark circles under her eyes and the tightness of the skin across her ribs and middle did not go unnoticed by Alex. It was clear she suffered much too during his illness. He remembered the fraught nerves and weariness he experienced when he cared for her. He could not blame her for being exhausted. He lay still, watching his bride sleep in the crook of his arm. He marveled at the realization that they were finally wed and sharing the chamber he had thought of as theirs for weeks but had not been able to share. He watched a peacefulness settle over her features as they relaxed when she drifted into a deeper sleep. He was fascinated with the slight pout her lips formed as her breathing deepened further. He ran his index finger across her forehead and down the bridge of her nose. Then he looked down at the hand that rested on his chest. He entwined their fingers, and his thumb stroked the spot where a ring should lay.

If I amnae able to take her to the kirk by the end of tomorrow, then the priest will be coming to this bed to wed and bless us. I amnae waiting longer than another day to be really and truly wed to this woman. I willnae have aught stand between us and our future. She is as much mine as I am hers, and it shall be that way always.

Those last thoughts floated through his mind as he drifted back to sleep.

Chapter Twenty-Three

righde found herself drifting back into the present when she heard a knocking at the door. She looked down at Alex who was still asleep.

"Come," she called softly. Wrapping the sheet around her chest, she sat up to see who was there.

She watched as her new sisters-by-marriage, she smiled at that thought, entered with a tray heaping with food.

"Sister, ye need to eat," Mairghread announced. Brighde could not put into words the joy she felt hearing her own thoughts vocalized. She was excited to finally have siblings who wanted her and appreciated her.

"Aileen says that Alex can have soup with vegetables today, and if he can hold that down, he might be ready for some meat tomorrow," Siùsan stated softly.

"I am ready for some meat now. Mairghread, I'm starved. Dinna feed me that watered-down broth I ken ye have. If ye willna fetch me real food, I will find it maself." Alex said with his eyes still closed.

"Is he back to being delirious? He must be because he kens a patient canna have something so substantial after being ill for so long. Arrogant, mon. Be glad we brought ye aught," Mairghread tsked at him but laid a kiss on his cheek before swatting at him. "Ye arenae getting aught more than this until ye can prove ye can keep it down."

"Aye and that gruel would be kept down more easily if there was some meat or bread to soak it up," Alex grumbled good-naturedly. He opened his eyes and attempted to sit up. Trying to keep the sheet tucked above her breasts, Brighde helped prop pillows behind him.

Once the tray was settled on a table near the bedside, the two women left saying they had their own pig-headed husbands along with a stubborn little boy to ensure were fed.

Brighde climbed from the bed and searched for her chemise. Finding it raffled up in the sheets, she pulled it loose and slipped it over her head. She came to Alex's side of the bed and picked up a bowl, but before she could bring it to his mouth, he shook his head.

"I amnae that hungry yet. Ye eat." He nodded toward the tray that had a full meal waiting for Brighde.

She looked between the tray and Alex but shook her head.

"Brie, ye've lost quite a lot of weight since I was wounded. I dinna like how thin ye are. It worries me."

"Alex, I am fine. Dinna be silly. There's naught to worry aboot me for. Ye're the one who needs to mend and get back on yer feet."

"Mo chridhe, I amnae taking a sip of that soup until I have seen ye eat to ma satisfaction." The words were said softly, but there was a hard edge to them. One look at his fierce expression and Brighde knew Alex would not back down until he was convinced she ate enough.

"Vera well."

She put the bowl back down and found a few things from the tray that mildly interested her. She picked at them until she looked over at Alex. Somehow, even in bed with a sheet slung low over his belly and a massive bandage wrapped around him, he managed to look intimidating with his arms crossed and legs apart.

"Ye arenae fooling me, so unless ye'd like me to feed ye, I suggest ye eat properly." Alex sounded like he was admonishing a wayward child, and it rankled, but Brighde could also admit that he was right. She would be of little use to his recovery if she fell ill too. She nodded her head and began to eat seriously. It was not long before she realized just how famished she was. She found cheese and bread along with cold chicken on the tray. She ate what she could, but days of barely eating at all shrank her appetite.

"Alex, I really canna eat more without making maself sick."

"Vera well. I ken yer appetite is nae what it was, but I am happy that ye are now well fed. I will have some of that soup now." He tried not to scrunch up his nose as she brought the bowl to his lips. After several long sips, he pressed it away. "I wouldnae tell anyone if ye were to give me a few bites of that chicken."

Brighde looked at it and seriously considered it before she shook her head.

"Brie, ye can either give it to me now, or I will find a way to get it when ye arenae looking. If ye would just give it to me, then ye would save us both the trouble of me getting out of bed."

Brie was not pleased with his announcement, but she also knew he was telling the truth. She did not want him to harm himself with his own stubbornness. Giving him a few bites of chicken seemed the lesser of the two evils.

After he had feasted on the five bites she was willing to give him, Alex looked up at her. He lifted her hand to his mouth and slowly licked the juices from her fingers and pressed kisses to the tips of each.

"If I canna walk to the kirk by tomorrow eve, the priest will come here to properly marry us."

His announcement took her by surprise since she was not expecting the topic, but she nodded her head without reserve.

"I dinna think ye should be trying to walk as far as that, so I will summon the priest maself."

"So ye are in agreement then?"

"Of course," she said indignantly.

"Vera well," he grinned wolfishly.

They could not help but laugh at one another. They finished the meal while chatting about what had been happening around the keep during his illness. She regretted to admit she really knew very little because she had barely seen --or heard-- from anyone. When she let it slip that she had not left their chamber since they walked in together, Alex bellowed for his father.

Laird Sinclair rushed through the door only to find what looked like a perfectly tranquil domestic scene, if not for the fact that his son was propped up in bed with bandages around his middle.

"Da, why did ye nae insist that Brighde take a break from caring for me? She has been trapped in this chamber for nearly a fortnight. Why didna anyone help her more?"

"Alex, dinna take that tone with yer father. It was ma choice to remain here. In fact, Callum tried to carry me out of the room, and I kicked him in the shins and vera nearly bit him. I amnae proud of that little scene, but it was me who refused to leave nae anyone neglecting me."

"Ye're a right pair, the lot of ye. Ye're both as stubborn as mules when it comes to caring for one another. He wasna much better during yer illness. In a moon, I think he left this chamber all of three times." Laird Sinclair shook his head. "By the by, ye brothers will help ye to the kirk as soon as ye're ready. Father Peter has agreed to waive the bans under the circumstances." His eyes skimming over the disheveled bedsheets.

"Since ye have already wed by consent, the banns seem a bit pointless." Laird Sinclair shrugged before walking back out of the room. He left husband and wife staring after him.

~~~

It was not long before Alex and Brighde became tired after eating more than they were accustomed to, so they retired after Alex had the opportunity to watch Brighde bathe. He was sorely tempted to try and help her, but even he had to admit that was beyond his physical abilities at the moment. While he was able to make love to her lying flat on his back, he knew he could not bend over the tub. Afterward, she sat on the bed between his legs and let her eyes drift closed as he ran the comb through her hair. It had been ages since anyone had done it as slowly and gently as he did now. It was lulling her to sleep, so when her head bobbed more than once, Alex set the comb aside and helped her ease over to her side of the bed. She had come to bed naked, and it had taken every last shred of Alex's self-control not to fondle her as he worked through the tangles in her hair. Now, as he leaned over her to gently set her head on the pillow and she turned on her side, his hand brushed across the side of her breasts. His cocked twitched. He knew she was aware of his arousal. There was no way she could not have been when she sat between his legs. He ran his fingertips down her ribs and splayed his hand across her belly. He had only found his release within her once, but he wondered if it had been enough to create a new life. He had always been so careful with the women in his past, never spilling inside one or only allowing himself to do so where he was sure he could not create a babe. The desire to build a family with Brighde was powerful, but part of him hoped they might have a little longer as just a couple. He prayed he would become the man his father was and be the type of father he was blessed to have.

"Are ye wondering if ye've planted a bairn in there?"

Alex looked over Brighde's shoulder to see she was wide awake.

"Aye."

She shifted to be able to see him more clearly.

"Is it wrong that part of me desperately wants to carry yer bairn, and another part of me longs to nae have share ye with another person?"

Alex pulled her flush to his chest and slid his arm between her breasts cupping the side of her neck. He held her close and breathed in the scent he had become so accustomed to he almost did not notice it anymore. He held her for so long she thought he would not answer.

"It isnae wrong at all. I was just thinking the same thing." His other arm slid beneath her, he hugged her from behind. "We can wait to try to make a bairn if ye wish."

"I dinna ken how that can be. I ken that when a man leaves his seed inside a woman there is always a chance she might conceive. And to be truthful, I dinna like it at all when ye pull out from me. I dinna like that feeling of emptiness just before I find ma release. It leaves me feeling hollow in some way."

Alex appreciated her candor and was pleased she felt comfortable talking about the more intimate parts of their relationship.

"There are ways to prevent getting ye with child that dinna involve me pulling out. There are sheep's bladders that can be used to keep ma seed from entering ye even though I am inside ye. There are different teas and tinctures ye can use, but I dinna care for that as I amnae entirely convinced they are safe. There is also another part of ye that I can come in."

"Ye mean ma mouth?" Brighde asked just above a whisper.

"There is that. But I didna mean that." Alex gently nudged her with his hard length. It slid between her buttocks and tapped her most sacred of spaces. Alex peered over her shoulder to see her reaction. His cock pulsed as he saw her mouth form a silent "oh." His mind immediately flashed to having her mouth around him. It was over a moon since their first trip to the beach. He almost choked when he felt her hand guide his tip to her rosebud as she tilted her hips back.

"This is what ye want? What ye like?"

"I have enjoyed it, but it isnae necessarily what I want with ye."

Alex never mentioned a past with other women before, and Brighde found it difficult to hear. She did not like the idea that other women had shared with Alex what she was just learning about.

"If that's what ye want, Alex, I am willing to try." Alex heard the tiny hitches in her voice. He pulled her back, so he could look her in the eye.

"I will never make ye do aught ye dinna want. If this doesnae appeal to ye, then it willnae ever happen."

"But if it's what ye enjoy, then I'm willing to try." She repeated the same refrain.

Alex searched her eyes and saw some curiosity, but there was worry there. He did not think it was about the actual act. There was something else.

"Brie, what arenae ye saying? What are ye holding back?"

"If this is something that ye like, then I would prefer ye do it with me." She whispered.

"With ye? Who else would I be doing it with? I--" It registered with him what she was really saying. "Brie, there will never be anyone else. Nae just because of ma honor and the pledge that I have made. I told ye as much that night on the wall walk. I dinna want anyone else. I havenae ever kept a mistress because there wasna any woman before ye that I would consider binding maself to in any way. Aye, I have been with other women, but that was the past. It doesnae bare thinking aboot because none of them mattered. It is nae them that I ache for. It isnae a single one of them that I crave like I do ma next breath of air. It isnae a single one of those women that I want to share ma life with. Ye ken I havenae ever brought a woman back to this chamber, but I didna think twice about bringing ye here. I kenned before I could have realized that ye were the only one for me. Brie, whatever we share in our bed and in this chamber is between only the two of us. It has naught to do with anyone else." He stroked the full length from her temple to the end of her hair as he looked down into her silver-grey eyes.

"That may be, but how can this nae be just the same as it has always been for ye? I've never done these things before ye. I ken I'm being peevish, but it smarts to realize that ma husband beds me just like any other woman he's already been with." As soon as the words left her mouth, she wished she could swallow them. The look of hurt was almost as severe as the one she caused all those nights ago when she nearly lost what mattered most.

"Is that what ye think? I told ye I havenae ever kept a mistress because there has never been a woman before ye that I cared aboot. I've told ye that more than once. Is that all this is to ye? Ye think I'm just tupping ye? Like I would a tavern wench or some whore who's been with a hundred men before me and will probably be with a hundred after me. I thought that I've been making love to *ma wife* every time we came together. I never took for granted what we shared, but it seems like ye just assumed I was fucking ye. Ye still think I'll go fuck someone else. Ye dinna trust me at all."

Alex struggled to get off the bed. He ran his hand through his hair in frustration before walking across the chamber to look out the window. He might have been an injured man, but he still had more strength as a Highlander than most men ever did.

Never hearing him speak like that before, Brighde watched him for only a moment before following him. She squeezed herself between the side of the window and him.

"Or have ye ever thought that mayhap I worry I amnae good enough for ye, that I maynae be enough? I canna compete with women with more experience than me."

"And ye dinna seem to understand that it's never been a competition. There isnae anyone to beat because there was never anyone else. There were warm bodies that may have pleasured me, but I never looked back once we each got what we wanted. I didna care once it was through. I walked away just as they did. Ye dinna have to try to be better than someone who doesnae exist. Ye are the only woman I have ever loved. Canna ye understand that? Dammit, Brie! If ye willna believe ma words, then I will show ye." He pulled her along with him until he got to the chair in front of the fire.

"Ye want to ken what it means to be fucked, then think back to that morning in the cave when I took ye against the wall." He wrapped her hair around his hand and pulled her head back. "Anyone watching us would have thought I was. But do ye ken what I was thinking that entire time?" He wrapped his arm around her, and she tilted her hips back in invitation. He plunged into her, thankful that she was already wet. "Do ye ken what I'm thinking now?" He thrust again. "The only thing in ma head then, and is in ma mind now, is how ma heart feels like it could burst from how much I love ye. I thought that it wasna possible to get any closer to ye or deeper inside ye than I already was. That I couldnae get enough of the one woman I already gave ma heart to. To the one woman I give it to now and will do over and over again till ma vera last breath. So mayhap I did fuck ye then, and mayhap I am now, but I believed then that I was making love to ye just as I am making love to ye now. I dinna ken how else to show ye how fierce and strong ma feelings are for ye."

Brighde was lost in his words and the sensations of him sliding in and out of her. As much as she liked it when they came together with tenderness and slowness, she craved this harshness, this base need to join together to demonstrate the power of their feelings for one another. She leaned further forward and spread her buttocks with her hands. She pressed back with her hips each time Alex's thrusts pushed her forward.

"I need this too. Harder. Ye will nae break me. Ye have me. Ye have all of me. Every part." She pushed back hard and reached back to find the grooves on his hips that fit her hands so perfectly. She pulled him to her and gripped tightly, digging her fingers in while she looked over her shoulder. The look of concentration and determination reminded her that there would always be a warrior just below the surface. She nodded her head once before she let go of his hips.

The temptation was strong, but he shook his head.

"I'm too close, ye're nae ready, and I canna bear nae looking into yer eyes for another moment."

He pulled out of her and spun her around. He lifted her, and she wrapped her legs around his hips still careful not to touch his injury. She could not believe the strength he possessed. He carried her to the edge of the bed and laid her down. He pulled her legs loose and placed one foot on his shoulder while he held the other close to his good hip. He braced himself on one arm as he pressed into her over and over. Brighde fisted the sheets as her moans came closer and closer together.

"Come for me. I canna last much longer." As if on cue, Alex felt the muscles of her core close in around him, milking him. He seated himself to the hilt and rocked until he felt her spasms calm and his own cock stopped jerking inside her.

Brighde pulled him down to her and pressed a searing kiss to his mouth. It was her turn to mark him as hers. She was awestruck that any man who had been battling a near-death illness only a day ago would do what Alex just did, but she also knew she never should have doubted that warrior in him or the love he felt for her.

They stayed together like that until Alex noticed she was starting to get chilled.

"Brie, climb under the covers," he said as he slowly pulled out. She whimpered at the loss, but the cool night air had her scrambling to pull the sheets over herself. As Alex moved onto the mattress beside her, she looked at his bandages and was relieved to see there was no blood on them.

"Alex, I dinna ken how to explain how I feel, but I ken I will always love ye. I havenae ever experienced aught as strong."

"This is all new to me as well. I dinna have the words to describe it. Sometimes I can only show ye. It hasnae ever been like that before ye. I love ye too."

181

They fell asleep in one another's arms.

Chapter Twenty-Four

They settled into married life over the next several weeks. Alex made good on his pledge to be wed before a priest and in a kirk. The afternoon following Alex's return to consciousness, Tavish and Magnus carried Alex down to the kirk. He was none too pleased to need his younger brothers to carry him anywhere let alone across the bailey but marrying Brighde properly outweighed any embarrassment. Alex healed quickly and was back in the lists before Brighde felt comfortable, but he allowed, and even encouraged, her ministrations when she fussed. They slipped off together and often as they could. When time permitted they went down to the beach alternating between swimming and making love. More often than not they ended up making love while in the water. They tried going to the loch a couple of times but found that Callum and Siùsan always beat them there. They snuck off to the storage buildings or up to their chamber multiple times a day. Never again was any doubt of their feelings for one another ever expressed.

Alex could not have been more in heaven until one morning he awoke to Brighde retching over the chamber pot. He hurried to her side and saw she had already cast up her accounts. He held her hair back until she wiped her mouth with the back of her hand.

"There isnae aught left to come up."

Alex handed her a sprig of mint to chew on and wiped her forehead and the back of her neck with a cool cloth. She held the compress against her neck.

Alex watched anxiously for the color to return to her cheeks. When it did not, even after a few moments, he pulled a fresh leine over his head and reached for his plaid.

"I dinna like this. I'm fetching Aileen. Ye need to be seen by the healer."

Brighde caught his wrist as she leaned over the pot to throw up what she could not imagine was still in her.

"I've already seen her. Yesterday."

"And ye didna tell me? How could ye nae tell me ye're ill?"

"Because I amnae exactly ill. I may feel poorly some days over the next few weeks, but it's naught that won't right itself. Da."

She watched as the news washed over him and finally settled. He was struck even more dumbfounded than when she announced all those weeks ago that he was going to be an uncle.

"A bairn. Our own bairn?"

"Ye had to ken it would happen sooner rather than later with the way we've been. We may have tried many other ways to couple, but we've done it the way that makes babes plenty of times."

Alex sunk into the chair and pulled Brighde into his arms.

"Aileen says so?"

"Aye. She actually thinks I'm a tad further along than would fit with when we announced we were wed and said our vows before Father Peter. It would seem our night, or rather morn, in the cave bound us together from then on."

She looked at Alex's face and worried her bottom lip.

"Are ye happy about this?" She asked softly.

"Happy?" He looked at her in awe and placed his hand over her belly protectively. He smiled at her before sharing a tender kiss that conveyed all the depth of love they felt for one another.

"I didna think I'd spilled in ya the third time even though I felt a short wave of pleasure. It certainly explains the tenderness in yer breast and why they've grown. Nae that I am complaining about the latter."

Alex grinned as she swatted him. He caught her hand and pressed it against his heart.

"This beats for ye and our bairn that grows inside ye. It may have taken me a while to unmask the mysterious woman who fell into ma arms, but ye have certainly been a prize worth winning."

Epilogue

I am a blessed mon in ma middle age," Laird Sinclair declared. "Ma eldest son has his first bairn aboot to be delivered. Ma second son has a wife who is nae far off from delivering their first bairn, and ma only daughter just announced that her second is on the way."

"Haud yer wheeshtt, auld mon," Tavish complained. "This family breeds faster than a fluffle of rabbits. There's naught to be excited aboot. This keep is already being overrun with weans."

To anyone who did not know him, they would think he was ill-tempered about children, but he did not hide well, nor did he ever really try to hide, that he thoroughly enjoyed being an uncle. He spoiled Wee Liam every time he visited Dunbeath or Tavish visited Varrich. Siùsan's younger half-brothers had returned with them and now fostered with Clan Sinclair, and while Magnus had appointed himself overseer of their training, it was Tavish that led them on the adventures that always got them in trouble but were always the most fun.

"If anyone needs to cool his heels, it's ye," chimed in Mairghread who was seated in her husband's lap while holding their sleeping toddler. "Just ye wait. Yer turn canna be that far off."

"Nae me. I dinna need to marry, and besides how would I ever choose? Nor why would I want to disappoint so many by making myself unavailable?" Tavish laughed at his own jokes but sobered when he looked around and saw four sets of eyes trying to contain their mirth. They were not laughing with him but at him.

"Little brother, ye are bound to see soon enough. Fate doesnae work on yer schedule. Ye follow hers." Alex watched at Brighde waddled towards them. He stood to offer her his seat. She was clearly showing and well into being uncomfortable. If Mairghread's son and the size bairn she expected Siùsan would soon deliver were any indicators, she knew she would be delivering a bairn big enough to swing a sword. Alex stood behind her and rubbed her shoulders.

She caught the end of what her father by marriage was saying.

"I just wish Magnus was here. It's a shame I had to send him off to court on our behalf, but with Siùsan so close to her laying in and Brighde so far along, I couldnae send Callum or Alex. And I need Tavish to stay to train the men."

"And he canna be trusted around all those ladies at court." Mairghread stuck her tongue out at her brother when he growled at her while Tristan sat back and laughed.

Brighde rubbed her ever-expanding belly and smiled as she felt Alex's hands slide over hers. She laced their fingers together as they both patted the life that grew inside her. She still could not believe her good fortune in finding and being accepted by such a family as the one she had been so warmly welcomed into. She counted her blessings daily. Now she wondered which brother would beat the other to the altar, Magnus or Tavish since it was simply a matter of time.

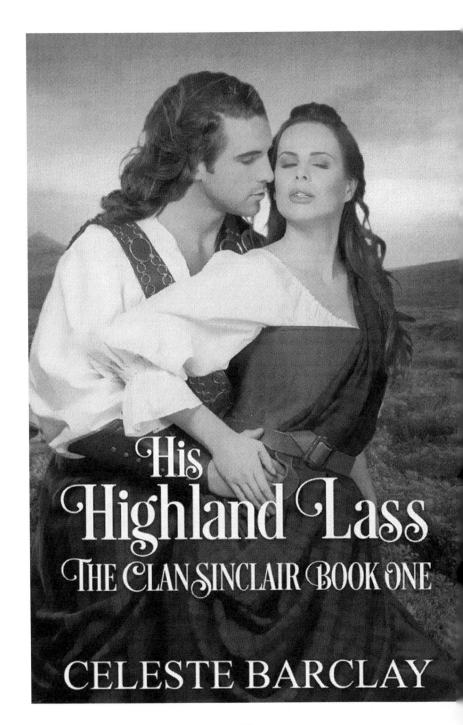

His
Highland Lass
The Clan Sinclair Book One

CELESTE BARCLAY

His Highland Lass
The Clan Sinclair, Book 1

An undeniable love... an unexpected match...

Faced with a feud with the Sinclairs that is growing deadly, Laird Tristan Mackay is bound by duty to his clan to make peace with the enemy. Tristan arranges a marriage for his stepbrother, Sir Alan, but never imagines that he would meet the woman he longs to marry. When things sour quickly between Tristan's stepbrother and Lady Mairghread Sinclair, Tristan is determined to make her his. A choice that promises to change his life forever.

Raised with four older warriors for brothers and as the only daughter of the Sinclair laird, Mairghread is independent resourceful, and loyal to her family. When her father arranges a marriage to a man she has never met for the sake and safety of her clan, Mairghread tries to accept her fate. Mairghread is betrothed to one man but it is the dark, handsome, and provocative laird who catches her eye. Arranged to marry Sir Alan, Mairghread finds herself drawn to Laird Tristan Mackay. After meeting her intended, Mairghread knows she cannot go through with the marriage, but she must find a way to end the feud that is tearing the two clans apart.

When the wedding is called off by Mairghread's father, Tristan and Mairghread see an opportunity to be together. Neither of them imagined that they would find the passion that grows between them. However, a spurned mistress and a jilted suitor stand between Tristan and Mairghread's happiness. Tristan and Mairghread must fight for the love they have found with one another.

Destined for another...

Mairghread Sinclair is not prepared for the danger that awaits her while visiting the Mackay clan. She must use her wits to keep herself alive when danger pulls her away from the man she loves.

Fated to be together...

Laird Tristan Mackay was not looking for a wife, but could Lady Mairghread Sinclair be the one to open his heart and bring peace to their clans, or will their passion tear the two clans apart?

Available purchase or download on Amazon

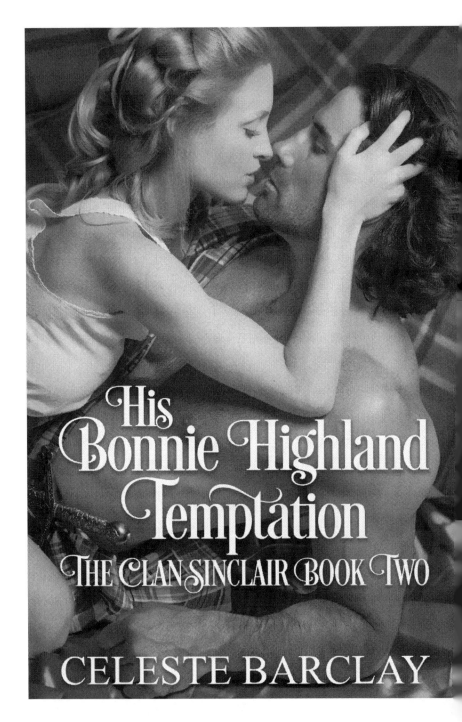

His
Bonnie Highland
Temptation
The Clan Sinclair Book Two

CELESTE BARCLAY

His Bonnie Highland Temptation
The Clan Sinclair Book 2

Unwanted and unloved...

Siùsan Mackenzie has spent a lifetime feeling unwanted and unloved after her mother dies in childbirth and her father abandons her for a new wife and new family. Forced to start her life in her clan's village and then brought to the castle as no more than a servant, Siùsan longs for the chance to escape her clan and the hurt of being ignored. When her father, the Mackenzie chief, unexpectedly announces her betrothal, Siùsan is filled with fear that her father is sending her off to an ogre who will treat her no better or possibly even worse. When she discovers who her intended is, she seizes the chance to leave behind those who sought to punish her and manipulate her.

Could Siùsan's father finally have done right by her? Will Siùsan find happiness in her new home, or is her future only to repeat her past?

Unaware and unready...

Callum Sinclair, the heir to Clan Sinclair, knows that he will one day have to marry to carry on his clan's legacy. He just did not know that his bride-to-be would arrive less than a week after his father announced the betrothal. Enjoying the company of women has never been a struggle for Callum, but as are all the men of Clan Sinclair, he is committed to being a faithful husband. When Siùsan arrives, Callum is unprepared for the gift his father has given him in his soon-to-be wife. Callum is eager to get to know his fiery haired bride who barely comes up to his chest, and Siùsan is tempted by Callum's whisky brown eyes and gentle nature.

But if only it were that easy.

A tangled web of jealousy and deceit is woven when members of Siùsan's clan join forces with outsiders to keep them apart.

Will Callum be able to reach Siùsan to prove to her that she will never be unwanted or unloved again? Can Siùsan put her trust in a man she desires but barely knows?

Available purchase and download on Amazon

Thank you for reading
His Highland Prize

Celeste Barclay, a nom de plume, lives near the Southern California coast with her husband and sons. Growing up in the Midwest, Celeste enjoyed spending as much time in and on the water as she could. Now she lives near the beach. She's an avid swimmer, a hopeful future surfer, and a former rower. When she's not writing, she's working or being a mom.

Visit Celeste's website, www.celestebarclay.com, for regular updates on works in progress, new releases, and her blog where she features posts about her experiences as an author and recommendations of her favorite reads.

Are you an author who would like to guest blog or be featured in her recommendations? Visit her website for an opportunity to share your insights and experiences.

Have you read *Their Highland Beginning, The Clan Sinclair Prequel*? Learn how the saga begins! This FREE novella is available to all new subscribers to Celeste's monthly newsletter. Subscribe on her website.

www.celestebarclay.com

Made in the USA
Middletown, DE
27 March 2019